Judgment Under Fire

His expression didn't change, but the gray of his eyes looked ever more silvery in the dim light. "It's Skinner, and those like him, that we're here to defend."

Bree felt her temper slipping. She held on to it with a mighty effort. "There's more clients like Skinner? Cordially loathed by everybody while they're alive? Demanding some kind of justice when they're dead?"

"Exactly," Gabriel said. He looked very pleased. "Skinner's soul has been sentenced to purgatory. He's filed an appeal. He claims his actions have been either misinterpreted or that they were legal to begin with."

"What," asked Bree, fascinated despite herself, "has he been convicted of?"

"Greed."

"Greed," Bree said pleasantly, "of course. Naturally. You bet."

"One of the Seven Felonies, as you know."

"There're only seven?" She smacked the palm of her hand against her forehead and answered herself. "D'uh. Sure there are. What could be more screamingly obvious? Pride, Wrath, Envy, Gluttony, Lust, Greed, and the Damn Lazy. And his defense?"

Gabriel grinned at her. He had a perfectly charming smile, and Bree, to her annoyance, found herself smiling back.

Defending ANGELS

Mary Stanton

BERKLEY PRIME CRIME, NEW YORK

THE BERKLEY PUBLISHING GROUP
Published by the Penguin Group
Penguin Group (USA) Inc.
375 Hudson Street, New York, New York 10014, USA
Penguin Group (Canada), 90 Eglinton Avenue East, Suite 700, Toronto, Ontario M4P 2Y3, Canada
(a division of Pearson Penguin Canada Inc.)
Penguin Books Ltd., 80 Strand, London WC2R 0RL, England
Penguin Group Ireland, 25 St. Stephen's Green, Dublin 2, Ireland (a division of Penguin Books Ltd.)
Penguin Group (Australia), 250 Camberwell Road, Camberwell, Victoria 3124, Australia
(a division of Pearson Australia Group Pty. Ltd.)
Penguin Books India Pvt. Ltd., 11 Community Centre, Panchsheel Park, New Delhi—110 017, India
Penguin Group (NZ), 67 Apollo Drive, Rosedale, North Shore 0632, New Zealand
(a division of Pearson New Zealand Ltd.)
Penguin Books (South Africa) (Pty.) Ltd., 24 Sturdee Avenue, Rosebank, Johannesburg 2196,
South Africa

Penguin Books Ltd., Registered Offices: 80 Strand, London WC2R 0RL, England

This is a work of fiction. Names, characters, places, and incidents either are the product of the author's imagination or are used fictitiously, and any resemblance to actual persons, living or dead, business establishments, events, or locales is entirely coincidental. The publisher does not have any control over and does not assume any responsibility for author or third-party websites or their content.

DEFENDING ANGELS

A Berkley Prime Crime Book / published by arrangement with the author

PRINTING HISTORY
Berkley Prime Crime mass-market edition / December 2008

Copyright © 2008 by Mary Stanton.
Interior text design by Laura K. Corless.

ISBN: 978-0-425-22498-4

BERKLEY® PRIME CRIME
Berkley Prime Crime Books are published by The Berkley Publishing Group,
a division of Penguin Group (USA) Inc.,
375 Hudson Street, New York, New York 10014.
BERKLEY PRIME CRIME and the BERKLEY PRIME CRIME design are trademarks of Penguin Group (USA) Inc.

PRINTED IN THE UNITED STATES OF AMERICA

10 9 8 7 6 5 4 3 2 1

For Harry, who listened to it,
and for Michelle, who believed in it.

One

"Hanged by the neck until dead, every one of 'em," Lavinia Mather said with enormous satisfaction. "Uh-huh. Got a pile of developers that'd give me a bundle for the place, if the Savannah Historical Society would ever let me dig 'em up. But nope, it's the only privately owned, all-murderers' cemetery in the state of Georgia and it's smack on the Historical Register." Her soft white hair formed a wispy halo around her mahogany face and she gave Brianna a smile of angelic sweetness. "You're a lawyer, Ms. Winston-Beaufort?"

"Yes, ma'am," Brianna said.

"Go on!" Mrs. Mather shook her head in admiration. "I've got great-grandchildren older than you."

Brianna, whose Southern upbringing gave her an instinctive respect for the elderly, merely said, "Surely not, ma'am. As for me, I passed the bar five years ago. I'm twenty-nine."

"If you say so, honey. Anyway. If you *are* a lawyer, maybe you could sue the pants off the Historical Society for me. You get those folks off my back, I'll give you a break on the rent." She twinkled roguishly.

Bree murmured an ambiguous "Hmmm."

She'd tried not to let her dismay at the decrepit state of her surroundings be too obvious to the feisty Mrs. Mather. But the cemetery was a weedy mess. Not something you expected to find off the trendy West Bay Street area in Savannah. The sole magnolia tree was dead. The azaleas were undernourished. Pigweed obscured the headstones. The only horticultural reminder that this was part of the most beautiful city in Georgia was the live oak trees. The branches drooped with Spanish moss that hung silvery over the graves.

She'd thought she'd misread the ad, at first:

> For Rent. Prime Office Space. 600 sq. ft.
> Exciting Riverfront Area. $300 mo. 555-1225.

She'd only been in Savannah a week, but it hadn't taken her long to discover that six hundred square feet of office space, anywhere near the Savannah River, in any condition, would run four times the rent asked for in the ad. She needed to work somewhere until the renovations on her Uncle Franklin's office space were finished. She'd called for an early appointment, and discovered the address was even better than she'd hoped for; the building was between Mulberry and Houston, one block off East Bay. She could walk to work from her town house on Factor's Walk to 66 Angelus Street.

"Thing is," Lavinia acknowledged sadly, "the cemetery kind of puts folks off." A breeze scented with the dank-water smell of the river stirred around them both. She shivered a little and drew her worn sweater tightly around her skinny frame. "Might not be so bad if I had the git up and go to tidy the graves up a bit. But my motor's kind of slow starting these days." She tugged at her lower lip a little sadly. "I suppose you've seen all you want to see, now."

Bree put her own warm hand on the old lady's shoulder, and said tactfully, "Nothing a few loads of mulch and a pile of azaleas won't fix. I'd love to take a look at the offices. And I did tell you I wouldn't need the space for long? Six months, at most."

Mrs. Mather smiled that sunny smile. "You might find yourself likin' it a lot more than you think right now."

The space for rent was the first floor of a small house built in the early eighteenth century; a time when the streets of Savannah had been paved with mud and horse manure, and the air shrill with the cries of slave auctioneers. The house stood flat in the middle of a tiny cemetery of ill-tended graves. The general air of decay and dirt would put any prospective renter off, Bree thought. As for clients—Phew! A wrought-iron fence surrounded both house and cemetery; par for the course in a city where every house in the Historic District was wrapped with the stuff. The design of this fence was different from the usual magnolia or ivy leaves, though. Each panel was made of spheres so artfully created, they seemed to spin in the sunlight.

The house was sided in chipped, dingy clapboard that badly needed paint. But the roof was intact (or seemed to be) and the window and door frames were solid. Maybe the interior wouldn't be as moldy as she feared.

Bree kept a steady hand on Mrs. Mather's arm as the two of them negotiated the crumbling brick steps to the front door. The old lady fumbled successfully with the key and Bree followed her in to face a sudden burst of glorious color in the foyer.

"I don't believe it!" she said, startled into rudeness. She bit her lip. "I do beg your pardon, Mrs. Mather."

Either Mrs. Mather was a little deaf, or she tactfully chose to ignore Bree's outburst. They were in a tiny foyer with a well-polished pine floor. On the right, a steep staircase led up to the second story. Brightly painted medieval angels covered the risers. Deep purple ribbons twined through the vivid crimson robes. Stiff gold halos stood up behind their heads like half-risen suns. Silver-gilt hair flowed over their shoulders to their booted feet. The angels marched in a stately parade up the stairs to a short landing, and then disappeared around the turn. Bree had a sudden, fervent desire to see the rest of the frieze. The contrast between this and the weedy mess outside was astonishing. She was halfway up the stairs before Mrs. Mather called her to her senses.

"Come on into the living room, honey."

Bree abandoned the beautiful stairway with reluctance and went through the foyer to a small, bare living room. A white painted brick fireplace sat against the far wall. The walls were paneled in beautifully polished oak.

"Mind your head," Lavinia cautioned from the living room as Bree followed her inside.

The ceilings were low, like the ceilings in Bree's own home in Raleigh. Although, Bree thought a little ruefully, the only rooms at Plessey that were as small as this one were the old servants' quarters on the third floor. And nobody used them anymore.

The living room was perhaps fifteen by fifteen. A brick fireplace with an Adams-style mantel took up one wall. The outside wall had one window that faced a tangled mass of weeds. On the wall opposite the window, two little archways led to tiny rooms on either side of a closed door.

"Kitchen's off to the left there," Lavinia said briskly, "and there's a nice little dining room right through the archway on the other side of this door. And this door leads to the bedroom." She opened the door to a space that could have held a single bed and a bureau, but not much more. "You could use this as your office, maybe. And put the sec-a-tary and what all in the front room and use the dining room as a meetin' place."

Bree walked around the small empty room and stopped in front of the one window. It had a head-on view of mossy gravestones. The dirt in front of the gravestones was sunken. Bree had taken an elective in forensic science at Duke; bodies that weren't en-coffined decayed so quickly that within a month the dirt on top would sink, sometimes more than a foot. Bree peered at the graves through the wavy glass. It looked as if all the bodies had been dumped unceremoniously into the pits, certainly without coffins. Perhaps even unshrouded.

Ugh. Not a happy view for prospective clients.

A whiff of hot breath on the back of her neck made her jump. "See anything moving out there?" Lavinia leaned her fragile frame into Bree and peered over her shoulder. "That Josiah Pendergast, especially."

"Moving?" Bree exclaimed, astonished. "Why, no, ma'am."

"Good," Lavinia said with a grunt of satisfaction. "Maybe the place is takin' to you already."

"What exactly," Bree said, after a long, unsettled moment staring at the grave marked RIP J. PENDERGAST, "do you mean by 'moving out there'?"

"You got to ask that kind of question, I don't need to tell you. Something you should know for yourself, honey. Seein' as who you are." Suddenly stubborn, Lavinia jutted out her lower lip. "So. You're takin' the space?"

"I ... well ..." Bree turned away from the window, floundering. A cemetery! Her family would have a fit. "I didn't think I'd be looking for office space," she admitted. "My great-uncle Franklin died and willed his law firm here in Savannah to me."

"Franklin Winston-Beaufort." Lavinia ran one hand over her mouth in distress. "That fire 'bout done for him, didn't it? Poor soul. Poor soul. He reached beyond his grasp, that one. You salvage any of that furniture? Or did it all go up in smoke?" For a brief, hallucinogenic instant, the old lady appeared engulfed in flames. Her gray hair flew around her dark, wrinkled face in a fiery halo.

Bree took an involuntary step back, and the illusion disappeared. In a near-whisper, she demanded, "What do you know about my uncle?"

Lavinia shook her head slowly. "Accidents like that make headlines in a town like this," she said. "You can just imagine."

"I can just imagine," Bree echoed. She rubbed her eyes. She hadn't been sleeping well since she'd come to Savannah. She was overtired, that was all. "Nothing much was salvaged. His desk. A chair. The fire that killed him had been fierce, confined to the law offices. The rest of the building had escaped damage."

"It's that building over to Temple that you're talkin' about, isn't it? I hear some construction company's fixin' the whole place up."

She smiled a little ruefully, "A developer's doing some

major renovation to the building and I can't move in quite yet. His will was quite specific. It's the client list that I've inherited. So, I'm looking at several different venues, as a temporary measure, and this …"

"Ven-ues," Lavinia mused, tartly. "Huh. Any of these ven-ues just four blocks from where you live?"

"Well, no." Bree ran her fingers through her hair. How did this old lady know where she lived?

"And these ven-ues. They take dogs?"

Bree blinked at her. "Mrs. Mather. I don't have a dog. And I surely didn't mention where I live."

Lavinia pointed a skinny finger at Bree's beautifully tailored gray pin-striped suit, fresh from the second floor at the Saks Fifth Avenue in Raleigh-Durham. "Dog hair," she said succinctly, "or I'm a white-assed Dutchman. Single girl like you usually thinks more of her dog than her ma."

Bree brushed at her skirt. There was a collection of sunny fur around the hem, as if a large golden retriever had nudged its head against her knee. She opened her mouth to protest. She didn't have a dog. She hadn't run into any dogs on her way to this meeting. And why would Lavinia think it was dog hair, anyway? She rolled a bit of the fluff between her forefinger and thumb.

Actually, it looked and felt a great deal like dog hair. So Lavinia was right about that. Surely, she would have remembered running into a dog this morning.

"As for where you live?" Lavinia rolled on. "T-uh. My nephew, Rebus, made me get caller ID years ago. That 848 exchange means that old set of town houses on Factor's Walk. And it's an old exchange, too. Means you been here a while."

"Well, the family has been here a while," Bree admitted. "Owned a town house here, I mean. We used to come here in the summers, my sister, Antonia, and I."

"So here you are, fresh from your father's fancy law firm in North Carolina, ready to take on the world, and you don't want to rent this place for three hundred dollars a month?"

Had she mentioned her father's law firm? Bree didn't think so. "Well, I..." Bree floundered again. She wasn't used to floundering. If three years practicing law had taught her anything, it'd taught her to be decisive. "I'm just not sure, Mrs. Mather."

"Call me Lavinia, honey," she said. "One thing I don't approve of these days is youngsters' manners. But it's clear to me that your mamma taught you some. So you go right ahead and drop the Mrs. Mather part."

"I do thank you," Bree said, rather absently. From where she stood, she could see into the little kitchen. The refrigerator was the old, humpbacked sort that you saw in *Leave It to Beaver* reruns on the oldies channel.

"I mean to *say*," Lavinia continued, with quavering emphasis, "where you going to find a nice place as cheap as this?"

Bree surveyed the rooms more slowly this time. The secretary and the paralegal could share the living room. And there was enough space for a small love seat and a coffee table. The bedroom would suit her very well as an office. With the addition of a microwave, the small, 1950s kitchen would be fine as a break room. She hoped she wouldn't have to spend too much on setting the office up; the smaller the space, the less she had to furnish.

"I got my own rooms and my workshop upstairs," Lavinia said. "But I work mainly at night, so I won't bother you a bit. And I'll keep the small folks from coming down the stairs and hassling you."

Bree managed to keep the astonishment from her voice. "You have children?"

Lavinia's giggle was so infectious Bree found herself laughing, too. "And at my age, young Bree! No, no *children* upstairs at all."

Pets, then. Bree tended to trust people who had pets. She looked around one more time. Lavinia was right. The office space was a bargain, even with the hideous surroundings outside and the mysterious golden dog hair inside. A few dedicated gardening weekends in the old cemetery would make a dramatic difference.

Take it, the voice in Bree's head said. She trusted that inner voice. It'd been with her all her life. It'd led her to law school, to the job in her father's firm, and here, to Savannah. It had also warned her against her last lover, Payton the Rat. She hadn't listened to it then. And look at all the misery that had come from that.

She'd take it.

"I would very much appreciate the opportunity to rent this space from you, Lavinia."

"I would very much like to rent to you, honey."

Solemnly, they shook hands. Lavinia's fingers were dry and cool and felt like the bones of small birds.

The decision made, Bree stood a little taller in relief. "Now, if I could take a look at the lease?" A contract was familiar territory; she'd been feeling a little out of her depth until now.

"Lease," Lavinia snorted. "Honey, what would I need a lease for? You work out, you can rent this place from me as long as you like. You don't work out, we'll just agree to part ways."

"But I'll be making quite an investment, Mrs. Ma— I mean Lavinia. And I don't believe either one of us—"

"No lease." Lavinia shook her head. "Don't trust the courts. Don't trust the law. Trust in God. And," she added firmly, "my own good digestion."

Bree hesitated.

It's the right thing to do.

She *did* trust that voice; it was her own highly developed intuition, wasn't it? It had led her out of Raleigh and working for her nutty—if adorable—father, Royal Winston-Beaufort, and here to Georgia, where the very air smelled of freedom. She didn't have to take on her great-uncle's clients; his bequest had been "to see to their needs," and she could have parceled them out to existing law firms if she'd really wanted to. But Savannah was a chance at a life of her own and she'd grabbed at it.

"That's all right then." Lavinia, who seemed to have heard this internal dialogue, trotted out of the dining room, across the living room, and back to the foyer. Bree followed. Bree had long legs, especially measured against Lavinia's short ones, but she had to hurry to catch up. She found Lavinia wriggling the door latch impatiently.

"I've a lot to do upstairs, honey. So if you don't mind, you can show yourself out, as the saying goes. You can come back tomorrow and start moving in." She peered out the door, and up and down the street. "You be sure it's locked behind you. This here's a good neighborhood, but you just never know about kids these days. Not to mention the Josiah Pendergasts of this bad old world. This murderers' cemetery is the only place for a beast like that."

Bree's lawyer's conscience prodded her. "Don't you want to have a lease for your own protection, Lavinia? I mean, I'm surely flattered that you trust me on sight. But it *is* a hard old world out there. You're right. Just in case, why don't I bring a copy of a standard contract with me tomorrow?"

"T-uh," Lavinia said. "You can put your standard contracts where the sun don't shine." She reached up and curled a strand of Bree's long hair around one finger. "That's natural, isn't it, honey?"

"Well, yes." Bree blushed. She had very few vanities. Her luxuriant hair, long, white blonde, and as fine spun as sugar, was one of them.

Lavinia leaned in close. Bree caught the spicy scent of dried herbs and another, sweeter smell of exotic flowers. "You see those angels I painted on the stairs, don't you? Your hair's exactly the color of the bravest and the best one a-them." Her smile lit her face like a sun breaking over the horizon. "It's meant that you rent this place. Couldn't be clearer."

What *was* clear, Bree thought, was that her new landlady had a very small screw loose. But Lavinia's screws were definitely tighter than Aunt Corinne-Alice's or Great-uncle Franklin's. Both of those relatives had dabbled in some pretty weird stuff. And Bree had survived those eccentricities of her childhood just fine. "I'll see you tomorrow, then," she said. "And thank ..."

Lavinia whisked up the decorated stairs like a puff of smoke, leaving nothing but the scent of herbs and flowers behind.

"Mrs. Mather? Lavinia?"

No answer. Just the decisive slam of an upstairs door. Bree raised her voice a little, "I'll see you about ten o'clock, then?"

Not a word from her putative landlady. But the scent

of unfamiliar flowers drifted down and she caught the sounds of skittering feet. A cat, maybe, or a small dog. As for the perfume, Bree inhaled with pleasure. Roses, perhaps, and something more than roses. She waited a long moment to see if Lavinia would call down to her, then let herself out the front door.

Outside, the breeze had quickened and swung round from the west, bringing with it a foul odor of decay from the cemetery. Bree stopped short, horrified. She sneezed heartily. No wonder Lavinia perfumed the air. The stink was horrendous. Strange that she hadn't noticed it before.

She stood on the top step, irresolute, struck with the conviction that this rental was a really, really dumb idea. Unless Uncle Franklin's practice was limited to the smell-impaired, nobody would come back for a second appointment. And her clients would have to be really nearsighted not to disapprove of the derelict cemetery. The Historical Society wouldn't mind if she weeded and mulched, but she doubted sincerely that she'd be allowed to transform the place into something more habitable by moving the graves to a proper cemetery.

She thought suddenly of Josiah Pendergast. Lavinia didn't think he belonged in a proper cemetery at all. "This is the only place for a beast like that."

Phooey. Corpses didn't inhabit a place. They just occupied it. Like furniture. Highly unattractive furniture, from any prospective client's standpoint, and it was furniture that couldn't be tossed out in the trash.

On the other hand, the office was quiet. It was tucked far enough away from Bay Street that the noise of the city and the wharf was diminished to a mere grumble. And that was a plus, surely.

But the rotten scent hung around her like a dreadful cape. Bree pinched her nose shut, to see if it helped. Nope. The smell was everywhere. Quiet wasn't enough. This wasn't going to work. She turned to face the front door and stretched out her hand to knock again. She'd tell Mrs. Mather she was sorry. Somebody else would surely want the office space.

A scream of agony split the air.

Two

Vex not his ghost.
—*King Lear*, Shakespeare

Bree froze, hand upraised. The shriek came again, not, Bree realized almost at once, a human shriek, but the sound of an animal in pain. And it came from behind the decayed magnolia tree. She was off the steps and running toward the gravestones before she'd actually thought to move.

The howl trailed off to whimpers. Bree skidded to a stop in the middle of the graveyard. She took one deep, calming breath. It was stupid to rush into whatever it was. She stared intently at the magnolia tree. It was old and almost leafless, the bole the width of her shoulders. The terrible sounds came from behind it, she was sure of it. She set her briefcase down and slipped off her jacket.

"Hey!" she shouted. "Hey!"

The whimpers trailed off into silence.

A scrabble of dead leaves made her jump. She caught the back view of a skinny figure enveloped in a smoky mist. Bree blinked hard and rubbed her eyes.

"You, there," Bree called, "hang on a minute."

The figure turned at the sound of her voice. She caught

a brief glimpse of a white face, the mouth split in a terrible grin. The scent of decaying corpses was stronger now. Bree took an involuntary step back. She heard a thud, then another, and the sound of a bat or a stick falling onto flesh. The animal shrieked again. Bree shouted and sprang forward, fury almost overwhelming her common sense.

The shrieks stopped. Then whoever it was, whatever it was, jumped the wrought-iron fence and disappeared behind the brick warehouse that sat next to 66 Angelus Street. The whimpering remained behind and trailed off into a hoarse, painful panting that struck at her heart.

Bree raced back to her briefcase and slipped her cell phone into her skirt pocket. She grabbed one of the thick, dead branches that littered the pathway. She ducked under the Spanish moss that hung from the magnolia like hair, brushing the damp tendrils aside with an impatient hand.

A dog lay huddled against the far side of the trunk. It raised its head as she approached, its teeth drawn back in a snarl. Bree crouched a short distance away and used the voice that had calmed both foals and lambs when she was home at Plessey. "There now," she said. "There now."

The dog struggled to sit up. It was large, perhaps the size of a Labrador retriever. The dingy gold coat was snarled with burrs and twigs. It was horribly skinny, as if it hadn't eaten for days.

Bree put the branch down. The dog's hind leg was caught in a steel-jawed trap. At least it couldn't lunge far, if fear and panic drove it to bite.

"Easy," Bree said in a calm and cheerful voice. The dog sank back into the pile of leaves. Its tail gave a feeble thump. Bree edged forward on her knees, half-singing a constant "there now, there now." She laid one hand on the dog's head. It licked frantically at her wrist. She ran the other hand over the dog's matted ribs and down to the trapped leg. She knew this kind of trap. Her grandfather had banned it from Plessey years before, but not before he'd taught both Bree and her sister, Antonia, how to release animals captured in its teeth. She pressed the spring release and the jaws relaxed with a sudden twang. The dog jerked away from her soothing hand and struggled to its feet. *His* feet, Bree realized after a moment.

"Well, boy," Bree said. "You just steady on, now. Steady."

The dog's dark brown eyes met her own, briefly. Bree cupped her hand around his muzzle, and gently probed the injured leg. "It's broken, for sure," she said softly. "I'll have to carry you, pup. You going to mind that?"

The dog looked up at her, as if to deliberate. Then he sank limply back into the leaves. Bree slid one arm under his chest, and supported his hindquarters with the other. She struggled to her feet with a whoosh of effort. She hauled a hundredweight of horse feed around the barns at home, and the dog weighed less than that, but not by much. She staggered slightly as she left the cemetery and headed to the curb where she'd parked her little Fiat. No good at all to drag Lavinia into this. She'd call the police and the Humane Society from her car.

The dog just barely fit into the backseat. He lay quietly, not, as she feared, unconscious, but simply accepting her attempts to make him comfortable. She settled him as best she could, then went back to retrieve her briefcase and her suit jacket. Should she take the trap for evidence? Better to leave it, perhaps. The police usually wanted crime scenes undisturbed, didn't they? The trap was new; the stainless steel jaws blotched with the dog's blood. And it rested on a toppled gravestone. She knelt and brushed aside the leaves that covered the inscription, careful to avoid adding more of her fingerprints to the trap.

OLIVIA PENDERGAST
I CHRONICLES 29:15

"A relative of the restless Josiah," Bree mused aloud. "Yikes."

She rose to her feet and looked beyond the fence for the white-faced thing, or at least some trace that it'd been there. She found nothing, and after a second, even briefer search of the area around the magnolia, she keyed 911 into her phone and requested police presence to investigate a case of animal abuse, just off East Bay at Mulberry.

A squad car turned the corner almost before she'd slipped the cell phone back in her pocket. Bree lifted her hand and stepped off the curb. The siren was off, but the red lights flashing red-orange-red were scarier than the siren would have been. She cast a worried look up at the second story of the little house, but the curtains remained drawn and motionless. She wanted to keep this from Lavinia, if she could. The old were fragile. And there was something particularly horrifying about animal abuse. As tough as she was, it'd likely scare poor Lavinia into the next county.

The squad car drew to a noiseless stop next to her. The officer inside was young, pink-faced, and alone.

Bree smiled at him. "Thank you for coming so quickly, Officer."

"I was just around the corner, ma'am."

She looked past his shoulder to a tray of Starbucks coffee on the front seat next to him. He followed her glance and blushed. "The guys sent … that is, I volunteered for the coffee run. Since I was right close when the call came in, I said I'd take it." He put the cruiser into park and emerged from the driver's seat. His uniform looked as if it'd just been unwrapped from the box it came in. His black shoes were shiny and new. And he carried a brightly painted baton, and no gun. He stuck his hand out, and said, "Officer Dooley Banks, ma'am."

Bree took his hand a little dubiously. She hadn't much experience with the police. But this guy surely didn't behave like the cops on *Law & Order*. "Brianna Winston-Beaufort," she said. Then added, "Attorney-at-law."

He touched his cap, "Miss Beaufort. You had some complaint about animal abuse?"

—◆◆◆—

"I suppose," Bree said into the phone some hours later, "that I was purely lucky that Officer Banks had been on the force all of oh, five minutes. Maybe less."

"Lucky?" her mother echoed. "Lucky? I don't want you anywhere near that place, Bree honey. It sounds dangerous. And you said it's in the middle of a cemetery?"

"It's a very pleasant cemetery," Bree said, fingers firmly crossed. "And Mrs. Mather's as sweet as can be. In her late seventies, if I'm any judge. Just a nice old lady, Mamma."

"And what do you mean, lucky?" her father demanded. "You have any trouble at all getting the right kind of attention from those people in Savannah, you let me know, hear?"

Even on the extension, two hundred miles south of the town house, her father's nosy concern set Bree's back up. And she'd edited out the truly eerie parts of her day's adventure. But she said mildly, "Well, a dog with a broken leg's more a case for the ASPCA than the police. But Officer Banks filled out a report just as nice as you please. So if it was a malicious act, and I do catch the guy, they can charge him."

"You took the poor thing to the pound, didn't you?" her mother said. "You know the town house rules about dogs."

Bree gazed at the ceiling. She was calling from the living room. The Oriental carpets on the pinewood floors were faded with age. Her grandmother's grand piano occupied the corner closest to the fireplace. Floor-to-ceiling bookshelves lined either side of the French doors to the balcony. Beyond the balcony, the Savannah River drifted by. It was all familiar, and much beloved. "The crown molding's getting a little chippy," she said. "Do you think I should have the painters in?"

This diverted her mother's attention, as she'd hoped it would. "Why, we just had the whole place repainted not five years ago," she said indignantly.

"Ten," her father said impatiently. "It's been ten years or more, Francesca. But maybe we should have the painters in, Bree honey. We can hurry right down and see for ourselves, if you like. We can be in there in five hours. Less."

"No need," Bree said hastily. "Now that I look a little closer, it's just cobwebs." She got a firmer grasp on the phone. "Now, look. I'm so glad y'all called. But I've a couple of résumés to look over tonight."

"It's well after eight," her mother protested.

Bree didn't say anything. This kind of intrusive, loving, crazy-making concern was one of the reasons she was here in Savannah, and not practicing law at home.

"You know how you get." Francesca pressed on. "You've been sleeping okay, Bree darlin'? She hasn't been eating again, Royal. I just know it."

"I've been eating just fine," Bree said firmly.

"You're going to keep on working after the kind of day you had?" Francesca demanded.

"I'm going to need someone to answer the phones, at the very least," Bree said. "I've been getting some pretty good responses to the ad I put in the *Savannah Daily*. And since I'll be moving into the new offices tomorrow, it'll be a good thing to have someone around to give me a hand sooner rather than later. So I need to start interviewing."

"For all of that, sweetie," her father said instantly, "we can come on down and give you *four* hands."

"Yes, indeed," her mother said. "And you'll want someone to help you pick out the right color paint. And what about drapes?"

Bree suppressed a groan. "I appreciate that. I truly do. But I have to go now. And thanks for calling, y'all. I'll talk to you later in the week."

"But Bree . . ." her father said.

"Now, Royal," her mother said. "Don't scold. Bree, you just let me know what your color scheme is going to be and I can bring down a couple of samples . . ."

In desperation, Bree jiggled the call button in the handset and shouted, "Hello? Hello? Mamma? You're fading on me!"

"We're losin' you, Bree!" her mother shrieked. "Royal,

it's that cheatin' phone company again! I swear that company has it in for you, Bree."

"Sorry, Mamma! You're breaking up! Bye, Mamma!" Bree set the phone into its rest and sank into a nearby armchair with a sigh of relief. "Woof," she said.

"Woof," said the dog at her feet.

She sat up. "And *you*," she said to the dog, severely, "are an illegal alien, pup."

The dog looked into her eyes and gently wagged his tail. He lay nested on an old duvet she'd found tucked in the back of the linen closet. A neat acrylic cast encased his injured leg from hock to ankle. The veterinary clinic she'd taken him to had bathed and clipped him, too. Free of burdocks and dirt, his coat was a yellow that would deepen to burnished gold once she got him onto healthy food.

"The town house covenants don't allow pets over forty pounds," she added. "So you're looking at a temporary stay. Just till you get on your feet."

The dog flattened his ears and cocked his head sorrowfully. Bree suppressed a stab of guilt.

"When you get a bit better we see about taking you home to Plessey. Mamma and Daddy could use a project other than me and Antonia."

The dog cocked his head in the other direction, looking, if possible, even more sorrowful than before. Bree scowled at him in exasperation. "For heaven's sake, dog. I'm just—" She stopped in mid-sentence. Was she really sitting here trying to justify her actions to a dog?

She rose briskly from the armchair. "Think you can eat a bit more, pup?" The vet had been gravely shocked at the animal's condition. A few ounces of digestible food every three hours was the most the dog could handle for the first few days. Bree had given him a cup of cooked rice and hamburger when she'd brought him home a few hours ago. It was time to give him another.

The dog struggled to his feet.

"No, no. You lie back down. You don't want to jiggle that leg any."

The dog sank back against the duvet with a resigned sigh. The vet had guessed he was a cross between a Russian mastiff and a golden retriever. "That round skull is a characteristic of the golden, Miss Beaufort. And the square, rather intelligent face is wholly mastiff."

"Rather intelligent," Bree said aloud, remembering the conversation. "You smart dog, you."

The dog grinned, reminding Bree of her own long-dead golden, Sunny Skies. He'd smiled at her in just that way until the day he slid into a final peaceful sleep.

"You sweet old thing," Bree said affectionately. This dog did remind her of Sunny, at least a little. "I'll just bet you had a good owner at one time, didn't you? You surely do respond to people. And I can't just keep calling you 'pup.'" Bree tugged thoughtfully at her ear. "What about Sam?"

The dog looked at her, tongue lolling.

"No? What about Goldy? That's what color your coat's going to be when we get you all cleaned up."

The dog closed his eyes, and then opened them again.

"Well, I don't suppose *you* have any ideas," Bree said with some exasperation.

The dog sneezed twice. It was an odd sort of sneeze. Almost sibilant.

"Sneezy," Bree said instantly. "Like one of the Seven Dwarves."

The dog curled his lip in a truly expressive sneer. Bree laughed. Her little sister, Antonia, would love this dog. And she'd come up with a good name, too. But Antonia was many miles and a state away at the University of South Carolina. "So I'll just have to come up with something all on my own."

The dog sneezed again, almost deliberately. "Sha! Shaa!"

"Sasha," Bree said. "That's it. For the Russian in you."

Sasha gave a great sigh of relief and settled his head on his paws. Feeling pleased with herself, Bree brought him another small bowl of food, and settled down in the armchair next to him with the stack of résumés and her own meal of salmon and salad.

The ad she'd placed in the *Savannah Daily* was straightforward:

Pleasant office ass't for one-man attnys office.
Computer-literate. Some bkping.

The responses ranged from the hopelessly hopeful: "I think it would be, like, very cool to work for a lawyer. I can come every day after school" to the comically desperate: "I've got a PhD in English literature from the University of North Carolina. Will work for food."

Bree sorted through half a dozen replies, and set aside two. She held her first choice aloft for Sasha's inspection. "This one seems likeliest, pup. A widow, poor thing. And she worked in her husband's law office until he died. All the right credentials, I think. And this one ..." She reread the cover letter again. "This one's so interesting I might just call him, too."

Sasha raised his head and gazed at her.

"He's a window-dresser, or was. And he wants to change careers. He's been going to night school to better himself, he says. Just the kind of person you want to give a hand up to."

Sasha looked politely interested.

"On the other hand, the widow's experienced. And she doesn't come right out and say it, but it appears she's fallen on hard times."

Sasha growled quietly.

"That's right, pup," Bree said, amused. "Tough section of town. So she might need a hand up, too."

Sasha growled again. This time he meant business. Bree set the résumés on the end table and got to her feet. The dog had propped himself up on his forelegs. He stared at the French doors to the balcony, his lips drawn back from his teeth. His growl snarled into a bark.

"Hush, now, Sasha." Bree went to the glass doors. She braced one hand against the bookshelf to the right of the door and peered into the dark. The moon was a quarter full in the misty sky. The lights of the city glittered on the banks of the river. "There's nothing out there. Nothing except the moon."

Suddenly, Sasha leaped at the doors, knocking her aside and snarling like a demon.

A white face grinned at her through the fragile barrier of glass. A white face enveloped in a column of smoke.

Three

Hated by fools, and fools to hate,
Be that my motto, and my fate.
—"To Dr. Delany, on the libels written against him,"
Jonathan Swift

Sasha whirled around and thrust himself at Bree. Both of them fell backward onto the sofa. The dog jumped awkwardly into her lap and for a moment, between the hundred-plus pounds of dog on her chest and stomach and her astonishment, she couldn't breathe. She placed both hands on the dog's muscular chest and shoved hard. "You're goin' to screw up that leg! Will you *get off*!"

Sasha stuck his nose under her arm and growled.

Bree made a huge effort to pull herself together. "I'm close to losing my temper," she said mildly. "I'm going to count to three. By the time I get there, you'd better settle *down*."

Sasha brought his head up and panted heavily into her face. Bree found herself panting, too.

Abruptly, the door buzzer shrilled. Sasha turned his head, hopped onto the rug, and limped to the front door, his ears pinned back. The buzzer sounded again. Bree got to her feet, tugged her T-shirt into place, and followed him. Her heart thudded hard in her chest and she was dismayed to find her legs trembly. There had been something horrible about that face. Just like the face in the grave-yard. She took a deep, deliberate breath and quelled the impulse to root around in the closet for her baseball bat before she opened the door. She looked through the security hole. She snorted and looked down at the dog.

"It's the UPS man. Or woman, rather."

Sasha's ears went up.

"You might guess from the tone of my voice that I'm not all that pleased about your behavior. Now, the poor girl shouldn't have tapped at the French doors like that, to be sure. But don't you think you overreacted just a little bit?"

Sasha's tail wagged back and forth.

"If you're thinking that maybe *I* overreacted a bit, you're darn right."

Sasha cocked his head.

"Will you lie down and behave?"

Sasha flopped awkwardly to the floor. Bree opened the door. The outside air was soft, damp, and smelled strongly of burnt matches. A large cardboard box sat on the doormat. The girl from UPS was already halfway down the walk, headed back to her truck. Bree called "thank you" after her retreating back.

Hesitantly, she stepped onto the small cement square that served as a front porch, and peered into the dark. Nothing. Familiar noises from Market Street drifted up toward her. She rubbed both her arms, to drive off the un-natural cold, then picked up the box and brought it in.

It was fairly heavy. When Bree shook it, the contents slid very little. She placed it on the dining room table. The address read: Brianna Winston-Beaufort, Esq, and the return address made her exclaim with pleasure. "Pro-

fessor Cianquino," she said. "You know who that is, dog?
My law advisor, from Duke. He retired the same year I
took the bar. He's got a nice little apartment just outside
Savannah, on the river. If you behave well enough for me
to keep you around, you'll meet him."

Sasha pawed at a dining room chair and poked his
nose inquisitively into the air. Bree peeled the packing
tape back from the edges and opened it.

The contents were tightly packed. There was a small
envelope on top, and a brand new cell phone still in the
package. The rest of the box held stationery. She opened
the envelope first. The card inside had Cianquino's name
embossed on the front: Armand Cianquino, Triad Professor of History of Law Emeritus. A line of small print at
the bottom read: Act Uprightly, 5:11. The handwritten
message inside merely said: *So battle is enjoined, my
dear Bree! With affection, Armand.*

Bree pulled the contents out, one by one. There were
two reams of letterhead, a package of number ten envelopes, a shrink-wrapped set of preprinted address labels,
and a hundred legal-sized envelopes with the return address on the upper left hand corners. She opened the small
square box that held the business cards and looked
thoughtfully at the design.

Brianna Winston-Beaufort
66 Angelus
(555) 567-9561

The font was attractive, if a little stuffy; a variety of
Edwardian script, maybe. She wasn't at all sure about the

raised gold logo. Should a lawyer even have a logo? It was a pair of feathery wings cupping a justice scale. As for the cell phone that was obviously the source of the telephone number on the stationery ... Professor Cianquino was clearly eager to give her a running start on an actual caseload.

This was just plain weird. Professor Cianquino wasn't into encouragement of his students before or after they graduated, and was, in fact, notoriously unsympathetic to human emotion of any kind. His twin gods were logic and reason. And here she was, his dear Bree? With a pile of expensive, unwanted stationery as a sort of office warming gift and a quote from the Koran from a guy who subscribed to the sayings of Confucius if he had any kind of religion at all. And how did he know her temporary office address? She'd just rented the space this morning.

And then there was the gift of the cell phone.

Bree picked up the package. It was the latest Apple, equipped with the kind of bells and whistles that encouraged messing around with the hot technology instead of getting any work done. She'd had her eye on this model, but she had a perfectly good cell phone of her own. Unlike the stationery, she could give this back to Professor Cianquino with heartfelt thanks for the thought. And a little white lie that she had one already.

The cell phone box played the opening bars of "O Thou That Tell'st Good Tidings to Zion," which Bree could identify only because she'd had to sing it at the St. Christopher's Episcopal Church Christmas pageant when she was sixteen. The first few bars played over and over again. *O thou that tell'st ... O thou that tell'st ...* until Bree stuck her fingers in her ears and yelled "Aagh!" so that she didn't have to hear it anymore.

The ring stopped, finally, and through the layers of cardboard, Bree heard the automated message reply: *You have reached Ms. Winston-Beaufort's message service. Please leave your name, number, and a detailed message after the tone.*

Then the quavering, confused voice of an old, old man. "Damn! Where in hell do they put the people?" He cleared his throat and bellowed, "Is there a confounded human bean at t'other end of this line? This is Benjamin Skinner. And I want me a goddamn *person*. And after I get that person, I want me a lawyer!"

The dial tone sounded. Benjamin Skinner hung up.

Bree stared at the box. Benjamin "Blackheart" Skinner—if it actually *was* Benjamin "Blackheart" Skinner—was Georgia's most reclusive billionaire. He had a lifelong habit of relieving major corporations of closely held assets. "Which makes him, dog, the richest man in Georgia, if not the entire United States of America, as well as the meanest. At least for right now. So why is he calling me?" There wasn't any friendly "woof" in reply. Bree looked under the table. Sasha was curled up on the carpet, fast asleep.

Not more than a week away from her family's clutches and reduced to asking a dog for advice. "And even if you could give me any, you look so plain pitiful it'd be a shame to wake you up." She got up. She needed a glass of wine and a to-do list, in that order. The wine would calm her down, and the to-do list would help make sense of the questions banging around in her head like so many bumper cars at the county fair.

Or she could call Mr. Skinner back on Professor Cianquino's cell phone and get the two biggest questions answered right now:

Why did you call me, and not some white shoe law firm that's been practicing law in Savannah since the Civil War?

And what do you want?

She glanced at the clock over the fireplace mantel; nine thirty. Too late to call Professor Cianquino, although clearly not too late for Mr. Skinner. She remembered an article about him in *Forbes* magazine. In addition to being pathologically camera-shy, he was a notorious night owl, supposedly existing on two to three hours of sleep at night. "Not that I believe that for a New York minute," Bree muttered. All that told her was the man had a PR firm so powerful it could spin the toughest journalist. She sat at the table, sliced the cellophane covering the box with the tip of her fingernail, and opened it up. She paused and bit her lip.

The cell phone was wrapped in its component parts, just as it'd come from the factory.

The charger was in a sealed plastic bag. So was the phone. And so was the battery.

So how had the call come through? For that matter, why had she heard the automated reply?

She pressed the "send" button through the plastic bag. The little screen stayed dark. The phone itself was mute. Very curious now, Bree put the phone together and turned it on. The screen glowed. A text message appeared: "Missed Call." Bree clicked on "send" and a phone number appeared on the screen, identified as "The Skinner." She pressed "send" again. It rang three times before it was picked up, and a young male voice demanded, "Who's this?"

"This is Brianna Beaufort," Bree said, with more than a trace of annoyance. "I'm an attorney. Who's this?"

"Jesus," the voice said in disgust. Then, to someone near to him, "They're circling already." His voice came back on the line. "Call in the morning. Better yet, don't call at all."

Bree bit her lip, hard, which helped her manage to say politely, "I'm sorry to trouble you, sir. I'm returning a call from my cell phone, from a man who identified himself as Benjamin Skinner. May I speak to him?"

"This is Grainger Skinner, his son. Mr. Skinner isn't available," he said flatly. "If you have business with the family, I suggest you wait until tomorrow."

"Mr. Skinner wanted to talk to me right away," Bree said courteously. "Would you tell him that I returned his call as soon as I could?"

"Wasn't soon enough, Ms. Beaufort. Turn on the news. Mr. Skinner died this afternoon at his home on Tybee Island."

Bree's face went hot with an immediate, profound embarrassment. Skinner's call was a joke. A prank. Someone was jerking her chain, big-time. She wanted to crawl under the table and sit next to Sasha. Instead, she managed a deep breath and to stutter, "Sir, I am *deeply* sorry to have troub—" before the brusque and justifiably irritated Skinner, junior, shut her off.

It'd be rubbing salt in the wound to turn on the ten o'clock news and get the particulars of Benjamin Skinner's death. She poured herself a glass of wine and settled on the sectional to watch as a kind of penance.

All of the stations led off with the story. There wasn't any question about it. Eighty-four-year-old Benjamin "Blackheart" Skinner had keeled over from a catastrophic heart attack while sailing with his son and daughter-in-law and drowned in the coastal waters of the Atlantic.

They'd hauled him back to the thirty-thousand-foot mansion he'd built on Tybee Island, but, as the perky news anchor said energetically, "All efforts at resuscitation failed."

Enough time had gone by for reporters to nail down a few interviews with Skinner's associates. Death hadn't done much to improve the business world's opinion of him. Comments came from Douglas Fairchild, his politely dubious partner in local construction projects, "You're sure he's really gone? Bennie's a tricky son of a (bleep!), God bless him." Carlton Montifiore, the overtly hostile plaintiff in Skinner's latest and most notorious lawsuit, snapped, "A heart attack? Fat chance. The (bleep!) didn't have a heart."

On the other hand, Skinner's departure was sincerely regretted by a silicone-enhanced blonde occupying the penthouse at a condo development called Island Dream. These multimillion-dollar luxury condos fronting the ocean on Tybee Island were one of Skinner's newest projects. "He loved me," Chastity McFarland breathed at the TV cameras. "And he would have wanted me to have the best. This apartment, f'instance. When he left me this morning, he was on his way to the lawyers to get me the deed. What I've got here is a verbal contract." She glared into the cameras. "And I'm not moving one (bleeping!) inch. I got my rights, see. And if you ask me"—she leaned forward, giving the person behind the camera a good look at her cleavage—"it was murder!"

The station ran a months-old clip featuring Skinner himself—a thin, blue-suited figure with a newspaper held up his face to keep the cameras away. He'd emerged victorious from the Chatham County Courthouse after yet another class action suit over lead paint in his New York slums. His lawyer, John Stubblefield, offered "no comment." Skinner dropped the newspaper, his bright blue eyes glaring into the camera. He snarled, "You want a comment? I'll give you a comment. I told those bozos they could shove it up their (bleep!) when they first tried to sue the pants off'n me." The newspaper shielding his face quivered as he chuckled. "So our great justice system done it for me."

The camera cut to the perky blonde reporter standing on the beach at Tybee Island. Behind her rose a multistory condominium. The pink stucco wall at the entrance sported a sign that read: ISLAND DREAM. "Benjamin Skinner's death is only the latest in a series of problems that have plagued the multimillion-dollar Island Dream. Early this morning, county building inspector Rebus Kingsley plunged to his death from the penthouse ..."

With a brief "poor soul" for the unfortunate Rebus Kingsley, Bree switched the TV off and thought about Benjamin Skinner.

He had a distinctive voice. Raspy, high-pitched, easy to imitate. She frowned at the blank screen. Who'd set her up? And why?

The "who" part was easy. There was only one person who made a part-time career out of making her crazy.

"Antonia," she said crossly.

Her tone of voice jerked Sasha out of a sound sleep. He raised his head, thumped his tail anxiously on the floor, then thudded over to the couch and put his head on her knee.

"You haven't met her, dog. Antonia's my adorable little sister."

She had Antonia's number on speed dial. She glanced at her watch. Quarter to eleven. Antonia had a bit part in

the current revival of *Oklahoma!* at the Richmond Hill
Community Theater. The cast should have finished up the
final "Okla-Okla-Homa-Homa" fifteen minutes ago. She
caught her sister on the third ring.

"Breenie!"

"Don't call me Breenie," Bree said automatically.
"Where are you?"

"At the theater."

"I know you're at the theater. Where are you *in* the theater?"

"Headed out to Tybalt's for the cast party. This was
our last night. We only had one curtain call, Bree. And I
thought they were going to give us a standing ovation, but
no-o-o. Do you know why half the audience stood up?"

"To get a head start on the traffic," Bree said.

"To get a head start on the *traffic*," Antonia agreed in
indignation. "I mean, here we are, dancing and singing our
little guts out, and all those folks want to do is get to bed
early. I ask you. Whatever happened to common courtesy?
Whatever happened to decent manners? Doesn't anybody
care about craft anymore? On top of that, it's not even
nice."

"Speaking of common courtesy, speaking of good
manners, speaking of *nice*," Bree said, suddenly furious.
"I do *not* in any way, shape, or form appreciate the little
joke you played on me."

"What little joke?"

"I have two words: Benjamin Blackheart Skinner."

"That's three words. And who's he?"

"I suppose that you and Professor Cianquino couldn't
know he was going to up and die on me," Bree said, con-
ceding that, at least. "But the old geezer did, this afternoon, and of course I called him back, and of course I got

somebody from the family and I was absolutely, totally humiliated." Bree felt herself choke up. She wasn't surprised. What with the tortured dog, the weird little old lady at the cemetery, the police, and the scare put into her by the UPS delivery woman, she'd had a pretty bad day. "It wasn't funny!"

"Are you *crying*?" Antonia demanded. "Bree, I can count the times you've cried because you were sad since high school on one hand. Well, maybe two," she conceded. "There was the breakup with Payton the Rat. And when the old dog Sunny passed on. Now, if you count the times you cry when you're totally pissed off, that's another kind of crying altogether and doesn't truly count. I'd have to be a centipede to keep count of those."

"Just chill for a minute, okay?" Bree scrounged in the pocket of her jeans for a tissue and blew her nose. "I've had a long day, that's all. And I wanted to let you know that your little joke backfired."

"I have no idea what you're talking about. Honestly. Whatever it is, you want to tell me about it? You want me to skip the cast party and drive on over?"

"It's hours to Savannah and it's going on to eleven. No, I don't want you to drive on over. Besides, haven't you got class tomorrow?"

"School," Antonia said thoughtfully, and then clammed up.

Bree rolled over the silence on the other end of the phone, noting, in passing, that it was a guilty kind of silence. Her aggravating little sister had probably dropped out of another school. This would send their parents into fits. Bree wasn't going to worry about that now. "You're telling me you didn't get together with Professor Cianquino and set this up?"

"You mean that old geezer from law school? I haven't seen him since you had the third-year reunion out at the house."

"Don't call him a geezer," Bree said. "And that's exactly who I mean. And why did you think I wouldn't want to pick out my own stationery?"

"Why don't you start by telling me what's going on," Antonia said, suddenly practical.

Bree told her.

"No! Of all the skunky things to do. And the old fart kicked off this afternoon? Holy gee. Well, it wasn't me. I'm insulted that you thought it was." Antonia sighed, her voice gentle. "It was a mean old trick to play on you, sister. I'm truly sorry."

"If it wasn't you, who, then?" Bree demanded.

"Gee, I don't know. Try Payton the Rat? Nothing like an ex-boyfriend with vengeance in his heart."

"Payton," Bree said. "Good glory. You might be right." That relationship had ended badly. It even went some way toward explaining why Professor Cianquino let Payton buy the phone, as he must have done. Payton graduated magna cum laude the same year she did. Professor Cianquino had a genuine respect for brilliance. And he wouldn't have known about the breakup, which had been all of three weeks ago.

"You still there?" Antonia demanded. "If it was Payton, are you going to get mad and go after him with a garden rake?"

"I'm still here. And if it was Payton, I'm not going to go after him with any kind of gardening tool."

"You went after that shoplifter at Home Depot with a garden rake," Antonia reminded her.

"He knocked over that little kid on his way out the door," Bree reminded her. "And I'm so over losing my temper these days it isn't funny." She stuffed the tissue back into her jeans pocket. "Sorry about bein' weepy. I guess I lost my professional cool."

"Save it for the clients," Antonia advised. "Nobody's better at professional cool than you. But you can cry into my ear any old time."

"Okay. Thanks."

"Of course, nobody's better at losing it than you, either."

"You can stop there right now," Bree said.

"Forget the garden rake. Remember that time you dived over the desk at that guy in moot court? Had him by the throat in two seconds flat, that's what I heard."

"You heard wrong."

"And they suspended you for how long?" Antonia asked innocently.

"A day. And I apologized. Actually, I crawled like a slug and ate dirt," Bree said ruefully. "But that was years ago, and have I pulled a stunt like that again? No, I have not."

"And I think I will drive on over, if you don't mind. I was thinking about comin' to stay with y'all for a few days anyhow. And it sounds like you need a hand settling in."

"I do mind. And I don't need a thing," Bree said firmly. "I'll stop in to see Professor Cianquino tomorrow, and he can clear this up. And then I've got a pile of people to interview to set the office up. You get on back to UNC."

"School," Antonia said in that thoughtful way. "About school."

"You drop out of UNC, you're going to have both Mom and Dad on your back like fleas on a hedgehog. And don't count on me to stop them."

"So much for sisterly solidarity."

"You finish up your degree," Bree said, "you might end up knowing how to spell it, at least."

Antonia clicked off with a derisive shriek.

Bree swallowed the last of her wine, and addressed the dog. "We're going to think about this tomorrow."

She took a hot shower, pulled on an oversized T-shirt, and got ready for bed. She was drifting off to sleep when the face at the French windows popped up in her mind's eye like a card trick. She sat up, suddenly chilled. It hadn't been the UPS woman. She was sure of it. It'd been a man's face on the other side of the glass, with the coldest blue eyes she'd ever seen, wrapped in a graveyard shroud.

Four

Grrr—there go, my heart's abhorrence!
—"Soliloquy of the Spanish Cloister," Robert Browning

She slept. And as she slept, the old nightmare came back to haunt her.

Bree dreamed of drowning, and the shrieks of drowning men. She woke up with a shout, just as the birds were stirring in the trees outside her window, her right hand stretched out to pull the shrieking figures from a dark and turbulent sea. She wrapped the duvet around her shoulders, then rubbed her face furiously with both hands.

She'd had this dream when she was young. It was always the same. She floated in an ocean she'd never seen before. Someone loomed over her. A woman, she thought, with black hair and pale eyes, whose features were hidden by a smear of dark shadow. A sound of wings disturbed the air. No—not a sound. A percussion of wings that beat inside her head, chest, and lungs.

And then, suddenly, there was a creation-splitting explosion in the vastness of the sky and the sea rose up to take her. Sometimes the heavens burst with dark and deadly looking fire; sometimes with a light so brilliant that she wept at the beauty of it.

Both fire and light foretold the deaths. The bodies rose

up from the depths of the sea and fell from the storm-cloud sky. They swirled soundlessly, lightly around her, their fingers trailing across her cheeks, their hair brushing her hands. They fell like leaves in a forest. And she dived and dived again to save them, and each time the bodies slipped away and the faceless woman with the black hair called "Bree!"

She hadn't had the nightmare for years.

It was back? Now, after all these years, here, in this luxuriously comfortable bed where she felt so safe?

Bree shuddered with panic and drew the duvet closer around her shoulders. When she was very young, and Antonia a toddler, her mother would come to her in the night and bring her hot, sweet tea to drink, and talk away the nightmare. But the dream had gone away when she'd turned twelve, gone, she'd thought, for good.

And now it was back.

"Well, *that's* a hell of a note," she said aloud. She pulled on a robe, then stared at her face in the bureau mirror. Her own adult face stared back at her. There was a furrow between her eyebrows and her lower lip trembled. And behind her, looking over her shoulder was ... what? She whirled around to see nothing at all except the canopy bed with its rumpled bedclothes and pillows scattered on the rose-carpeted floor. "Too many weird things all at once," she said aloud. "So just straighten up, Beaufort. And lay off that third glass of wine from here on in." She ran her hands through her hair, then tugged hard at it.

She went into the kitchen to make a cup of strong coffee. She helped Sasha into the backyard and back into the house again. Then she pulled on a pair of sweats and went for a jog by the river. By the time she came back, pleasantly loose from the exercise, she'd pushed the nightmare memory back where it belonged, all the way back to her childhood. She would forget it. She absolutely would forget it.

She spooned a can of dog food into Sasha's bowl, put two cartons of yogurt into a bowl for herself, added a huge handful of Sugar Crisp, and sat down at the kitchen table. The two of them ate in a companionable silence. Sasha finished first, then limped over to the table and looked up at her with an expression that said as clearly as anything did: Now what?

Bree looked back at him. "Now what, is work. You're going to want more of that dog food as time goes on, I expect, and it doesn't come free."

She decided to spend the first half hour of her day on the phone and set up an initial round of employee interviews. She'd use the rest of the morning to shop for office furniture and supplies.

Both her choices were at home. Ronald Parchese was pathetically eager for a chance to leave window-dressing at Dillard's for the more sterile environs of a law office. ("It's Par-chay-zay," he said earnestly, "like the board game, only more aristocratic.") Rosa Lucheta mentioned rather diffidently that she'd been taking evening paralegal courses and she missed the excitement of the legal life. Bree set up interviews with both for Wednesday afternoon at the Angelus office, confident she could at least partially equip the place by then. She left a message on Professor Cianquino's answering machine, thanking him for the gift. She also suggested lunch as soon as he was free, at the restaurant of his choice. Then she sat down at her computer and dashed off a polite form letter to the others who'd responded to her ad for an assistant and addressed the envelopes. She showered, changed into one of the elegant suits that was her work uniform, and at nine o'clock sat down for a second cup of coffee. She'd accomplished quite a lot already.

"Except for what to do with you, Sasha."

He looked up alertly when she spoke his name aloud. He was curled up on his duvet. His bandaged hind leg stuck out at an awkward angle and the healing sores on his flanks looked itchy. She was mindful of the vet's orders of small amounts of food every two to three hours for the next couple of days. How could she do her interviews, get her office set up, and take care of him, too? She didn't know how women with kids handled them and a career, too.

She couldn't skip the feedings. The sores on his haunches had begun to clear already. His eyes were bright and hope-filled. Even his coat looked less scruffy. Amazing what a good night's rest and the right kind of food could do.

A mental review of the state of her checking account made her drop the idea of day boarding. "I could take you in the car, I suppose," she said doubtfully. "The weather's just fine." The day had dawned bright and cool. October in Savannah meant the end of the enervating heat, and if she put his improvised bed on the backseat, he'd be comfortable enough. The alternative was dashing back to the town house at intervals during the day.

A third option suddenly occurred to her and she smiled. She should have thought of it before.

⚬⚬⚬

"You make no never mind about that dog," Lavinia said confidently as Bree set the dog at her feet with a grunt of effort. "I'll see to those nasty scratches right enough. And

you feedin' him that store-bought dog food?" She clicked
her tongue disapprovingly. "I got me some stewed
chicken and rice. That'll put a spring in his step, no doubt
about it." She looked at Sasha sternly. "You know what
they put into that canned stuff? If I told you, it'd turn your
stomach for sure."

Bree went back to her car, and returned with the rolled
up duvet, the water bowl, and a cardboard box filled with
dog food, ointment, and fresh bandages. She set them at
the foot of the stairs in the foyer. Sasha limped once
around the living room's perimeter, then came back and
curled up at the foot of the stairs.

"I truly appreciate this, Mrs. Mather."

"Lavinia. You need to go back to callin' me Lavinia."
She'd changed her soft wooly gray sweater for a soft
wooly lavender sweater. Her black skirt drooped around
her slippered feet. A bit of what looked like chamomile
was stuck in the hair piled into a knot on the top of her
head. She crossed her arms and beamed at her scruffy-
looking patient, like some raffish fairy godmother.

"Lavinia," Bree said obediently. "You're certain it's
not too much of a bother? You said something about your
own pets yesterday morning, and I thought you might not
mind giving him a bit of a hand." She looked up and past
the brightly painted stairs, where her landlady's apartment sat overhead. The pleasant herby smell was much in
evidence, but no sound came from the second floor. "I
surely don't want to take advantage."

"Tougher folks than you have tried," she said. "This
here's nothing at all."

"Thank you." Bree took the rent envelope out of her
briefcase and handed it over. "I've written out a check for
one month's security deposit and two months' rent. And

you'll find a lease in there. I wish you'd take a look at the terms and think about signing it."

Lavinia took the envelope with a pleased expression.

"I'll be off now, to find office furniture and make a start on supplies."

"Can't do better than that Second Hand Rows for furniture," Lavinia said. "That there's a charity for the Sinai Temple. You'll find those folks right off of Whitaker Street, near Montgomery. Got them a bunch of good bargains. You'd be amazed at what folks just throw away. Perfectly good sofas and all, just tossed out for the poor folks, God bless 'em."

Bree thanked her for the idea, not sure whether Lavinia had blessed the poor folks or the folks at Second Hand Rows. The few pieces of office furniture her uncle left her were in storage while the offices were renovated. She planned on using his chair and desk for herself. But she needed to equip the place for her assistant. "I'd like to start moving in tomorrow morning? And then I've scheduled some employee interviews for tomorrow afternoon."

"Be good to have live people around the place again," Lavinia said.

"I'll be off, then." She bent down and ran her hand gently over Sasha's head. He flopped back against the second tread with a sigh of pleasure. One of the brightly painted Renaissance angels with silver gilt braids peeked out between his ears.

"Guarding him, like," Lavinia observed of the painted figure. "You hurry up and get better, dog, so she can get back to guarding the rest of us."

"I'll be back for him before six," Bree promised. "You and the angel take care, now."

She jogged down the brick steps, smiling at the old

woman's fancies, delighted that her day was beginning so well.

Her landlady was right about Second Hand Rows. She found a comfortably worn leather couch and chair, an old chest that would make a useful coffee table to put magazines on—for all those waiting clients—and a big oak table only slightly foxed from age. "Picked that up from when the old library over on Hudson Street closed down," the laconic cashier said. "You don't find tables that size no more. Gotta be twelve foot if it's one." He shifted his toothpick from the left side of his mouth to the right with an expert roll of his tongue. "Anything else I can do you for?"

"A desk," Bree said, "if possible."

He shook his head. He was tall and skinny, with the concave chest of a smoker. Bree could barely make out the Grateful Dead logo on his faded T-shirt. A paper label with a sticky back sat on his right sleeve that read: HELLO, MY NAME IS HENRY. "Fresh out of desks."

Bree pulled out her credit card. "Then we can settle up, if you wouldn't mind, Henry."

He nodded, punched the totals from the price tags into the register, and slid her card through the machine.

"You think you could deliver these things for me?"

"Free-delivery-on-large-items-less-than-ten-miles-from -the-store," Henry recited, clearly having said it before. "You setting up a new apartment or what?"

"Or what," Bree said. "It's an office. In a terrific old house by the cemetery on Angelus. I'm a lawyer, just starting out."

He stared at her. "That a fact. Angelus, you say. Mrs. Mather send you?"

"Are you familiar with it? It's that little old place right

in the middle of the cemetery. Kind of an odd place for a law office, I thought, but then, it's close to the Market, and the rent's about right. I'm making the living room into a client waiting area. It's got wood floors, a fireplace, wainscoting. It's really quite, quite *professional*."

"It's not *me* you need to convince, lady."

Bree smiled at him, and laughed a little. "You are absolutely right. I think I'm a little nervous about it. It's my new clients I have to convince, if," she added anxiously, "I'm to have any."

"Angelus Street, huh? Got something over here you might want to see." He slouched toward the jumble of boxes and racks of clothes, pots and pans and dishes at the rear of the store. He scrabbled in the pile farthest in the back, and emerged with a picture in his hands. He held it high, the cardboard back facing Bree. It was quite a large frame, at least forty inches square. Bree took a breath, prepared to be charming about her absolute refusal to have clown faces, or black velvet Elvises, or dogs playing poker over her vintage fireplace.

Henry flipped the painting around to face her.

Bree stumbled backward, as if from a blow. A fierce rush of light and sound crashed down upon her like a stupendous wall of water.

It was the landscape of her dream. The dark and bloody water roiled among the out-flung hands of the drowned and drowning. The dim hulk of a ship heaved on the horizon, and on the deck, the dark-haired, pale-eyed woman with her face obscured in shadow flung her hands out in despair. Over all, a giant bird spread its wings, a call to death and destruction. It was a cormorant, she realized, the Fisher King of birds. And for some, an avatar of the devil.

Bree fumbled for her cell phone in her purse with shaking hands. She had to call someone, she had to ... what?

Get a grip, get a grip, get a grip! She pinched herself hard, then again, hard enough to draw a bead of blood from her forearm.

Henry, oblivious, peered down at the painting. "It's the ocean," he said. "Kind of a shipwreck, I guess, with all them hands in the water." He looked up. "Kinda gruesome?"

Bree sat down on a battered metal chair and put her head between her knees. The first time and only time she'd fainted, she'd won a bet with her sister about who could bike up Market Hill the fastest. There wasn't going to be a second. Not if she could help it.

"You ain't pregnant or nothin'," Henry said in a kindly way. "Took my wife like that with our first kiddie. Just the first coupla months."

"I'm fine," Bree said as evenly as she could. She smiled a little. "And I'm perfectly unpregnant."

He flourished the painting. Bree faced it, the nightmare ocean in her dream, and said steadily, "Thank you kindly, Henry, but I think I'd better wait until I get all the furniture in place before I start adding ... art."

"Had some fella in here the other day, said this painting was by some guy named Turner. Or a copy of one, anyways."

"He must have meant *The Slave Ship*," Bree said. She was proud that her voice was level. "It's a very famous painting by J.M.W. Turner, an English artist. In the late eighteenth century, the captain of a slaver threw all the slaves who were sick or injured overboard to drown. It was a terrible tragedy. Turner immortalized it." She forced herself to look more closely at the painting. Maybe it was a copy of that grave and terrible work of art, and not the nameless ocean of her dreams, after all. The sky flamed with hellish red, orange, and yellows. The sea boiled with angry color. The ship looked like a coffin.

No. It was *her* ocean. *Her* nightmare. She was sure of it. For one thing, there was that shadow of a huge bird with outspread wings hanging in the sky. If fear had a form, it was that bird. And the drowned and drowning faces in the sea were all the colors of mankind. Not *The Slave Ship*, but something very like it.

She turned around and walked out of the store on trembling legs.

Ten minutes later, she found herself sitting outside the School of the Arts coffee shop at Liberty and Abercomb with a cup of Java Jolt. It was too early to order wine. A glass of wine before lunch didn't mean she was a raving alcoholic, did it? Of course it didn't. She wouldn't even think about trying to find a bar this early in the day. Even though she was pretty sure Hooligan's on Liberty Street was open and would serve her something even stronger. She took a shaky breath, laughed at herself, and ignored the concerned, sidelong stares of the two students sitting at the table next to hers.

When her cell phone rang, she grabbed it with hands that felt arthritic, and the sense that somebody had just thrown her a life preserver.

"Miss Beaufort?"

"Professor Cianquino!" She sank against the back of the metal chair. Calm. She had to be calm. She dug her nails into her knee and the momentary pain helped her focus. "I'm so glad you called," she said cheerily. "I wanted to let you know how much I appreciate the thought behind your lovely gift."

"So it arrived last night," he said. He had a calm, light tenor voice. When something struck him funny—and not many things did—he had an unexpectedly high-pitched giggle. That, and his compact, perennial air of youthful muscularity, occasionally reminded her of that action star, Jackie Chan. Mostly, though, he made her of think of Michelangelo's sterner representations of God. Professor Cianquino's commitment to intellectual discipline and rigorous scholarship was total. At law school, his public lectures attracted a standing-room-only audience. But only a handful of students dared to take his seminars. Those who did, and survived, usually went on to become distinguished scholars in their own right. Bree squeaked through his courses with gentleman Cs, and felt lucky to have done that.

"UPS brought the package right to my door," she said. "I hope you got my message thanking you? And I would just love to take you out to lunch."

"I'm afraid I'm housebound these days," he said. "A recurrence of an old problem."

"I'm truly sorry to hear that." Bree paused, slightly flummoxed. Professor Cianquino was a reserved and formal man. There was no way she could flat out ask about his health. But he'd said housebound, not bed-bound. He lived at Melrose, out on the river. She'd been there once before at a group seminar, and despite Professor Cianquino's courtesy, she hadn't liked the place, which was stupid, because it was gorgeous and the professor an excellent, if reserved, host. She shook off her hesitation. "May I drop by to see you?" His apartment, she recalled, had a garden patio out back. "If it doesn't come on to rain, I might come by today with a small picnic?"

"I'd like that," he said, a little distantly. "It sounds quite pleasant. About twelve thirty would be fine."

"And is there anything you don't care to eat these days?"

"It's my leg that's troubling me, Bree. Not my digestion," he said crisply.

Bree bit back a "yes-SIR" and fought an impulse to salute the cell phone. "About twelve thirty, then." She clicked off and made a face. Among the students at that long-ago Melrose seminar was Payton McAllister. Payton the Rat. She'd fallen in love with him while sitting in the rose arbor at the back of the house. He conducted a lengthy, erudite, impassioned defense of the Sullivan Anti-Trust Act, while pacing up and down the allée in a pair of shorts and a T-shirt that showed enough muscle to fire Bree's imagination about the rest of him.

She wasn't up to facing those memories now.

Not only that—something about the house itself had made her edgy even then. Maybe it'd been the last of her common sense trying to tell her Payton was going to break her heart. Maybe she'd been coming down with the flu, and she'd confused the fever and chills with a bad atmosphere. For whatever reason, she'd only been truly comfortable there in the presence of Professor Cianquino himself. The rest of the place gave her the creeps. And did she really want to talk to him about the events of the past twenty-four hours while dodging memories of Payton's lips, eyes, and hard, muscular chest?

Maybe she could help Professor Cianquino and his limp into her car and take him out for lunch. If he'd been housebound for a while, he'd probably appreciate it.

"Dimwit!" she said aloud. Lack of sleep, that was her problem. The return of the old nightmare, after she was sure she would never have it again—that was part of it, too. Not to mention having to confront Payton himself if he was the jerk behind the phone call from Skinner.

Wimp. She was a wimp. She shook her head in disgust, to the snickers of the students sitting next to her at the coffee bar, and went off to find a suitably delicious picnic lunch at the Park Avenue Market. If she got a case of the Payton willies or the Melrose blues, she'd either attach herself to the poor professor like kudzu or go straight on home.

Five

That to the height of this great argument I may assert
eternal Providence, and justify the ways of God to
man.

                                    —*Paradise Lost*, John Milton

And malt does more than Milton can to justify God's
ways to man.

                    —"Terence, this is stupid stuff," A. E. Housman

Professor Cianquino's apartment sat on the ground floor
of Melrose, an eighteenth-century plantation house that
faced the Savannah River. The original Melroses were
slave owners, cotton growers, and among the first to join
the Confederate Army during the War Between the States.
After Appomattox, Francis Melrose sold the house and
acreage to a banker from Chicago and flounced off to Ja-
maica with his wife, sister, and two daughters. There he
went into the sugarcane business and died a heartless old
man at ninety-six.

The banker from Chicago, finding Savannah society
icily unwelcoming to an unreconstructed Yankee, sold
the house to a suffragette Baptist who opened a Bible
school for gentlewomen. Melrose changed hands many
times after the school closed. In the sixties, an architect

from New Jersey meticulously restored the handsome old house and went bankrupt from the cost. A retired judge picked the house up at an auction for taxes and then divided it into six expensive apartments. He rented them to people like Professor Cianquino—tenants who valued the view of the river, the seclusion, and the quiet.

With a sackful of picnic food on the seat beside her, Bree drove up the long drive to the mansion and came to a rolling stop. It looked just like its photograph on the tourist postcards, with the air of a place that had come to a relieved and contented old age after a stormy past.

Of course, the house was haunted, although she refused absolutely to believe that her unease with the place had to do with ghosts.

Without having the slightest belief in the hereafter or in any of the departed who were supposed to live there, Bree loved Savannah's reputation as the most haunted city in the United States. Most of the ghosts drifted around the old houses and cemeteries of the Historic District, although a fair number occupied old plantations like Melrose on the outskirts of town. She couldn't remember the exact number of ghosts who were supposed to haunt Melrose, but there were at least two. There was Marie-Claire, the noisy one. She was the cast-off mistress of a river pirate and had drowned herself from grief when the pirate turned respectable and married a judge's daughter. Then there was the truly creepy son of the original Melroses, who'd ended his days in an insane asylum after a murderous rampage among the slaves. Of the two, she would prefer to meet Marie-Claire. The two of them could commiserate over their lousy taste in men.

Bree sat in the car, and fought a perfectly irrational desire to turn around and drive home to Raleigh. The drive

up to the house was lined with live oaks swagged with
Spanish moss. The gardens surrounding the house rioted
with late roses flowered into bursts of deep yellow, pink,
red, and creamy white. Saint-John's-wort bloomed in
huge spheres on either side of the brick walk leading up
to the green-painted front door.

The place was beautiful. If there was grief and misery
there, it was from her own heart and mind, and not from
wood and stones.

Bree got out of the car, went up the brick walkway,
juggled the paper bags from the Park Avenue Market
from her right arm to her left, and pushed the front door
open. The house smelled like lemon Pledge and old
books. The entryway was floored in wide pine planks,
polished to a honey gold. Huge Oriental vases filled with
dried hydrangea sat on either side of a beautiful old mahogany breakfront against the back wall. The sweeping
staircase at the back of the foyer led up to the apartments
on the second and third floors.

Professor Cianquino occupied apartment #2, the former ballroom, on her right. She pushed the doorbell,
wondering if she should try the door or wait for the poor
professor to limp across the wide expanse of his living
room to open it for her. She had her hand on the doorknob. Before she could know, it swung open to reveal
Professor Cianquino, not with a crutch but in a wheelchair.

She bit back a gasp of alarm. He looked very ill. Bree
had attended his lecture on Medieval Church Law not six
months ago with a couple of friends. She was shocked at
the change in him. He'd lost weight. His hair was completely white. And he'd grown a thin, elegant beard that
gave him the look of a Confucian ascetic.

Bree concealed her shock with a smile and a flurry of greetings. She walked with him as he rolled the wheelchair back across the living room to his kitchen. "I stopped at the Park Avenue Market and decided I'd like nothing better than their chicken-curry salad and some of that fruit sorbet that's so refreshin'."

He looked up at her and said dryly, "You're getting quite Southern on me, Bree. That only happens when you're off balance. You need to keep your composure, my dear. Particularly now that you're on your own. You're going to be presenting cases in court."

"Yes. Well." Bree set the bags on the kitchen table. "You're right, of course. I'm just a little concerned about you, is all. You do look a little poor ... that is, as though you've spent some time recuperating."

He frowned in a reflective way and asked with interest, "Have I changed so much since you saw me last?"

"You're quite a bit thinner," Bree said bluntly. "And your hair's gone all white. And then there's the beard." She bit her lip hard. Antonia had a T-shirt that read "Help me! Help me! I'm talking and I can't shut up!" She should have put it on this morning to remind herself not to babble.

"Things have become a bit ... difficult. But we'll get to that in a moment." He eyed the grocery bags on the table. "There's a delicious smell coming from those bags. And it's a chicken-curry salad, you say? I have a Cabernet Franc that ought to go with it nicely. And perhaps a Pinot Gris with the sorbet?"

"That sounds wonderful," Bree said, because it did. "Shall I set the food out in the garden?"

He smiled up at her. "I'm sorry to say that we won't be able to linger over the meal. Perhaps you wouldn't mind setting up in my office. We've quite a bit to discuss, and not a great deal of time. I've some information in files I'd like you to see. I have a client I want you to meet."

Bree was surprised. "I didn't know you actually practiced law."

He smiled faintly. "I've kept my hand in, over the years." He wheeled his chair around with an expert twist of his wrist. "You know the way?"

"I don't believe you invited us into your office when we were last here."

"At the far end of the living room. To the right of the fireplace. The carved wooden doors. I'll return with the wine in a moment." His gaze met hers for a brief instant. There was kindness there, and a fierce intelligence, and something she had never seen from him before. Regret, maybe? She wasn't sure. And what would he have to be regretful about?

Bree gathered up plates and cutlery, and a pair of wineglasses. With some difficulty, she managed to carry all of it plus the food across the living room. If the professor had furnished his place anything like her Aunt Cissy, who was fond of whatnots, piecrust tables, and tufted hassocks, she wouldn't have made it without dropping the lot. But Professor Cianquino had simple tastes. A cream leather sectional in front of the fireplace. A reading chair with a good lamp. Uncarpeted pine floors. At the farthest end of the living room was a set of carved double doors that led to his study.

The journey across the floor was long. Time felt elastic, almost flexible. It was a disturbing feeling, an intensification of the unease she'd felt when she had visited the place. She reached the double doors with a sense of having come a long way.

She didn't want to go into the study.

She stopped herself from looking over her shoulder; she thought of Professor Cianquino's face, with its strange combination of sorrow and determination. She focused instead on the doors. They were made of rosewood, and carved with an elaborate design of spheres so artfully shaped they seemed to spin the quiet light.

She had seen those spheres before. On the fence surrounding 66 Angelus Street.

Intensely curious, now, she opened the doors and went in.

The simplicity of the living room made the chaos of his office all the more surprising. Taken aback, she stood for a second and just looked at it, whatever she'd expected, it wasn't this. She had a curious sense of homecoming. She had a stronger sense of the need to run.

Not sure where to put the load of food and dishes, and even less sure of what she felt, Bree forced herself over the threshold.

The room was completely lined with bookshelves that ran from the twelve-foot ceiling to the floor. And the shelves were stuffed to overflowing. Books were everywhere. Leather-bound, paperback, hardcover, skinny, enormously thick—it was overwhelming. Bree recognized a complete edition of the *Oxford English Dictionary*. Underneath it were rows and rows of books bound in tan leather with a red band across the spine. That weird sense of being pulled in two directions went away, to be replaced by a feeling of total contentment. This was a library, and Bree had always loved libraries. A leather chair stood in front of the bookshelves. She dumped the armload of dishes and food onto the seat, and ran her hands over the books. The thick gold lettering on the red band was familiar. It seemed to be a complete set of the *Corpus Juris Secundum*. Bree smiled with pleasure. Nobody but huge, white-shoe firms carried actual bound copies of the *Corpus Juris Secundum* anymore. It was much easier, and more profitable, to access case law online through Lexis, or any of the other online research services.

Bree chuckled to herself. It was time to introduce Professor Cianquino to the ease of online research. It'd be pretty amazing to browse case law with an actual book—but it took forever. The global search function alone saved hours.

She looked around for a place to set up lunch. An oak table that had to be fifteen feet long—maybe more—ran right down the center of the room. It was piled high with curiosities: clay pots, a pair of scales, a heap of clothes made out of what looked like fusty sacking. There was even a bulky scabbard with a banged-up sword.

And in the middle of the table was a large cage with a bird in it.

Bree blinked at it. The bird blinked back, then said, "Hello."

"Hello," Bree said.

"Hello."

She heard the soft whisper of the wheelchair behind her and turned to greet Professor Cianquino with a smile. "I suppose he'll go on all day like that?"

"I suppose not," the bird said.

"Is it an African gray parrot?" Bree asked with interest. "I read somewhere they can have a vocabulary of over two hundred words."

"Parrots!" the bird said, and spat. "I suppose not!"

"Quiet, Archie." Professor Cianquino held two bottles of wine in his lap. He gestured toward the corner where a card table was shoved against the wall. "I think we can settle in over there."

Bree cleared the card table of a ream of paper, a couple of file folders, and the day's edition of the *Savannah Daily*. She wedged them into the nearest bookshelf on top of a series of books titled The Annotated Koran.

"Not the blue file, and not the newspaper. I want you to read both while we're eating."

Bree looked at him in surprise.

He smiled. "You've rented the office space and hung out your shingle?"

"Well, yes. Or very nearly. I bought some furniture today. And I've arranged for the office space, but the landlady doesn't want a lease."

He shrugged. "Perhaps you don't need one. When you're ready, I have a case for you, if you'll take it. But we won't discuss the details until after we eat."

Bree served the chicken-curry salad on split brioches, and accepted a glass of wine. She sat down on a truly uncomfortable carved wooden chair, plate in her lap, wineglass in hand, and decided it was now or never. "I appreciate the thought behind the gift of the stationery, Professor Cianquino. And the cell phone! It's just wonderful! Although I do have one already, and I'm not sure I can break the contract with Verizon to switch over to it. I thank you kindly all the same."

His smile broadened. "I do like Southern manners. They are quite Chinese sometimes, a people whose courtesy is exquisite. I, of course, hear the 'but' behind your civility."

"That takes the wind out of my sails," Bree said ruefully. "It's just that ..."

"You can, of course, turn the gifts down. But I would

like you to consider all the consequences your decision has before you do so. Particularly the cell phone. It is a means of communication you may not wish to abandon."

"I'm not sure I understand you," Bree said.

He rested his elbows on the wheelchair arms and steepled his fingers. "To be frank, it's difficult to decide where to start." He thought for a moment, and then said, "Did you take the call from Bennie Skinner?"

Bree paused, her filled brioche halfway to her mouth, and said, "Excuse me?"

Professor Cianquino waited, his head tilted a little, as if listening for something.

Bree set her sandwich on her plate. She hadn't been all that hungry to begin with. "Well, no. I didn't." She looked at him narrowly. "You know he up and died yesterday afternoon."

Professor Cianquino gestured at the copy of the *Savannah Daily*. The headline read: "Famed Billionaire Dead."

Bree took the sandwich up again, and peered at it rather doubtfully. "Now, UPS didn't deliver the package until eight thirty. I opened the cell phone up around nine. The call came in about ten minutes later. What I think is, the call from him must have been delayed somehow." She waved the brioche in the air, scattering bits of chicken into her lap. "Some technical glitch, I expect, because of course, the poor man couldn't call after he was dead."

"He was allowed just one call," Professor Cianquino said in a reflective way.

Bree swallowed, choked, and laughed as airily as she could. "The other option, of course, is that some joker called and pretended to be him. I even thought that maybe you had some help picking the gift out." She faltered.

"From, you know, someone who knows me pretty well. And then maybe that someone thought it'd be hilarious to jerk my chain a little."

"You mean Payton McAllister?" Professor Cianquino smiled. "No. I had some help, but not of that kind. And it wasn't a technical glitch."

Bree abandoned the sandwich and grabbed the glass of wine. Had everyone in the southeastern states heard that she'd been dumped by Payton the Rat? She took a healthy slug to hide her irritation. Professor Cianquino winced. It was, she silently agreed as it went down her throat, far too nice a wine to belt back, but so what? Then the rest of what Professor Cianquino said registered and she gulped at it again. She said politely, "Then what you're telling me is that Benjamin Blackheart Skinner called me after he died? The call was from a ghost?" She kept her tone gentle and very reasonable. Clearly, whatever ailed poor Professor Cianquino wasn't limited to his leg. A line from *Hamlet* entered her head (and exited almost immediately), *Oh, what a noble mind is here o'erthrown!*

He looked at her sternly. "What is the single most valuable piece of information you learned from me?"

Bree didn't even have to think about that. He'd drummed it into all of his students. " 'You will find truth in experience.' "

"And what can you conclude from that?"

Bree looked at him, not sure where this was headed. "Well, I guess it means that you can talk yourself blue in the face, but you won't know for sure until you try it yourself."

He nodded, "That the only way anyone truly *knows* is through direct experience. So I can talk myself blue in the face, about whom that phone call was from and why I would like you to take on this case, but until you have direct experience, you aren't going to believe me." He reached across the table, laid his hand lightly on hers, and withdrew it. "I can assure you, I do know a hawk from a handsaw."

"*Hamlet, Hamlet, Hamlet*," the bird said.

"Be quiet, Archie." The bird subsided sulkily onto its perch. "I would like you to take Benjamin Skinner's case, Bree. The start of your new practice is what this is all about."

Bree looked at the glass of wine in her hand. It was empty. She set it carefully on the table. "With all due respect, sir ..."

In the distance, the door chimes rang. Professor Cianquino activated the wheelchair. "Our client's early."

Bree stared at him. Benjamin Skinner was dead. Three C-SPAN reporters couldn't be wrong. Could they?

"If you'll excuse me for a moment, I'll bring her in. I may be some time. Please wait for me. And finish your lunch."

He rolled out the door and shut it behind him. Bree poked at her food. She poured another glass of wine. She tried not to think that the most respected teacher in her law school was stark raving bonkers.

She applied logic.

He did say "her" when he referred to the client.

If he said "her," he couldn't be bringing the spook, ghost, haunt, revenant, decaying body, whatever, of Benjamin Skinner in for a case conference. Benjamin Skinner was a "he" as his pneumatic blonde sweetie had so breathily stated in her television interview.

She sat back. This was stupid. Professor Cianquino wasn't crazy. *She* was crazy. She'd built a few bad dreams, a prank phone call, and a couple of half-seen shadows into perversity. Had the professor said one word about ghosts? The afterlife? The undead?

Not one.

Bree picked up the blue folder and opened it. It was background information on someone named Liz Overshaw who, Bree realized, as she skimmed through the pages, was the surviving majority partner in Skinner Worldwide, Inc. Ha. Not only a rich client, but a client right up Bree's particular alley. Bree thrived on corporate tax law. She tossed the folder back on the table and began to walk restlessly around the room. "You know what my major concentration in law school was, don't you?" she said to the bird. "It was . . ."

"Business," said the bird. "Corporate tax law."

Bree swallowed, took a breath, then moved to the table to get a closer look at—What did the professor call him? Archie.

"Hey, Archie," she said.

The bird blinked one beady eye, shifted on its perch, then pecked frantically at a bit of cuttlefish hanging in his cage. If it was an African gray parrot, it was unlike any African gray parrot she had seen before. It was large, as such parrots are, but its plumage was a soft sepia brown mixed with streaks of black and gold. If it looked like any kind of bird at all, it was an owl. But, she knew (and why she knew this was a total mystery; she had an affinity for odd bits of facts) that owls didn't talk. Furthermore, contrary to conventional wisdom, they were among the stupidest birds in the avian hierarchy.

"Who's stupid?!" Archie demanded and clicked his lethal-looking beak with the sound of a scythe through flesh.

Bree noticed, first, that the door to the cage had been removed, and second, that Archie had two-inch talons on each claw. She backed away. She went to the door and hesitated at the murmur of voices beyond. Getting Liz Overshaw as her first client was quite a coup. Professor Cianquino had told her to wait. She would wait. She moved back to the bookshelves, whistling idly, and trying not to cast nervous glances over her shoulder.

She picked up the first volume of the *Corpus Juris Secundum* and admired the soft feel of the calf leather. She ran her fingers over the raised gold lettering on the spine, and looked at the title in the soft office light. It wasn't the *Corpus Juris Secundum.* The gold letters clearly spelled out:

CORPUS JURIS ULTIMA

The last, the ultimate in case law?

A familiar bookmark leaped out at her. It was a copy of an old woodcut, a rubber stamp of a man in medieval dress, a pointed cap on his head, and a quill pen in his hand. Beneath the caption at the bottom, the words:

FROM THE LIBRARY OF
FRANKLIN WINSTON-BEAUFORT

This set of books had belonged to Uncle Franklin? Bree ran her hand through her hair. Her memories of her uncle were of a stern, remote old man who treated everyone in his life with the same gentle courtesy. He'd sat on the seventh circuit court as a judge for many years. She couldn't imagine anyone less interested in an elaborate, fantastical joke.

Maybe it was just cases that had been heard in the Supreme Court? She flipped the book open and read:

Lucifer v. Celestial Court (Year 1)

Bree stared at the pages. What kind of lunacy was this?

Uncle Franklin's edition of the *Corpus Juris Ultima* was formatted exactly like the *Secundum*.

Except that the cases cited were totally nuts.

The cause of action in the case of *Lucifer v. Celestial Court* was wrongful dismissal. The plaintiff alleged rank prejudice, arguing for the enforcement of one of the Seven Celestial Virtues, *caritas*, which, if Bree recollected her Latin correctly, was the highest form of caring love. The arguments for the defense included all of the Seven Deadly Sins, but rested heavily—and most successfully— on the sin of Pride. Bree scanned the summary of the defense with mild astonishment; Lucifer had quite a rap sheet. Bree read on, chuckling—a forced, panicky sort of chuckle—but a chuckle nonetheless. As pastiche, this was pretty funny. Elaborate, but pretty funny. The disposition of the case was no surprise; Lucifer was remanded into custody, and sent back to hell for all eternity, with little, if any, hope of an appeal.

Somebody had spent years putting this together. Probably a whole group of somebodies. And this sort of elaborate fantasy wasn't without precedent. She could walk into any Borders bookstore and find scholarly volumes dedicated to unicorns, dragons, and witches. Not to mention vampires, fairies, and werewolves.

Celestial law might even be a saner subject than most. It certainly had more academic heft than, say, elves, if one were inclined to whimsy. She looked up and down the rows of gorgeously bound volumes. Uncle Franklin's collection was just more elaborate than usual. Clearly, this was a man who hadn't done things by halves.

The door from the living room opened. Bree jumped, as guilty as if she'd been caught reading personal mail.

"Put-it-back, put-it-back, put-it-back," Archie squawked.

Bree gave the bird a nasty look, closed Volume One carefully, and slipped it back on the shelf.

Professor Cianquino said, "We're ready for you, Bree. If you would join us, please?"

Bree picked up the blue folder containing the background information about Liz Overshaw, and followed his wheelchair into the living room.

Six

I do not ask to see
The distant scene; one step enough for me.
—"Lead, Kindly Light," John Henry Newman

Liz Overshaw sat on the cream leather couch in front of the fireplace, one thin leg crossed over the other. Bree had seen pictures of her in newspapers and magazines. She was the chief financial officer of Skinner Worldwide, Inc. Corporate America flung her achievements in front of the media every time a gender discrimination suit was filed in federal court. She was in her late forties, too thin, with the polished, sort of tightened-up look of someone with a lot of money to spend on age-denying surgeries. She was dressed in Armani—a conventional, skirted suit of beige gabardine. She wore a sapphire and diamond Rolex, and her pearl drop earrings were huge and obviously real. Her graying hair was short, uncombed, and she was in need of a shampoo. She'd also chewed off most of her lipstick. And, as Antonia would have said had she seen them, you could put groceries in the bags under her eyes.

Liz stared pensively at the floor and turned the Rolex she wore around and around her wrist with an agitated forefinger. She looked up as Bree approached her, then cast a sideways glance at Professor Cianquino. "She looks like some kind of albino."

"It's her hair, Liz," he said. "That silver blonde is, of course, unusual."

"I'd dye it, if I were you," Liz Overshaw said to Bree. "But then, you probably like the attention. I'll tell you something, young woman. You don't want to stand out in a crowd if you want serious people to take you seriously. You especially don't want to look like a dimwit model. Business life is hard enough for women as it is, especially in the South."

Bree drew a deep breath, opened her mouth, and then got a fit of the giggles. Talking owls, a multivolume encyclopedia of celestial law, and now positively the rudest woman she'd ever met in her life. It wasn't memories of Payton the Rat that made Melrose an uncomfortable place to be; it was the lunatics in it. "Oh my," she said. "I do apologize. I can tell you, Ms. Overshaw, I haven't modeled a thing since I handled Play-Doh in kindergarten twenty-five years ago. As for the dimwit part, you'll just have to judge for yourself, after we talk."

Liz Overshaw looked at her coldly. "Cianquino, this is a mistake."

"You'll find that she's exactly the lawyer you need for this particular case." He turned to Bree and nodded at the far corner of the couch. "Sit down, please, Bree."

Professor Cianquino's cool professionalism doused her fit of hilarity like a dash of cold water. Bree sat down.

"This is Liz Overshaw."

Bree nodded. "How do you do?"

"Not goddamned well, as you might guess." Liz cleared her throat with an irritating sort of gargle. "This business with Skinner ..." She cleared her throat again. "We've got to do something about it."

"You were—and still are, I imagine—a senior partner with his most well-known company, Skinner Worldwide, Inc.?" Bree asked. Bree's mother was fond of reminding both her daughters that honey was a far more effective flycatcher than vinegar, so Bree added, "And an admired and effective CFO, as all women in business know."

Liz ran both hands through her hair. "Yeah. Actually, if I can come up with the funding, I'll be the majority shareholder, too. Skinner left options on his stock to his partners. We—that is, I—just have to decide whether I want to buy him out, or find an appropriate buyer."

This kind of arrangement wasn't unusual when the stockholder in a corporation wanted to bar family heirs from getting control of a company. Bree made a note in the file. "Is that going to be a problem?"

Liz flung her hand up irritably. "Christ, no. I'm not here about that. If I needed business counsel you think I'd be talking to you?" She glanced at Bree sideways and pursed her lips. "Not that you aren't perfectly competent, I'm sure. Cianquino doesn't deal with idiots."

"Then how can I help you?"

"I told you. I've got to do something about Skinner before I end up in the ha-ha room at the sanatorium." She glared at Professor Cianquino. "You *sure* I can trust her?"

He smiled and shrugged. "There isn't anyone else I can recommend to you. Her qualifications are unique."

"All right," she said crossly. "Just fine." She inhaled, and then let her breath out with an explosive "Pah!" "You've read the reports of Skinner's death?"

"The newspaper account, yes," Bree said. "And of course, the television news channels covered it quite extensively."

"The coroner's office is calling it a heart attack. He had a heart attack and drowned. Skinner didn't drown."

"Heart attacks take a lot of assertive men in their early sixties," Bree said in a mild way. "And is it likely that the medical examiner would make a mistake? Especially with such a prominent man as Mr. Skinner?"

"Prominent son of a bitch, you mean," Liz said. She made that hawking noise in her throat, like Felix Unger in those endless reruns of *The Odd Couple*. Bree looked down and studied her own toes. Liz Overshaw couldn't help it if she had postnasal drip. But she sure could be less noisy about it.

"He was murdered."

Bree looked up. "I beg your pardon?"

"He was murdered. He won't tell me how. He can't tell me how, because the next thing he knew after getting kicked in the chest with a heart attack, he was floating over his own corpse on a mortuary slab wondering what the hell happened. Did you see the interviews the press did after his death? One of those four is a murderer."

Bree didn't say anything for a long moment.

"Carlton Montifiore, Douglas Fairchild, John Stubblefield, and Chastity McFarland," Liz said impatiently. "Did you see it?"

"Yes, I saw the interviews." Bree refused to look at Professor Cianquino. If she looked at the professor, she was going to make a horrific face at him. "That's what the young woman who's his current companion seemed to feel," Bree said diplomatically. "That he was murdered."

"That little idiot," Liz said without heat. "Hell, maybe she actually knows, too." She clamped her mouth shut and stared at her hands, apparently unwilling to say any more.

"And you know he was murdered because . . ." Bree let her voice trail off.

"Because he's haunting me!" Liz burst out. "The bastard won't leave me alone!"

You betcha. Liz was being haunted. Right. Quite a Savannah-like circumstance, that was for sure. Best place to claim a haunting was in the most haunted city in America. If nothing else, her admission explained some of her rude behavior. It'd take more confidence than Bree possessed to tell a perfect stranger this kind of hooey. No wonder she was defensive.

Bree didn't comment aloud. Instead, she nodded thoughtfully, and said, "I see."

"I can damn well tell you don't believe me," Liz snarled. "You think I'm crazy."

The first thing a lawyer learns in law school is that representation is sacred. A lawyer has an absolute duty to defend her client, and to represent that client's interests with every legal weapon at her disposal. There isn't an equivalent of the Hippocratic Oath for lawyers, but Bree knew that if there were, it would run something like: *I swear to uphold the interests, rights, and well-being of the client to the last drop of my blood, without personal prejudice or bias of any kind.*

But she was stuck with a nutcase, that was clear. If Professor Cianquino hadn't been in a wheelchair, she'd whack him over the head with something large enough to get his attention. He wanted her to take this case. He'd recommended her to one of the most influential women in Georgia business circles. If Bree had sat down and made a laundry list of the type of clients she wanted for Beaufort, LLC, this crazy woman was it.

Unless she stood up and told her no. Which would be professional suicide before she even had her desk delivered and her phone lines put in. She thought ruefully of her stationery. At least she was set up with that. So Bree said merely, "I think you're under a tremendous amount of stress. I'm truly sorry for that. And I'd like to help you if I can."

"Cianquino says you can." Liz took a deep, shuddering breath. "I can't take much more of this. I haven't slept since it happened."

Bree looked at her bitten nails, her unwashed hair, but most of all her air of desperation. She was truly sorry for her. The woman was at the end of her rope. If nothing else, maybe she could persuade her to see her doctor and get a few sleeping pills. She said with genuine kindness, "I'll certainly try to help. What kind of outcome were you looking for? What can I do?"

"Stuff Skinner back wherever he came from, for one," Liz Overshaw said. "But Cianquino says that can't be done. At least not right now?" She lifted an eyebrow inquiringly.

"Not right now," Professor Cianquino agreed.

"Stuff him back?" Bree said.

Professor Cianquino gave her an admonishing glance. Bree took the hint and shut up.

Liz was back at her watch turning. "So if we can't stuff him back where he came from, I want you to prove he was murdered. That's what he wants *me* to do. Catch his murderer. He wants revenge. He wants justice. And like he did all the time when he was alive, he won't get off my behind until I do find out who killed him, or at least hire someone to do it." She closed her eyes briefly, and then opened them. "This is the brief: I'm retaining you to find out who murdered Bennie Skinner." She bent down, drew her checkbook from the briefcase at her feet, and uncapped her pen. "What's your usual retainer?"

Bree opened her mouth. Absolutely nothing came out. She felt like Alice, falling down the hole to Wonderland. Finally, she managed, "I've haven't quite settled on . . ."

Liz waved her hand in a "shut up" gesture. "I'll make it for ten thousand. That should be enough to get you started with a private investigator and pulling all those reports from the cops and the coroner's office." She narrowed her eyes. "I just want one thing from you and that's that you keep your mouth shut about me. I can see from your face that you're wondering why I don't hire a private eye myself. God knows we pay enough to those leeching corporate security firms already." She leaned forward, and pointed at Bree like an irate traffic cop. "Because I don't want anyone to know I'm behind this. The *Wall Street Journal* gets hold of the fact I'm taking orders from a dead man, I'm never going to find anybody to buy Bennie's stock. Worse than that, the board will fire me for moral weakness, or whatever."

"Unsound mind," Professor Cianquino said. "And I must say, Liz, you have one of the finest minds I know."

Bree pulled a pen from her jacket pocket and pretended to take notes on the margins of the file.

"Is this perfectly clear?" Liz demanded. "My name's kept out of this."

"Absolutely."

"Cianquino said I can trust you."

"Yes," Bree said simply, "you can."

Liz ripped the check out of the checkbook, tossed it onto the coffee table in front of her, and collected her briefcase. "I'll be off then, Cianquino." She stopped halfway across the floor and frowned at Bree. "Call me when you've got something, and not before."

She banged the door shut when she left.

Bree picked up the check. There it was: *Pay to the order of Brianna Winston-Beaufort Ten Thousand Dollars ($10,000.00)* and drawn on the First Bank of Savannah. On the little line on the lower left hand corner Liz had written, In Re: *Skinner.* There was a very long pause.

"Well," she said. "I'd like to know what's going on here."

"It's as you see."

Bree cleared her throat. "I have a couple of questions."

"I'll try to answer them."

"You don't believe Benjamin Skinner is haunting Liz Overshaw. Do you?"

"She's your client. You have an absolute duty to act in her best interests."

"Does that include setting up a visit to a good therapist?"

Professor Cianquino frowned. "Liz is very much in her right mind. She's under a great deal of stress. That's obvious. I would suggest that you take the responsibilities of the case more seriously. I would hate to think I was wrong in referring you to her."

This from a man with a truckload of angelic case law in his office? Bree opened her mouth to ask about it. She wanted to know about the parrot/owl/whatever. She wanted to know if any of this had to do with the painting that had terrified her into a faint. She wanted to know if this man who intimidated future Supreme Court justices was as crazy as a June bug.

"Your first case," Professor Cianquino said, with a clear air of dismissal. "If you run into any problems, you'll call me?" He turned his wheelchair and rolled toward the front door.

Bree's early training in Southern girl politeness held. That, and the feeling that you just didn't ask sassy questions of a powerhouse professor emeritus from one of the world's leading law schools. She slung her purse over her shoulder and rose to her feet. "It's actually doable, you know," she said to the back of his neck. "Liz Overshaw may be crazy, but the case itself isn't."

He pulled the front door open, and then turned aside to let her through. Bree was about to mention her uncle Franklin's books but Cianquino looked stern, and highly unapproachable.

"I mean, I can certainly pull together the resources to do a private inquiry into Skinner's death. Do you suppose that she'll be satisfied if I prove he did die of natural causes?"

"Anything is possible," he said coolly. "Oh. If you need a good investigator, I can recommend this agency." He pulled a business card from his suit coat pocket. "The principal is named Gabriel Striker."

She reached out and took it, then tucked both card and check into her purse. The professor smiled at her. "Good. Excellent." Then, "Good luck to you, my dear. Do you have an idea of what you want to do first?"

Bree ran her hand through her hair. Dimwit model, my foot. "You bet I do."

⋙⋘

"Thing is, honey, there's just too much of it." Fontina gathered the mass of Bree's silvery hair into her hands and tugged at it. Bree was willing to bet that the hairdresser's given name was something good old Southern like Ashley or Sarah-Anne. But the name in small, discreet lettering on the front door of the salon was Fontina, and she'd been recommended by Bree's chic Aunt Cissy as the best hairdresser in Savannah.

Bree wasn't about to tell Fontina she'd chosen the name of an exceptionally good cheese for her salon; she was willing to bet more than a few customers had sniped at her already. Fontina was tall, skinny, and her hair was shot through with bright purple streaks. "Don't be put off by the gum chewing or the color she's dyed her *own* hair," Aunt Cissy had said. "She's a genius. And if you tell all your friends about her and I end up havin' to wait months for an appointment, I'll put a curse on you and you'll be bald before you're thirty."

"Honey?" Fontina said. "You're not tellin' me you want me to cut this off?"

"Sorry." Bree sat up a little straighter in the cushy chair. "I had a short night and a very weird day and I'm a little drifty. About my hair—I don't know what to do, except not have it be a distraction for clients. I got my first case today, did I tell you that?"

Fontina nodded. "You sure did. And you told me it was an emergency."

"Well, it is. I don't want anyone thinking that I look too young, or too unserious to do my job, and I'm going to be dealing with private detectives, the police, and the coroner's office for the first time in my professional life. I want to look like I count for something. Something serious, because my first case is a little ... a little ..."

"Offbeat?" Fontina suggested kindly.

"Offbeat. That's it. So I called Aunt Cissy and then I called you. Aunt Cissy said to put myself totally in your hands. What do you think?"

"About your aunt Cissy or your hair?"

Bree rolled her eyes.

"I do like your aunt Cissy," Fontina said. "Sends me more work than I can handle most weeks. Next thing you know, I'll be having to expand. And if there's one thing I don't want to do, it's expand." She said abruptly, "So you don't want to cut this off, praise be."

Bree poked despairingly at her head. "I just want it to behave. I'm opening a law practice. I want to look cool and professional. I'm interviewing prospective employees tomorrow morning. I've got my first case. I'm planning on being ready for more clients by the end of the week, if I can. Doing something about this hair is kind of a necessary first step, if you see what I mean." She sighed. "I thought that a short bob might work."

Fontina shook her head. "No way. I'll show you what's gonna work."

Seven

"Braids!" Lavinia Mather exclaimed when Bree walked into the foyer half an hour late, to pick up her dog. "Don't you look like something. Hm, hm. I surely like that effect, Bree."

Bree patted her head a little nervously. "Are you sure you like them?" Fontina had divided her hair into four thick braids, and then wound them artfully around her head. She felt extremely professional; better than that, she felt armored.

"You look like a queen," Lavinia said. She put her hand on Bree's arm and turned her gently toward the stairs. "You're lookin' more like Her every day." She pointed at the Renaissance angel with the crown of silver hair.

Bree shook her head and laughed. "I'd forgotten about your painted angels, Lavinia. Well, I'm not an angel, but I do think the hairstyle suits me."

"Noble," Lavinia said. "You look noble."

"Thank you," Bree said meekly. She bent and patted her happy dog. "And thank you for taking care of Sasha. He's looking better by the minute."

"He had him a good day, too," Lavinia said. "Made sure that those men who delivered the furniture didn't take any advantage of this old auntie."

"The furniture's here already?"

"Step in and see."

Bree followed Lavinia to the entrance to the living room. The leather sofa and chair made a nice ell in front of the fireplace. And the oak table took up just the right amount of space in the dining room. "It looks just great. But what did you mean when you said the delivery men tried to take advantage of you?"

"They almost forgot that picture, didn't they?"

Bree stepped all the way inside and froze. The picture was there, propped against the mantel. Her head swam. Her senses darkened. For a minute, it looked like the water was moving. As if the hands were beckoning to her. And in the raging crimson sky above the wrecked ship, the great bird flew with a slow, deadly "snick" of his wings. She staggered, unsteady on her feet, and Lavinia gripped her arm again, with both hands.

She stood on tiptoe and whispered in Bree's ear. Her words were almost lost in a rising sound of wind. "They tried to tell me you hadn't paid for it. But I knew better, and so did Sasha. You've been payin' for that picture for years." She looked at Sasha. "You told him, dog. Didn't you, boy? Growled like some movie monster until they went back to the store and brought it in."

Sasha barked, sharply, and Bree came to herself with a start. She stared at Lavinia. The old woman stared back, her black eyes unreadable. "Thing is, honey," she said after a long moment, "those things you want to hide from sight? They'll get bigger and bigger all by themselves in the dark. You want to look those things right in the eye.

Put 'em out there where the light can get at 'em. Only good things grow in the sunshine."

Bree walked up to the painting and put her hand on the surface. Paper and paint. That's all it was, paper and paint.

"That all right with you, Bree?" Lavinia's voice was soft.

For one, wild moment, Bree didn't dare to turn around. Lavinia didn't stand behind her. Something else stood there. Something so big, it filled the room and shut out the afternoon light streaming in the windows. It grew and grew again, and then with a rush of giant wings, it was gone.

"All right?" Lavinia repeated.

Bree didn't turn around. If she did, she'd demand the rent check back. She'd walk out of here without that dog, without an office, and leave the damn painting behind. She'd drive the three hundred and fifty miles to Raleigh-Durham, sit at her old desk in her father's law firm, and think seriously about marrying a nice guy and starting a family. Instead, she reached up and took the painting down. "Well, if that's true, there's a lot more light at home, Lavinia. This painting will be the last thing I see at night, and the first thing I see in the morning."

Lavinia gripped her arm. "No. No, Bree. That's something you're going to want to leave here."

"Nonsense." She hefted it in both hands. It was lighter than it looked. "I can always burn the damn thing if I want to."

"If I were you, I'd burn the damn thing," Antonia said. "What was wrong with that mirror that was over the mantel? That's been in the family for a million years?"

It was Uncle Franklin's mirror; Bree remembered the day he hung it over the mantel. The frame was curiously worked in gilt. When she moved it to put the painting in its stead, it'd been unexpectedly heavy.

"I liked it," Antonia complained. "And I don't like that thing."

"I stuck the mirror in the hall closet. And I don't want to talk about the painting." Bree turned, looked at her sister lazing on the chintz couch, and made a heroic effort to keep her temper. "I cannot *believe* that you waltzed in here without so much as a phone call."

Antonia sprawled at ease on the sofa. Her backpack was on the rocker by the fireplace. A large, overstuffed duffel bag stood by the front door. Bree'd practically broken her neck stumbling over it when she'd come home.

"Last time I looked, no one gave *you* the deed to this place," Antonia said rudely. "I've got a set of keys just like everybody else in the family." She swung herself flat onto the couch with her head at one end and her feet at the other. Bree stood at the fireplace with the painting propped at her side. Sasha hopped back and forth between them.

"Lie down, Sasha," Bree said. She pointed at the floor.

With a heavy sigh, he settled by the coffee table.

"You ought to be ashamed of yourself. You're upsetting the poor dog." Antonia patted the cushions and made a chirping sound. "Come on, sweetie. Lie down here with me."

"As if he can jump up on the couch with that leg." Bree

tossed Antonia's backpack aside and sank into the rocker by the fireplace. She looked at her sister and sighed with a sound so like Sasha's that both her sister and the dog jumped a little.

Antonia was six years younger than Bree, and they looked nothing alike. She had brown eyes to Bree's green, chestnut hair to Bree's silver blonde, and she barely topped five feet three. The only familial resemblance was in their voices, which one of Antonia's more chuckle-headed boyfriends described as mellowed honey.

Antonia decided she was going to be an actress when she was fifteen, after sitting through five consecutive performances of a touring company's production of *Grease*. Years of voice training had deepened Antonia's speaking voice and amped up the volume, but even now, it was easy to mistake one for the other on the phone.

"You must have set a record for dropping out at UNC," Bree said. "Classes have been in session how long? Two days?"

Antonia flattened herself on the couch, then raised both legs over her head, keeping her back perfectly flat. "A couple of weeks. And I got the tuition money back." She lowered her legs, and then repeated the exercise effortlessly.

"And your reason was what again?" Bree asked rhetorically. She smacked her forehead lightly. "Of course. Silly me. A chance at an audition with the Savannah Rep. Not a for-certain-please-show-up-at-six-o'clock appointment, but a chance."

"It's a chance at a call-back," Antonia corrected her equably. "I auditioned this afternoon. Bree, they *loved* me!"

"Of course they loved you. You're absolutely sensational. Not to mention gifted. Although it looks like you're going to be sensational, gifted, and semiliterate if you keep dropping out of school. And what's the part again?"

Antonia swung herself upright. "The actual part is for Irene Adler in this fabulous new play about Sherlock Holmes."

"THE woman for Sherlock Holmes." Bree had read all of Arthur Doyle in high school. "The most beautiful woman in London."

"Yep. Now, the *career* part of it all is a chance to become a member of the permanent repertory."

Bree didn't say anything. She didn't have to.

"So, okay. The chances of that are, like, one in ten."

"Factor that by a hundred," Bree suggested.

"But the chance of a job as assistant stage manager is more, like, one in two."

"Really?" Bree said. "Is that a paying job?"

"Yep."

"And it would pay how much?"

Antonia told her.

"Which means you'd be staying here?!"

"It's either that or a park bench." She looked anxious. "You don't mind, do you? I mean, even when you were dating Payton the Rat and we were sharing the apartment in Raleigh, we managed to stay out of each other's way."

"It's not that."

"Well, what, then?"

Bree stared at her. How could she tell Antonia of this feeling she had—a feeling getting stronger by the hour— that she was getting into something she couldn't control. Something strange. And dangerous.

She shivered, suddenly, convinced she was being

watched, that both of them were being watched, that the sound of wings had followed her here, to the only place where she could be safe. She turned her head away, and encountered Sasha's grave, unblinking gaze.

The cormorant. It lies in the cormorant.

"I don't understand," Bree said aloud. "I don't get it. What do you want from me? What?!"

"Hey! Bree! You okay?" Antonia was halfway across the room, her face pale.

"Of course I'm okay. I'm fine."

"You don't look fine." Antonia rubbed her forehead, and then sat back down on the couch. "You scared me half to death."

Bree got up and turned the painting so it faced the wall. "Don't be a smart-ass. What's the matter with you, any-way?"

"Nothing's the matter with *me*. You looked like the last act of *The Duchess of Malfi*."

"What's that supposed to mean?"

"You know, it's that perfectly grisly revenge play by Webster. Where everybody ends up covered in blood and screaming with horror."

Bree rolled her eyes dramatically. "You're imagining things."

But she'd turned the painting to the wall. So who was imagining things now?

She'd take it back to that shop in the morning.

"I don't know," Antonia muttered. "Maybe it's the braids. I'm not sure if I like the braids. You look fierce."

"The braids are so I don't look like a dim-witted model."

"Somebody said you looked like a dim-witted model?"

Antonia's giggles were infectious. "Is that the coolest insult ever, or what?!"

Over pizza at Huey's, Bree gave Antonia an edited version of the last thirty-six hours. She left out the spooky stuff, and talked a lot about Liz Overshaw and Benjamin Skinner.

"It's an omen," Antonia said through a mouthful of thin crust four-cheese pizza. "I mean, how cool is this? I'm auditioning for a Sherlock Holmes play. And your first case means that you get to play at being Sherlock Holmes. It's prophetic, that's what it is. Not to mention that you're starting off with a pretty fancy client, right off the bat. I mean, if Overshaw's even halfway as loaded as Benjamin Blackheart Skinner, you'll be able to retire before you're forty! As long as you catch the murderer, that is." She levered a third slice from the plate sitting between them, paused with the slice halfway to her mouth, and said, "Oh. My. God. Nemesis. That's what it is. Nemesis."

"The beer's gone to your brain." Bree moved the pitcher of Stella Artois out of Antonia's reach.

"Here!" Antonia grabbed the oversized menu and shoved it into Bree's hands. "Pretend you're reading that! Put it up higher! Higher!"

"What in the world are you doing?" Bree asked crossly. "Have you lost your *mind*?"

"It's Payton the Rat!" Antonia hissed. "No! Don't turn around! He's right behind you!"

Huey's was right on the riverfront, the trendiest of the trendy stores and restaurants that occupied the old Cotton

Exchange on the wharfs. And if there was one thing Payton was good at, it was finding trendy spots.

"What's he doing?" Bree asked tensely. She kept her eyes studiously on the list of appetizers.

"He is standing at the bar with an absolutely foul-looking drink in his hand. It's pink."

"A girly sort of a drink?"

"Very girly. There's fruit in it."

"Then he's waiting for somebody. Payton only drinks twelve-year-old or older single malt whiskies."

"What a jerk," Antonia said briefly. "Wait. Yep. You're right."

"He's with somebody?"

Both of them knew what she meant.

"Yeah." Antonia's eyes met Bree's. "Under thirty, but just. And a hard-body. A gym rat. I mean, she's got arms like wire cables on a suspension bridge. You can look. He's got his back to us."

Bree turned halfway around and then back again. "She's gorgeous," she said flatly.

"In a Bionic Woman sort of way, yeah." Antonia shook her head in mild disgust and refilled her glass from the pitcher. "Didn't take him long to hook up."

"He was hooked up before we broke up." Bree decided to refill her glass, too.

"Oh, bummer. Look happy. Look busy! He's seen us!" Antonia broke into a trill of laughter, and said very loudly, "I hope you told the guy where to get off! Really, Bree, you've had to beat guys off with a stick since you dumped that fat—" She broke off and her voice dropped several degrees to an icy chill. "Why, Payton! If it isn't the fat-head himself."

"Hey, Bree," Payton said. "You're lookin' good."

Bree looked up from her menu and said casually, "So you've found this place, too. How've you been, Payton?"

He held a glass of what was probably Laphroaig in one hand, and the shoulder of Ms. Suspension Bridge of 2007 with the other. He gave the woman a pat on the back, and said, "Got a little business, here, Sean. I'll meet you back at the bar." Then he addressed Antonia, "Shove over, Toni. Let me sit and talk to Bree here for a second."

Antonia smiled sweetly at him and moved farther into the booth. Payton perched comfortably on the outer edge and looked into Bree's eyes with a warm sincerity that was as genuine as a blizzard in Tahiti. "You're looking well," he said, and sighed. "And it's *good* to see you, Bree." He cocked his forefinger and thumb to make a pistol. "Love the hair. Found any office space yet?"

"On Angelus," Antonia said, "right on the river, practically." Then she added, loyally, if inaccurately, "Gorgeous view."

Bree took a small sip of beer. Payton was gorgeous. A lot of the gorgeousness emanated from his eyes, which were a brilliant sort of blue violet (due, she had discovered, to the kind of contact lenses he wore)—and a lot more due to the chiseled line of his cheekbones and his incredibly fit body. His hair was clipped short, and he had an attractive line of stubble on his chin. Her stomach was fluttery. Her heart was a little sore. But she didn't want to cry, scream, or throw things. Most of all, she didn't want to be sitting in this booth looking at him.

"I hear you took on an offer with Stubblefield, Marwick," she said. "Congratulations. Looks like we'll be seeing each other in the courtroom now and then."

His smile widened, which meant he was aggravated.

"I didn't realize until just today that you'd decided to open a practice here, too."

Bree wondered at the speed with which the word had gotten around. "You remember my uncle Franklin."

"The weirdo?"

"The judge," Bree corrected, coldly. "He had a small practice after he retired from the bench. He left it to me. Certainly nothing like Stubblefield, Marwick," Bree added sweetly.

"Couldn't have surprised me more, when I got the offer," Payton said. "Not that I would have turned them down—I mean, honestly, Bree, the best law firm in the Southeast . . ."

"The most profitable, anyway," she said dryly. Stubblefield, Marwick specialized in class actions. Infomercials soliciting dying smokers, brain-damaged children, and breathers of asphalt ran routinely on late-night television.

"We've got a pretty impressive list of clients," he said easily. "Yes, we've made a reputation standing up for the rights of the unjustly oppressed . . ."

"For forty percent of the settlement fee," Bree said. "Really, Payton." She bit off the rest of what would be quite a harangue, if she let herself go, and said only, "So they made you an offer you couldn't refuse."

"Over three hundred K a year," he said.

Antonia made a noise like a fork in a food grinder. "You are such a *tacky* fathead, Payton."

"I hope you're very happy," Bree said politely. You certainly won't have to worry about your Am-Ex bill."

". . . and our client list, as I was about to tell you, has some of the best people in Savannah."

Bree frowned. This was leading up to something.

"Among them," Payton said easily, "Dr. and Mrs. Grainger Skinner."

"And they are?" Bree said. Then the penny dropped. "Benjamin Skinner's son and his wife."

"His son," Antonia said doubtfully. "Oh! The guy who answered the phone when you called Mr. Skinner back."

Payton shrugged in a deprecating way. "Grainger Skinner himself isn't that big a deal—it's not money that counts in Savannah. But his wife is a Pendergast, and that does count for something."

Antonia paid no attention to this. "Huh. That was such a weird thing to have happened, Bree. I mean, I had no idea cell phone calls were stored like e-mail." She forgot, temporarily, that she hated Payton the Rat and said to him. "Some glitch in the cell phone tower made Bree get a phone call from Skinner *after* he died. Isn't that bizarre?"

"That's bullshit, is what it is," Payton said. "You know, Bree, there's ways of soliciting clients, and then there's ways of soliciting clients. You kind of stepped over the line, there, if you don't mind my saying so."

"Oh, I mind," Bree said. The small, regretful ache in her heart was rapidly turning into a large urge toward violence. She hadn't dumped beer over anyone's head in years. Maybe it was time she took it up again.

"I'm glad I ran into you here, instead of having to look you up in that place on ..." he stopped, dug into his suit coat pocket, and pulled out his BlackBerry. He tapped it, then said, "Angelus, you said? I can't find it."

"Very edgy," Antonia said loyally. "That location is the start of a new trend."

"Not if your clients don't know where the hell it is."

Antonia glared at him. "She's going to be the hottest lawyer in town in no time."

"That's good to hear," Payton said smoothly, "because I certainly wouldn't want anything to stand in the way of that rush of new clients."

"Anything like what?" Bree asked.

"Like a totally futile investigation into the death of Benjamin Skinner." He hunched forward, his hands folded on the table, his brow furrowed in earnest concern. "Trust me on this one, Bree. Liz Overshaw is a well-known crank. Sort of the epitome, if you don't mind my being frank, of the postmenopausal, hysterical female."

"Oh, I mind," Bree said politely. She smiled.

Antonia looked at the smile and said nervously, "Uh, Bree?"

Payton's tone became even more confiding. "I mean, what possible good can it do you to begin your career in this town by antagonizing the biggest player in the city?"

"I don't know," Bree said, with dangerous calm. "What good do you think it can do me?"

"Well, that's just it. No good at all. Look here, Bree. We're in a position to send a lot of good cases your way. You did pretty well in corporate tax law, as I recall. And that can be a gold mine for you if"—he tapped her wrist with an admonitory forefinger—"you decide to play ball."

Later, Bree figured it was the tap on the wrist that did it. She didn't really remember anything too clearly. She was furious, that she recalled. She jumped up with some idea of grabbing both Payton's ears and banging his head sharply against the table. The next thing she knew, she was on her feet in the middle of the room, and Payton was on his back against the bar ten feet away, looking dazed.

A tall, powerfully built man with colorless eyes had his hand on her shoulder. Antonia sat huddled at the back of the booth, her face pale.

"You *really* shouldn't have done that," the man said.

Bree wanted to say, "Done what?" but she didn't. The glass doors to the restaurant swung wide open. Most of the customers huddled under the tables. Dishes, glasses, bits of pizza, salad, and napkins littered the floor. It looked like the aftermath of a hurricane. Instead, she said, "What happened?"

Two policemen walked in the door; the one in the lead, a surly-looking guy with a potbelly and a shock of greasy blond hair, shouted, "Everybody freeze!"

"This way." The man with the colorless eyes, which were not, Bree realized, colorless at all, but silvery, put his arm around her shoulders and pulled her without effort into the hall to the kitchen.

"Wait a minute." Bree tried to duck out from under his grip and get back into the restaurant. Somehow, she kept on moving, down the back hall, out the back door, and into the alley that led to the parking lot. It wasn't that she couldn't resist. It was that her resistance didn't make any difference. He was very strong, not at all rough, and smelled pleasantly of the outdoors. Once in the alley, he closed the door to the kitchen behind them, and let her go.

"You live up there." It wasn't a question. He looked up at Front Street, which was one level above the shops and restaurants on the wharf. This part of the River Walk was constructed entirely of brick walls that rose twenty feet to the street above.

"Well, yes, but I should real—"

"Go home."

"I can't leave my sis—"

"I'll let her know you've gone."

"Who *are* you?" Bree asked indignantly. "And what do you think you're doing pushing me around like this?"

"Am I pushing you around?" He stepped back and looked at her, amused. "Sorry." His eyes were very silvery in the half light from the streetlamps. And he didn't look sorry at all. "My name's Striker. Gabe Striker."

Bree's mind went blank for a minute, then, suddenly furious, she said, "The PI."

"Yes. Armand Cianquino thought I could give you a hand with the Skinner case. I just happened to be in the area when this little fracas with Payton the Rat blew up."

"Is there anyone in Savannah who *doesn't* know Payton dumped me?" Bree demanded through gritted teeth.

He backed up, his hands held up in mock surrender. She barely could make out his face in the gloom. "Hey. Sorry. I seem to have stepped out of line."

"No kidding."

"I do apologize." His voice drifted toward her. She had the oddest sensation that he was suddenly bodiless, a mist in the air, liable to disappear with a breath. "Go home. I'm going to do what I can to make this go away."

Then she was alone in the alley.

Eight

Bree squashed the impulse to make a rude gesture after Gabriel Striker, PI. Instead, she walked past the Dumpster to the edge of the sidewalk and peered around the corner of the building. A police cruiser headed the wrong way down the one-way street sat in front of the restaurant, red lights flashing. Either the crowd gathered outside had come from the restaurant or from the street, probably both. A pair of teenage boys held their cell phones up, taking pictures of the scene. Bree recognized the bartender, a cheerful woman in her midforties who didn't look very cheerful at the moment. The shorter of the teenagers recognized the bartender, too. Huey's was a popular place. "Hey, Maureen! What the heck happened in there?"

Maureen shrugged, her face bewildered. "What started it is some woman dove over a table to get at this guy."

Bree cringed.

"And then this freak wind came upriver and blew the place apart. Well," Maureen amended, "not apart, as such.

But it burst right through the doors and made one hell of a mess in there." She looked up at the sky in a confused way. "And then it sort of sucked itself out."

"Anybody hurt?" The kid shouldered his way through the crowd to Maureen, his cell phone aimed at her. "Can you give me a quote?" Maureen held her hand in front of her face. "Will you cut that out? The two of you get on out of here."

"Anybody dead?" the other kid asked. He had a gold ring in his nose.

"Not so's you'd notice." Maureen dropped her hand and made a hideous face at the cell phone. "Go on, you two. Get out of here. What are you hanging around making trouble for?"

"Huh," the shorter kid said self-importantly. "You know how much the TV stations pay for pictures of this kind of stuff?"

"It'd be a lot better if there was a couple of bodies, Pauly," said the kid with the nose ring. "Who wants to see pizza all over the floor? I can see that at home."

"You getting the message, Pauly?" Maureen said rudely. "You two, beat it. I already called the insurance company and the fewer people hanging around when they get here, the better." She scowled at them. "Maybe they'll figure *you* two had something to do with it." She watched the two boys disappear into the thinning crowd, then shook her head and went back into the restaurant.

A small breeze stirred in the street. Bree looked up at the sky. A thumbnail moon hung low on the horizon. A few clouds scudded past the stars overhead.

It was as quiet as the grave.

She trudged up the stairs to the town house, shaken, bewildered, and longing for sleep

The phone sounded inside as she fumbled with the keys to the town house door. Sasha barked. Somewhere in the distance, sirens sounded, and Bree had a sudden, irrational conviction that the police were after her. Her mental equilibrium tipped further toward a genuine fit of the willies as she got past the front door and nearly fell over Sasha. She saved herself—and the poor dog's leg—with a hugely athletic leap over his body and dived toward the phone.

"Bree, darlin'!"

"Mamma," Bree gasped.

"You all right, honey?" Waves of concern flowed over the phone line.

"I'm just fine. I was rushing through the front door to get to the phone and tripped over the dog."

"Dog? You still have that dog?" Francesca asked.

"Ah," Bree said. "Things have been so hectic here, I forgot to tell you about the dog." Holding the receiver to her ear, she put her back against the wall and sank to the floor. This pleased Sasha, who promptly tried to settle in her lap.

"I think you should tell us about the dog," her father's voice said.

"Well. He's a rescue." This was a guaranteed path to her mother's soft heart. "And he's a wonderful animal. Just wonderful. Antonia just loves ..." Bree bit her lip so hard she almost yelped. "I mean, if Antonia could meet him, she'd just love him, too. Here, he wants to say hello." She put the receiver near Sasha's muzzle and without much hope of a response said, "Speak!"

Sasha barked.

Bree put the phone to her ear again. "There! What do you think of that?"

"I think he sounds big," her mother's voice said dubiously. "You remember the town house covenants. If he's too big, Bree, you need to bring him on home to Plessey. As a matter of fact, when your father and I come in next week, we can take him back with us if we have to. Poor thing."

Bree looked at Sasha, who was getting healthier-looking by the hour, it seemed. "I don't know. I really like having him around." Suddenly, the rest of her mother's message sank in. "You're what?! Coming here?"

"For your open house, Bree, for heaven's sake. I knew you had too much on your mind getting your office set up. But now that you've found this darling little place, it's time to let the professional community know you're up and running."

"Now's really not a good time, Mamma," Bree said. "I mean, I appreciate the thought, but I'd really rather—"

"We knew you'd say that. So your father and I have already sent out the invitations. He still has a lot of good contacts in the law community, don't you, darlin', and they'll all turn out for him. It'll be a wonderful send-off, Bree honey. You'll see."

"You sent the invitations out?" Bree said.

"We did," her mother said firmly. "Next Thursday afternoon from five to seven at the Mansion."

"The Forsyth Mansion?" Bree said weakly. The hotel on Forsyth Park was rated five stars, and the restaurant, 700 Drayton, was fabulously expensive.

"That gives you a week to get the caterer and the florist set up. The bills are to be sent to us, aren't they, Royal?"

"Mamma," Bree said, "I really wish . . ."

Her mother's voice rolled over her protests like Sherman through Atlanta. "Now, you know how proud we are of you! You'll let us host this little reception, won't you?"

"You bet," Bree said, suddenly exhausted. She couldn't handle one more thing. Not one. All she wanted to do was take a long, hot shower and go to bed. "I appreciate the thought. Thank you, Mamma. Thanks, Daddy. You let me know before you begin the drive down, won't you?"

"Of course we will." There was a long pause. "You sure you're all right, dear? Royal, you think she's all right?"

From her position on the floor next to the phone, Bree could see into the darkened living room, but not around the corner to the fireplace. Suddenly, Sasha scrambled to his feet. His ears went forward and he stared intently into the living room.

As she watched him, part of her mind still struggling with the incident at the restaurant, the other part listening to her mother's light, pretty voice, still another longing for the total oblivion of sleep, a thin river of water seeped around the corner wall and headed toward her. Sasha barked once, and then fell silent.

"I've got to run, Mamma. I think I left the water running." She dropped the phone into the cradle and stumbled to her feet, her heart thumping. The water glowed with a yellow phosphorescence. It inched forward, changing direction every few feet as if encountering unseen obstacles.

Sasha turned and looked at her, his eyes glowing with reflected light.

It's looking for something.

Bree fought the impulse to run. Sasha looked up at her; then, tail set low, ears flattened against his skull, he moved cautiously forward.

Bree went with him. The source was somewhere in the living room ...

The painting.

She moved quietly, but with an intensity of purpose that heightened her senses. She could hear the soft hiss as the fluid crept across the floor, the slow beat of Sasha's heart, the up and down sweep of bird's wings. She gave the water a wide berth and rounded the corner into the heart of the living room.

The painting was alive. More than alive, it was absorbed in itself, with soft whispers and sly, low-voiced laughter. The flame red sea overflowed the frame, ran down the brick surround, and spilled onto the floor. The waves moved back and forth in slow, ominous swells, like a giant creature, breathing. The dark-haired woman with the pale eyes was gone. The shrieks of the dying were faint, almost inaudible. She heard them, though with that preternatural enhancement of her senses that let her hear the up and downward sweep of the bird's great wings.

Sasha growled and dropped to the floor.

The cormorant is on the move.

Not stopping to think, not *wanting* to think, Bree snatched at the first heavy object that came to hand: a bronze statue of a Chinese horse. She swung it around her head once and then let it fly, straight at the painting.

The statue hit with a *cr-a-a-ck* of sound and a spray of sickly yellow light.

The vision disappeared with a blast of wind.

The lights in the living room snapped on.

Suddenly, Bree was among familiar things, with no

trace of what she'd seen except the chips of marble mantel on the living room rug and the dented statue of the T'ang Dynasty horse.

From behind her, Antonia said, "It's not enough that you, like, skipped out on me in the middle of a natural disaster, you've got to trash the living room, too?" She marched in, threw herself flat onto the couch, and stared at the ceiling. "I'm here to tell you, Bree, I think you've totally flipped out."

Bree stood rooted to the spot. Her whole body was icy. Sasha nudged her hip, and then thrust his nose under her hand. She stroked his ears without thinking; then, her knees shaking, she sank into the chair next to the fireplace.

"Bree? Did you hear me? You swore you'd given up whacking people up the side of the head. I mean, the little creep deserved it . . . but you took down the whole restaurant!" She chuckled to herself. "Pretty darn impressive, though."

"Yes," Bree whispered.

Something in her voice alarmed her sister. Antonia sat up and looked at her, genuine concern on her face. "Hey! I was kidding about you flipping out. You look awful." She jumped up and twisted her hands together. "Can I get you something? A glass of water?" She moved halfway across the rug to the phone. "Maybe I should call the paramedics or something?" Her voice trembled. "Bree, you're scaring me."

"No." Her throat was tight. She cleared it and said loudly, "No. I'm fine." She ran her hands through her hair. "I'm going to bed. I don't want to talk about it."

Antonia bit her lip. "Fine," she said nervously. "That's just fine."

Bree got to her feet. She felt a hundred years old.

"You want a hand, or anything?"

Bree shook her head. "I just ..."

"Just what?"

Bree looked at her in despair. "I just want things to make sense."

Antonia's face whitened. Bree suddenly realized that her little sister, for all her brave talk, wasn't all that tough. It took everything she had, but she breathed deep, relaxed her shoulders, and sat back down. She crossed her legs and said with a fair assumption of carelessness, "It looks like I settled Payton's hash good and proper, don't you think?"

Antonia smiled, tentatively. "You sure did!"

"What happened to Ms. Suspension Bridge of 2007?"

Antonia giggled. "Who knows? I'll bet she ran like a rabbit. I'll bet she's halfway to Topeka by now."

Bree smiled and nodded.

It was going to be all right.

It *had* to be all right.

Nine

And we are here as on a darkling plain
Swept with confused alarms of struggle and flight,
Where ignorant armies clash by night.
    —"Dover Beach," Matthew Arnold

Bree folded the Wednesday edition of the *Savannah Daily* into neat thirds and dropped it into the recycling can.

On a second thought, she retrieved it and set it neatly on the trunk that served as a coffee table in her new offices. She hadn't had time to pick up any other reading material and the top of the trunk looked pitifully bare. Fortunately, nothing in the short news story titled "Freak Encounter Busts Up Huey's" identified her as the woman who started it all by diving over the table at Payton McAllister, attorney-at-law. There was a brief quote from a meteorologist about the likelihood of a sirocco-like wind sweeping through the heart of the Market District ("infinitesimal") and a longer op-ed piece about climate aberrations due to global warming. That was that.

At least it'd happened too late to make the late news on KWYC, for which she was thankful. It had, however, provided a virtually inexhaustible topic of conversation for

Antonia, who had been stuck with the bill for the pizza and demanded Bree pay her half.

Bree had paid up and offered her a choice: shut up about the incident at Huey's, or she, Bree, would get on the phone to their parents and rat her out about UNC. Antonia snapped, "Fine," then asked for the name of her martial arts teacher; Payton had spun through the air like a Frisbee, she'd said, which was not only totally cool, but a skill that was bound to come in handy at some point. Especially if her sister kept persecuting her.

Bree ended the conversation by going to bed.

She'd risen early after a disturbed and restless night, bundled up Sasha, lifted the painting from the wall, and left the town house for the office while it was still dark outside. Antonia almost never got up before eleven, but there was always a chance that she'd bounce into the kitchen, full of questions Bree couldn't, wouldn't answer.

Halfway down Montgomery, she stopped behind a Chatham County municipal garbage truck. Maybe she could bribe the driver to throw the accursed canvas into the grinder. She imagined the frame splintered, the torn canvas, and the red and maddened eye of the bird glaring at her from the mess of orange peel, decayed vegetables, and sodden paper towels.

Sasha whined from the backseat, and then barked.

It'll find its way back to you.

"Dammit!" Bree said.

The truck engine roared clumsily down the street. She let it go. And the first thing she did when she got into the office was hang the thing back over the fireplace.

She sat on the couch and stared at it. Mrs. Mather hadn't come down yet, and the place was silent. The

painting hung there, malign, awful, a haunt if there ever
was one. She desperately wanted it burned, cut up, ground
to ashes, destroyed. And she just as desperately knew that
she couldn't do it alone.

She curled her hand into a fist and banged herself on
the forehead in sheer frustration. The painting was just
that. A painting. It was a bad copy of a painting she must
have seen before, years ago, when she was little. She'd
seen the original as a kid, been petrified by it, and had
nightmares for years. Sort of a post-traumatic stress kind
of thing. She couldn't remember being scared by it, but
people frequently forgot traumatic events, while still suf-
fering the consequences of them. She remembered reading that somewhere. She hoped that this was true, and that
it wasn't something she picked up in the Your Health section of some half-baked popular magazine.

Maybe her mother remembered what had started her
nightmares. She could call and ask her.

Or maybe not.

She set up Sasha's water bowl, left him some kibble,
and went out to complete her furniture shopping. When
she came back, hours later, Mrs. Mather had been down
to brush his coat and tend to the healing wounds. He
greeted her at the door with a happy swish of his tail and a
contented sigh. She followed him into the living room,
walked up to the fireplace, and stared defiantly at the
wall. The painting still hung over the mantel, a sullen mix
of gray, black, and the crimson of that hellish fire.

"I'm going to take this thing outside and burn it, Sasha."

Sasha lay down with a thump on the floor, put his head
on his paws, and looked up at her sorrowfully.

It won't burn.

Bree stared resentfully at it, then dropped down on the couch and rubbed her forehead. She hated the thing. She looked at her watch. Her first interview wasn't due for an hour. She could keep on sitting here like a dormouse with her thumb up her nose if she wanted to. If dormice had thumbs, which they probably didn't.

On an impulse, she got to her feet and ran lightly up the colorful front stairs to the second floor. Lavinia had seemed to know something about the horrible thing. This wasn't all in her imagination. It couldn't be.

The landing was dim; there was no window here to look over the cemetery and no ceiling light. Lavinia's door was in shadow.

The march of painted angels went up one side of Lavinia's door, over the top, and down the other. The door itself was painted a sheer white that glimmered softly. Bree hesitated a moment, then tapped on the frame.

There was a soft, shuddery movement on the other side of the door, as if something large and feathery slid across the floor. The door opened, and Lavinia stood there in a flood of pale, silvery light. A gauzy shawl enfolded her, and her dark skin seemed to glow. "Well, child! This is unexpected!"

"I'm sorry to bother you," Bree apologized. "I had a couple of questions I thought I'd ask."

"No bother," Lavinia said equably. "Come on in and sit yourself down for a spell."

Hesitant, Bree stepped inside. For a moment, a very brief moment, the second floor seemed larger than she'd expected. *Much* larger. A velvety gray mist veiled the floor. The ceiling soared above her. A wall fixture lit with the softness of moonlight cast a gentle shine over a variety of large and small shapes. Lavinia's voice was a soft whisper in her head:

"Some of my littlies. You know what a lemur is? I have me a few. And these here are a couple of baby owls that lost their mamma."

A ring-tailed lemur curled its tail over the back of a rocking chair and stared at her with huge golden eyes. Bree stared dreamily back. The entire apartment seemed to rock to a slow, sleepy rhythm. The chair rocked with it. The lemur purred. She swayed lightly back and forth on her feet, as though on the deck of a ship.

The rocking, the lunar light, the scent of strange flowers all made Bree dizzy. She shut her eyes and opened them again.

The moonlit scene was gone in a flash, evaporated like mist in the hot sun. Lavinia stood in ordinary light on wide pine floors in a small, shabby room that smelled of lavender and roses. She pulled her sweater around her bony shoulders and smiled sweetly at Bree.

The rocking chair was there, though, swaying wildly as if something had jumped up in a hurry and pushed the chair away. A bit of soft gray fur still clung to it.

Bree pressed her hands to her ears and took a deep breath. "Please keep on with your chores. I've got ... quite a bit to do downstairs. What I wanted to ask you ... it'll keep just fine."

She walked downstairs at a much slower pace than she had going up. Sasha waited for her at the foot, ears up, tail wagging gently back and forth.

"That," Bree said with a great deal of puzzlement, "was very confusing. Lemurs? Baby owls? Where do these things in my head *come* from, Sasha?"

Sasha yawned, walked back into the living room, and went to sleep.

Bree rubbed her temples hard. She needed more sleep. She needed to rid herself of nightmares. She'd dumped a pile of unopened mail in her briefcase before she left; she'd it tackle now, before her first appointment of the day. Uneasily aware of the painting looming at her, she settled down to go over her unread issues of the *ABA Journal.*

Sometime later, a polite knock at the front door roused her from an infuriating essay complaining about tort reform. Bree got up to answer it, making a mental note to ask Mrs. Mather—Lavinia, rather—about a door chime. Or maybe an intercom. She'd decided after last night that she wasn't going to leave any doors unlocked, anywhere.

Sasha gave her an encouraging sort of bark as she walked by. She bent down and fondled his ears, then stroked his forehead. "If you like this one, give me some kind of sign, okay? It's Rosa Lucheta, the lawyer's widow."

But she opened the door to a short, thickset man with a black beard and a cane.

"Miss Beaufort?" He rolled the "r" slightly.

"Yes," she said. "May I help you?"

"I am Petru Lucheta. Rosa's brother." The accent was Slavic; beyond that, Bree was at a loss. It could have been Russian, Latvian, or Serbo-Croatian for all she knew.

"How do you do," Bree said politely.

"I am ke-vite well," he said. "Rosa, she is, alas, not so well."

"I'm sorry to hear that. But there was no need for you to come all this way to cancel the appointment. She could have called."

"Rosa is not so well permanently," he said. "She is unable to work, alas. I, however, am ke-vite able to work. I have come in her stead."

"I see." Bree considered Mr. Lucheta for a long moment. He had very black eyes. The beard covered most of his face, but what she could see of it had a benign, almost avuncular expression.

"You are willing to consider a man for this position?" he said anxiously. "The advertisement did not make a reference to gender."

"Our laws don't allow us to do that, Mr. Lucheta. Forgive me, may I ask? Are you a citizen? Of the United States, I mean?"

"Oh, yes. I mean, yes, I understand you. No, I am not a citizen. I have a g-r-r-reen card and I will be eligible for citizenship quite soon." He cleared his throat, glanced from side to side, and shifted his cane from his right hand to the left in the politest possible way. "May I come in?"

"I'm sorry, I didn't mean to keep you standing here on the stoop. Yes, please come in." She turned, hearing the shuffle-*thump* as he walked behind her. She felt like Ishmael listening to the one-legged Ahab roam the decks of the *Pequod*.

"We'll have more furniture soon," she said over her shoulder. "I ordered a desk and some filing cabinets from Office Max this morning, and they'll be here sometime tomorrow. And our phone lines will be installed by Friday afternoon, at least that's what Southern Bell promised, and they're usually pretty reliable."

The shuffle-*thump* came to an abrupt stop. "I see you have the *Rise of the Cormorant*."

Bree whirled. "I beg your pardon?"

He used his cane to point at the picture. "That. I haven't

seen it in many, many years." He limped closer. "T'uh. One of the copies, I see. Hm."

Bree sat down. Her knees were a bit trembly. "*One* of the copies?" she said. "As if, I mean, are there a whole bunch of copies?"

He folded his hands on his cane and gazed affably at the leather chair.

"Please, of course. Sit down."

"Thank you." He sat in a very formal way, with his back straight and his cane placed horizontally over his knees.

Bree tried to behave calmly, but she knew her voice was shaking. "You've seen this painting before? And you said something about a whole bunch of copies? Is it famous?"

"Do you mean, are there a whole bunch of copies, as there are a whole bunch of copies of Vincent's *Sunflowers* or Pablo's *Dove of Peace*? Art that has been carelessly replicated in volume? Is this a piece of art that is famous in that way? That is what you are asking me?"

"Yes," Bree said, finding this intimate way of referring to dead artists a little disconcerting. "Although I don't know this picture at all and I do know those others, of course. Everybody does. It can't be *that* famous. Or not as famous as the other pictures you mentioned."

"In some circles, it is *that* famous. As for copies, there are not so many. But you already know this, I think."

Bree shook her head. "I don't know a thing about it. I wish I did. It's called what? The *Rise of the Cormorant*?"

"Yes. It refers to the bird, you see, who flies over the ship."

Bree bit her lip. For some reason, the answer to this next question was critical. "Who painted it?"

"The Patriarch, of course." He turned to her. "You didn't know this?"

"What Patriarch? Who's the Patriarch?"

Petru tugged at his beard. "I'm sorry. Perhaps I've said too much for the moment. I was under the impression that ownership of the painting has passed to you."

"I hate the thing," Bree said. "Own it?" The depth of her fear and hatred surprised her. "I'd rather own a rabid dog. I don't want it. I loathe it. I've tried to wreck it and I can't. I can't even give it away."

"No?" Petru said with interest. "You've tried this? To pass it along to someone else?"

Bree shuddered. "Never. How could I foist that thing on someone else? I meant I can't see myself having the gall to give it to somebody." She took a deep breath and burst out, "It's wicked!"

Petru tugged at his beard. "The subject is wicked," he agreed. "The painting itself is not wicked—it merely is what it is." He tilted his head, considering, "What is the worst thing you feel when you see the *Rise of the Cormorant*?"

Bree stared at it defiantly. "I dream about the damn thing, you know. And the dream's always the same. If I could just swim fast enough I could keep the people from drowning. That's what I feel when I look at it; balked, angry, and helpless." To her extreme annoyance, tears sprang to her eyes. Antonia was right, Bree cried from rage and frustration much more often than she should.

Petru patted her hand in a comforting way. "This is very Russian, you know. To feel as deeply as this. It's a good thing."

"I don't believe there are any Russians in our family," Bree sobbed, "but I appreciate the thought."

Petru chuckled a little, dug into the pocket of his suit coat, and emerged with a clean tissue. Bree accepted it with thanks and blew her nose. It smelled of lemons. She leaned against the couch back and looked up at the ceiling rather than confront the painting again. "I just want it out of here."

"The only way to remove the painting from your life is to find someone else to accept it."

"That's ridiculous," Bree said, a little crossly. She was embarrassed at breaking down in front of a man who might be going to work for her; then she was embarrassed at her testiness. "I do apologize, Mr. Lucheta. I'm not usually this volatile. Please tell me all you can about the painting."

"The Patriarch created the *Rise of the Cormorant* as a warning, and as a test. The warning is, of course, that the cormorant is always on the rise. The test—the test is most interesting. There are those, Miss Beaufort, who would gaze upon those drowning souls and sail as fast away from rescue as they could. And there are those who beat the bodies with their oars and hope to drown them faster. And there are those who scream with rage that they cannot help fast enough."

"You forgot those who're scared pea green," Bree said with painful honesty.

Petru laughed a little. "Fear, like tears, is very Russian." He twinkled with satisfaction. "All deeply felt emotions are very Russian."

"But which Patriarch? There's a Patriarch in the Greek Orthodox Church, and in the Russian one, too, isn't there?"

"And for my people as well," Petru said. "I am a Jew.

But no, the Patriarch of whom I speak is one of the Patri-archs of Angels."

"I haven't heard of that religious sect before," Bree said. "Does it come from Western Europe or Eastern?"

"God is universal. The Patriarchs of Angels are uni-versal, too. There are no artificial divisions in the Spheres."

"I see," Bree said somewhat dryly. There was a look in Petru's eye she didn't like at all. Religious cranks were not her favorite kind of people. She balled the tissue in her hand and looked around for a wastebasket. She'd for-gotten to buy a wastebasket.

"And of course, there's the cormorant."

"Of course," Bree agreed. "A large diving bird, isn't it? You can train it to fish, I think."

"It is a fisher of men's souls," Petru said. Then, in a sonorous voice that rolled through the little room like a kettledrum, he quoted: *"The angel ended, and in Adam's ear / So charming left his voice, that he a while / Thought him still speaking, still stood fixed to hear."* He beamed at her. "Like the painting, the Patriarch commissioned this. John's greatest work, I believe."

"John?" Bree said, utterly baffled. "John who?"

"Milton. *Paradise Lost.* "

Bree bit her lip hard and said, "I see," in a strangled way.

"You are laughing," Petru observed without any sign of being offended. "La, la. There it is."

"I do apologize, but—" She stopped in mid-sentence. Petru looked at her. "But what?" he said encouragingly.

"Nothing. Nothing." She put her hand up to her eyes, as if to shield herself from a bright light. Nothing made sense. "I've been running around like a headless chicken, getting the office set up. I'm a little overtired, that's all."

Petru didn't move. But Bree had a sudden horrific fancy that he'd turned into something different. He wasn't a shabby, down-at-the-heels refugee, but a solid piece of the dark. She forced herself to open her eyes and look at him.

He smiled at her with such irresistible good humor that she had to smile back. "There is no need to hire me at all," Petru said, comfortably. "Sometimes it is difficult for those from different life experiences to adjust to one another. And many of you Americans are just a little bit suspicious of we Russians, are you not?" He shrugged. "I can assure you I am not a member of our mafia, or of our KGB, and that my heart no longer belongs to the Communist Party." He started to get up.

"Of course I'm not suspicious of Russians," Bree said. Only of people who referred to dead poets as if they'd had dinner with them last night, she thought. But she didn't say that aloud. "Please don't think that. It's absurd." She pulled herself together with an effort. She'd called this man in for an interview, dammit, and that's what she was going to do. Interview him.

Except she hadn't called him, she'd called his sister. She stared at him, eyes narrowed. That is, if he actually had a sister named Rosa. Suddenly, she wasn't sure of anything.

Sasha got up from his corner with a grunt, and hobbled past Bree to Petru Lucheta. He stuck his nose on the man's knee, accepted a pat, hobbled back to his corner, and went back to sleep. His message couldn't have been clearer if he'd spoken aloud:

There's nothing to worry about. A little eccentricity never hurt anyone.

Bree took a breath, held it, and decided to trust both her dog and her inner voice. "Do you have a résumé, Mr. Lucheta?"

"Call me Petru, please. I have here my passport, my sister Rosa's address in this city, where I live, and my license to practice law in Petrograd." He pulled a sheaf of documents from his suit coat, and placed them on the coffee table on top of the newspaper. The article about the wind damage at Huey's was uppermost. He looked at it, looked at Bree, and smiled like a bearded cherub.

Bree ignored the smile and examined the passport and the license, a piece of vellum with a gold seal. The vellum was in the Cyrillic alphabet. So he *was* Russian. And claimed to be a lawyer. She didn't read Cyrillic; for all she knew the poor man was licensed to sail three-masted schooners rather than practice law.

"I can't offer you a professional position," Bree began apologetically.

He held up one pudgy hand. "Of course you cannot! And I, I cannot practice law here, in your country, at least not for a great while yet. No, no. It's for the assistant to your good self that I come."

"A great while yet, you said? Do you mean that you're studying for the Georgia Bar?"

"Yes. At night. It is as well that I read English with much more adeptness than I speak it." He raised his chin. "Ah. I hear, perhaps, your delivery person at the door."

Bree jumped to her feet. There *was* a knock at the door, a modest rat-a-tat-tat. But Office Max wasn't due to deliver the supplies and the filing cabinets she ordered until tomorrow. And Ronald Parchese's appointment was for four o'clock; it was just after two right now.

Bree opened the front door to a pair of delivery men with DASHETT DELIVERY embroidered on their coveralls. The one with the name "Eustace" stitched above the Dashett logo held a clipboard and thrust it at her. "Mrs. Winston-Beaufort?"

"*Miss* Beaufort, yes," she said, as she scribbled her name on the sheet. "This is great. I didn't expect you guys until tomorrow. Please bring the desk on in here. The filing cabinets go in the dining roo— I mean, the conference room."

"No desk, ma'am," Eustace said. "We got boxes, we got bookshelves, but we got no desk."

Bree frowned and looked at the sender's name on the manifest. Professor Cianquino. "Oh, no," she said.

"This not your stuff?" Eustace asked with patient indifference.

"It's not my stuff," Bree said crossly. "But it is stuff that's been sent to me. I suppose it'd be really rude to send it back. Would you stack the boxes in the kitchen, I mean the break room, please? And the bookshelves can go along the wall opposite the fireplace. I needed some anyway."

"Your law library is arriving," Petru Lucheta said, as he got to his feet with some difficulty. "This is excellent. I am, of course, conversant with the computer, but it is a much greater pleasure to handle books."

He and Bree both stood out of the way as Eustace and his colleague brought the boxes in on dollies.

"I don't really have a law library, as such," Bree confessed. "I have a few reference volumes, like Black's and a few of my textbooks from school, but I depend on

Lexis for researching case law. This"—she gestured at the stack of cardboard boxes disappearing into the break room—"is a gift from an old friend, a retired law professor, who seems to have gotten it from my uncle. It's more of a curiosity than anything else, and," she added with considerable frustration, "I really don't have room for it."

Petru, who had ignored the latter part of this speech, stopped Eustace, withdrew a volume from the box at the top of the stack, and examined the spine. "Aha. It is as I had hoped! Lexis," he added, "does not have available the *Corpus Juris Ultima*. At least, not yet."

Bree closed her eyes. She heard Petru shuffle-*thump* to the kitchen. "Alas!" he called to her. "This version is not in Latin! We will just have to cope, dear Bree!"

<hr />

"You're not from Russia, or anything," Bree asked Ronald Parchese rather anxiously, several hours later.

"Russia?" he said, even more anxiously. "No. Do I need to be to get the job?" Ronald was slim, without being skinny, and had the sort of clean-cut looks that prompted her mother to talk longingly of grandchildren: blond, fair-skinned, with pale blue eyes and a boyish face. He was elegant, too; his black trousers were well-cut, and his striped shirt immaculate. He made Bree feel dowdy in her all-purpose trouser suit and white T-shirt.

"I didn't mean actually Russian," she said, to his further bewilderment. "I was just wondering if you were a Southerner like me, or if you've come to Savannah from somewhere else. But you say you've lived in Savannah all your life?"

"Every second, Miss Beaufort. Except for my little trips."

"Little trips?"

"I try to get to Italy every year. My people were from there originally, you know, but not for years and years and years."

"I see."

"You aren't looking for a foreign national for any reason? Because I would think that my trips to Italy would count."

"Oh, no, no." Bree felt herself beginning to stutter. "Forget I said anything about alien venues. Look, I'd like to take a second and read your résumé. Would you like a cup of coffee while I do that?"

"I'll take care of the coffee," he said. He rose lithely to his feet. "What sort of equipment do you have in the break room?"

"Just a Mr. Coffee. But the beans are from Starbucks."

"Tsk. Not good. We'll have to look into a Melitta. Right now, I'll see what I can do."

Ronald headed toward the kitchen, followed by Sasha, who'd taken to him immediately. Bree looked over his résumé. His word-processing skills were sensational. He'd taken a course at the Chatham County Community College in legal terms, and he had a two-year administrative assistant's degree from a local secretarial school. And she liked him. "Your braids," he'd said after they had shaken hands and sat down together for the interview, "are a stroke of genius. Who had the nous to pull that off?"

Ronald Parchese on paper was a nice all-American kid. She'd hired Petru. She hadn't really had a choice. In some obscure way, at such a remote level of consciousness that she almost didn't recognize it, a sorting process was going on and Petru was inevitable, like Mrs. Mather was inevitable and the sixty-volume copy of the *Corpus Juris Ultima* stacked on her kitchen counters.

She wanted somebody NOT inevitable. Like Ronald, who didn't have a clue about all the stuff that was gathering around her like a silken net. He hadn't even glanced at the *Rise of the Cormorant*, for instance, or if he had, he hadn't said a word.

So why not two assistants? One for whatever the Skinner job was really all about, and one for the Brianna Winston-Beaufort who was going to continue with a normal law practice long after the weirdness of the Skinner case was over.

The retainer from Liz Overshaw gave her a head start on expenses; and she'd saved enough before she'd made the move to Savannah to run her office for six months with an assistant. But she hadn't budgeted for two. She wasn't even going to have enough work for two until her practice built. If it ever did.

Ronald came back with a tray, which he settled on the trunk. He glanced indifferently at the newspaper headline about Huey's, handed her a cup of coffee, and settled comfortably into the leather sofa with his own. "What do you think? Are my qualifications okay?"

"I'd love to hire you," Bree said promptly. "But I'm not sure you'd be comfortable here."

He flushed a bright, angry red. "If it's because I have a domestic partner . . ."

"Of course it isn't that," Bree said indignantly. "Do I look like a bigot to you?"

"You'd be surprised at what bigots look like," he snapped.

"I probably would. But they don't look like me. Or my sister," she added.

Ronald's complexion returned to normal and the tremor left his voice. "Does your sister work here, too?"

"God, no! But she lives with me and she bounces all over. She's like a tennis ball loose in the room. You keep tripping over her. She's bound to bounce in and out of here several times a week."

Ronald's eyes brightened. "I know exactly what you mean! You love her, but brattiness rules."

"Exactly." Bree set her cup down and sighed. "The reason I'm not sure you'd like it here is because you're *too* normal. I can't tell you," she added passionately, "how much I want someone as normal as you are to be here every day when I walk in the door."

"There's a first," Ronald muttered. "If you could call my mother and tell her that, I'd appreciate it. So what's with me being so normal?"

"I'll show you what I mean. Let me just ask you something." Bree leaned forward, smiling. "You see that picture over the fireplace?"

"Do I not!" Ronald said. "I didn't want to say anything, but really, Bree, it's just hideous. How could you!"

"Ha!" Bree said. "I thought so! Please, please, please come here and work for me! The *first* thing we're going to do is get rid of that horrible thing. I don't seem to be able to get rid of it all by myself."

Ronald lowered his coffee cup and looked at her in dismay. "Well, my dear, you can't, of course. It's one of the copies of the *Rise of the Cormorant*."

A slight wind rose from the corners of the room and

stirred his hair. Bree wanted to scream, or smack herself in frustration.

Instead, she offered Ronald Parchese a pitifully low salary, which she promised to increase as soon as she was able.

Ten

Begin at the beginning...go on till you come to the end; then stop.

—*Alice's Adventures in Wonderland,*
Lewis Carroll

"Was Benjamin Skinner murdered?" Bree asked her new employees. She sat at the head of the twelve-foot table in the conference room. Ronald Parchese was at her left. Petru sat at her right. Sasha sat in the corner. Mrs. Mather perched on a chair at the end, a dust cloth in one hand and a can of furniture wax in the other. (Keeping the place clean, she'd told a skeptical Bree, came with the rent. Bree thought it was just plain nosiness.) "That question's at the heart of the case. Our client, Liz Overshaw, is convinced he was. It's our job to find out."

"Too exciting," Ronald murmured. "I watch *Law & Order*, but that's about it for my investigative technique."

"This Skinner fell off a boat and drowned, I thought," Petru said.

Bree rubbed her forehead. "Yes. I know. Maybe he was pushed? I don't know."

"If he was pushed, the son musta done it," Lavinia said. "That's all who was on the boat he fell off of. A disgrace, that's what it is. A chile killing his own pa."

"Liz doesn't think it was the son. Or rather," Bree corrected herself, "she believes the murderer is one of four people."

"There was somebody else on the boat?" Ron asked.

"Not as far as I know. We're looking at investigating these four people." Bree looked at her notes. "Douglas Fairchild, Carlton Montifiore, John Stubblefield, and Chastity McFarland."

"Who-ee," Lavinia said. "Some big names you got there."

Bree nodded ruefully. She referred to the extensive notes she'd made after a preliminary Internet search on Skinner. "Yes. Douglas Fairchild is a prominent investor here in Savannah and a partner in a lot of Skinner's local projects. This condo called Island Dream, for one. John Stubblefield is the senior partner of one of Georgia's most prominent law firms. They represent Skinner and his family." She paused. "We've already been warned off that guy. Which makes me wonder if there isn't something to Liz's suspicions. Anyhow—Carlton Montifiore is a local builder. He puts up a lot of Skinner's buildings here in Georgia, including Island Dream. And Chastity McFarland is, or rather was, Ben Skinner's mistress."

"Most times it's the wife," Lavinia said wisely. "This Ben got a wife? Olivia done for Josiah in just that way. He's got some grudge against women, that Josiah. You got to watch yourself with him, Bree."

It took Bree a minute to figure out that Lavinia was referring to the bodies buried in the cemetery outside.

"He's a widower," Bree said. "Skinner, that is."

"Any of them suspects on the boat?" Lavinia asked.

"No," Bree said firmly. "None of them were on the boat."

Lavinia subsided with a thoughtful air.

"We need to add the son and his wife to the suspect list, don't we?" Ronald asked. "I mean, I know it's screamingly obvious that they would be the murderers. So obvious that they might be after all, if you catch my drift."

"So obvious that it can't be them that it must be them," Petru said. "Hm."

"I guess we should," Bree said. "But Liz was pretty sure it was one of the four on the newscast."

Ron lifted both his eyebrows. "Did she say why?"

"Yes," Bree said.

"And?"

She sighed. "She said Skinner's ghost told her." She raised both hands to forestall the storm of skepticism. "I know, I know. It's totally insane."

"It's important to know *how* he told her," Lavinia said seriously. "In a dream? In a daytime appearance? All these things matter, with ghosts."

"I'll ask," Bree said dryly.

"I have to admit, this is ke-vite a good reason to ignore the relatives as suspects," Petru said. "It is not often that the dead are allowed to speak."

"Still and all," Ron said. "Skinner could be wrong. It's happened before. The dead aren't exactly infallible."

"Don't *I* know it," Petru grumbled.

Everyone nodded wisely except for Bree, who sighed and said, "We'll take a close look at Grainger and Jennifer Skinner. Actually," she added, "I know Jennifer Skinner, formerly Jennifer Pendergast, and if she's as much of a screaming pain in the neck now as she was in school, I wouldn't put it past her to kill her father-in-law." She wrote Jennifer's name in capitals at the bottom of her suspect list. "Now. The question is, where to start?"

"Perhaps we should recruit a professional," Petru suggested. "In my country, there are many unemployed persons from the KGB who would be ke-vite anxious to help. This is not so true here, perhaps. Has anyone recommended a good private eye?"

Everyone at the table looked expectantly at her. Bree thought of the card Professor Cianquino had given her with a flash of irritation. It was time she started making her own decisions. And Gabriel Striker was a little too bossy for her taste. This was her case, her client, her employees. "Let's see how well we do on our own first."

"You want to find out about those Pendergasts first thing," Lavinia said. "Hm, hm. There's bad blood in that family."

"Excellent suggestion," Bree said, with false enthusiasm. Positive reinforcement was a management technique she intended to use a lot, to help offset the lousy pay. And since Lavinia seemed to have joined the staff for free, she might as well roll with it. "But we need to gather some facts first. We need to get the coroner's report and everything the police have on the case. Ron, perhaps you can take care of that. And Petru, I'd like you to research Skinner himself. We need a complete picture. Google him. Start with magazine articles, books, newspaper stories, and make a list of his relatives, business partners. Pay special attention to anyone he's annoyed. There's a ton of lawsuits. He spent half his life in court either being sued or suing somebody else. Concentrate on the big cases, within the last year. Take a good look at those he won. I'd skip over anything with a corporate plaintiff or

defendant. Murder's usually a personal thing, and I doubt
that anybody on the board of Pepsi-Cola, for example,
would be out for Skinner's blood for real. If you need any
case references, go online with Lexis and hunt them up.
We're looking for connections between Skinner and our
four main suspects. Fairchild, Montifiore, Stubblefield,
and Chastity McFarland. And Google those guys, too."

Ronald made neat notes into his BlackBerry. Petru
scrawled on a legal-sized yellow pad in cryptic Russian.

"I'm going to tackle our suspects, one by one," Bree
said. "So if you guys come up with anything urgent ..."
she waved her cell phone. "Call me, okay?"

"Anything else, 'ma-am'?" Ronald asked, giving her a
mock salute.

Bree nodded. Her parents had called that morning,
with a whole raft of suggestions about the open house for
the firm the following week. Ron could take care of most
of them while she was out sleuthing around. And she'd
been worried about having enough work to keep Petru
and Ron busy full time.

"Oh, my. You do look grim," Ronald said. "Nothing
real to worry about, I hope."

"It's my mother."

Petru looked extremely mournful. Bree didn't want to
ask him why. She was sure Russians had strong feelings
about their mothers, along with everything else.

"She put a notice in the business journal about the
opening of the practice."

"So we may be getting new clients?" Ronald said.
"Excellent. That's nothing to be grim about."

"Of course not," Bree said. "I mean, that's the idea behind announcing a new practice. It's the invitations to the
open house."

"What invitations?" Ronald asked. Then, as the penny dropped, "Oh! Is that terrific or what! A party!"

"It's for next week. The tenth. From five to seven, and I will want to introduce you all, of course. My mother's booked 700 Drayton."

"The Mansion at Forsyth Park!" Ronald said. "Is this exciting or what!"

"So please, everyone, put it on your calendars."

"I'll have to see about flowers and food, of course," Ronald said. "You know, my own mother's absolutely delighted that I left Dillard's for a more professional career. But I still have the designer's touch, Bree!" He held up his hands and wiggled his fingers. "You leave all of that to me."

"I'd love to leave it all to you," Bree said frankly. "Use Savannah Designs for the florist. Talk to the party guy at 700 Drayton about the food. Knowing my mother, we should probably plan for sixty guests. And if there's nothing else?"

"Y'all want me to tell you about those Pendergasts?" Mrs. Mather said. "You got that Josiah laying in wait everytime you walk out that door."

Bree smiled at her and said kindly, "Let's the two of us sit down later today, Mrs. Mather." She glanced at her watch. "I have an appointment with Liz Overshaw at eleven. Okay, guys. Here we go."

⎯⎯∽⎯⎯

The headquarters of Skinner Worldwide, Inc., occupied fifteen of the floors in the twenty-story Skinner Tower in Atlanta. But from what Bree could gather, most of the top executives in Skinner's organization had followed Skinner's example and bought or built vacation homes on Tybee Island. "Most of the key decisions," Liz Overshaw said as she led Bree into her sunroom, "are made in the bar at the island country club." She pointed at a wicker chair facing windows that overlooked the shoreline. "Sit down."

Bree sat. Sunshine flooded directly into her eyes. She got up, moved the chair at an angle, and sat down again. Liz's house was old, built in the Southern Plantation syle with a wraparound porch and gray clapboard. The interior had a hasty look, with an indifference to color and style very much like Liz herself. The bones of the house were good, though, and the view of the Atlantic was superb.

Liz looked even more unkempt than she had when Bree met her at Professor Cianquino's. Her face was sallow. Her short, graying hair was swept back with a carelessly tied scarf. She wore a baggy pair of trousers and a light pullover top with the sleeves shoved up past her elbows. She paced up and down the length of the sunroom with short, agitated steps and shot a malevolent glance at Bree. "I thought I made it clear that I didn't want to be bothered with this until you had some results."

"I'm not going to ask you about ..." Bree hesitated a moment. In for a penny, in for a pound. So she said bluntly, "... the haunting. As far as I can tell, it has nothing to do with the case or what I can do for you." Unless, she added to herself, you're crazy as a bedbug and this whole thing's an exercise in nuttiness. "So let's set that aside."

Liz's shoulders relaxed a little; her restless pacing slowed.

"But I'm going to need some background material before I can go any further. And we can get on a little more efficiently if you wouldn't mind sitting down." She smiled. "I'm gettin' dizzy just watching you wear a path in the carpet."

Liz looked at her feet with a bewildered air. There was a dun-colored love seat at right angles to Bree; she sat in it abruptly, as if somebody had shoved her.

"Maybe a little coffee would help things along?" Bree suggested. "That nice housekeeper who let me in probably makes a pretty good cup."

Liz stared at her. A shadowy smile lit her face, and for a moment, Bree caught a glimpse of the pretty woman she must have been twenty years ago. She turned her head over her shoulder and shouted, "Elphine! Coffee!" She ran her hands through her hair and leaned back with a sigh. "Satisfied? Can we get on with it?"

Bree took a yellow pad from her briefcase and prepared to take notes. "Let's start with some possible business enemies. You've been with Mr. Skinner a long time, haven't you? Were you closely involved in his affairs from the beginning?"

"What's that got to do with anything?"

Bree shrugged. "I won't know until you tell me. But I'm walking into this absolutely blind, Liz. I've been thinking about how to wade into this case. If the police believe Mr. Skinner died of drowning secondary to a heart attack, there's not going to be a lot of forensic evidence against it. So I've sent for the coroner's report, the autopsy, and the rest, but it's all going to scream 'drowning secondary to a heart attack.' Don't you think?"

Liz pursed her lips. "Maybe. And maybe there's been a cover-up. Or just plain incompetence."

Bree shook her head. "The man's too well known for a botched investigation. The media's all over it. And if there's been a cover-up, the big question is why? The 'why' is what I'm after."

"And you think tramping around in the past is going to turn up a lot of maggots?" She bared her teeth in an unlovely grin. "Well, hell. You could be right." There was a soft rustling at the lanai doors, and her housekeeper came in with a tray. She was a motherly looking woman in comfortable shoes and a crisp housedress, with shrewd eyes. She handed Bree a cup of coffee and said, "You're Miss Beaufort?"

Bree smiled up at her. "I am."

"You know my auntie, I think. Miss Lavinia?" Her eyes, dark, unreadable, looked into Bree's for a long moment.

Bree wriggled a little under the scrutiny, then nodded, "Yes. I do."

"She thought maybe you could give me some he'p with a problem of mine. My stepson Rebus. Got himself killed, Rebus did."

"Of course," Bree said cordially. She didn't much like personal injury cases, but she couldn't turn down a relative of Lavinia's. She reached into her purse and handed her business card to the housekeeper. "Just call my office and either Mr. Lucheta or Mr. Parchese will set an appointment up for you."

"Anything else I can help you with?" Liz asked sarcastically. "A couple of new client referrals, maybe?" She looked over her shoulder at her housekeeper. "That'll do, Elphine."

Elphine left the sunroom with the same graceful dignity. Bree watched her go thoughtfully, then asked Liz, "She's been with you awhile? Mrs. Mather, I mean?"

"Who, Elphine? No. As a matter of fact, I signed her

on the day before Skinner died. My last housekeeper came down with some damn fool thing and quit. Or did she break a leg? I don't remember what happened. They all come from an agency. Anyway, the agency sent Elphine when the other one crapped out on me." She drummed her fingers on the chair arm. "I've got a meeting later this afternoon with some possible investors. Can we get on with this?"

"You'd started to tell me about Mr. Skinner's business enemies. Did you know him well early on?"

"I didn't start to tell you a damn thing. But there's no secret to my career, at least. God knows the business magazines have been over it enough. He hired me twenty years ago. I was just out of Wharton, and wanted to make CFO with somebody, anybody, as fast as I could. He was just starting to expand the business overseas, then." She fell silent, her gaze turned inward. "Skinner," she said after a long moment, "was not a nice guy. He was a user. He was demanding. And vengeful. If you crossed him, only the devil could help you, because God sure wouldn't. And he didn't give a rat's ass for his wife or kids or anybody else's."

"You have a family of your own?" Bree asked.

"Me?" She snorted. "What the hell would I do with a family? Business is all I need. It was all Skinner needed, too." She shook her head admiringly. "I'll tell you something, Miss Beaufort. He was one hell of a businessman. Everything he touched turned green. I left Wharton with a hundred thousand dollars in school loans and the clothes on my back. Within five years, I was worth two million. In twenty, I became really rich." She lifted her hand and held it palm out. "I've got a place in Palm Beach, a flat in London ..." She trailed off. "What are you looking at me like that for?" she snapped. "Do you have any idea how much I'm worth? I've got ..." She stopped and bit her lip. Then, with a defiant air, "everything I've ever wanted out of life."

Bree looked down at her yellow pad, where she'd absentmindedly doodled a weeping face. She didn't know if she felt sorry for Liz Overshaw or not. She for sure didn't like her much. "It's an impressive achievement, surely." She took a deep breath. "In all that time, Mr. Skinner must have made a lot of enemies."

"You know," Liz said with an air of surprise. "I don't believe he did. Oh, there were a half dozen people over the years who might have wanted to see him dead. But not many more than that. He was a son of a bitch, but he was an honest son of a bitch. He never shafted anybody, or at least," she amended, "anybody who didn't deserve it."

Bree blinked a little.

"Yeah," Liz shifted in her chair. "I know what his reputation is. I didn't say he was nice. He wasn't. But he wasn't a crook. And he didn't tolerate crooks."

"You said maybe half a dozen sincere enemies over the years. Let's start with the most recent ones. And the ones who were around Savannah when he passed on."

"On the theory that the ones in the far past would have knocked him off by now?" Liz shook her head. "You don't need to look there. I told you where you need to look. Skinner was murdered by one of those four. Fairchild, Montifiore ..."

"Stubblefield and Miss McFarland," Bree finished for her. She took a deep breath. "Okay, then. What about motive?"

"Beats me."

"Is there an ongoing connection among the four of them?

"Of course." Liz frowned with exasperation. "I thought everybody in Savannah knew about it."

"I've only been in town a week or so." Bree had practiced law in her father's firm for five years. She'd been exceptionally good at handling difficult clients. She called on those skills now. "So if you could fill me in, I'd appreciate it. Let me guess. I know they were working on a project together?"

"That's right. Island Dream. It's a fifteen-story condominium about three miles from here. Beachfront. Fairchild and Skinner bought up the twenty acres surrounding an old fort on the channel quite a while ago. Skinner was thinking about restoring the fort—well, turning it into a family home, anyway. But Lyn died, his wife, and his son wasn't interested, so Fairchild bought him out. Tore the fort down and built Island Dream. Skinner was livid."

The Savannah Historical Society was fiercely protective of historic buildings. Bree was surprised that the county had allowed the demolition of the building and said so.

"There was a bit of a stink about it. But Fairchild's able to twist a lot of arms in town. Or maybe it's because his family's been around for ages and he knows where the bodies are buried. Anyhow, he got around the Historical Society. Skinner was bound and determined he wasn't going to get around him.

"So, Skinner had his knickers in a twist because Fairchild told him he was going to rebuild the fort into six town homes, and the project turned into a hundred and fifteen multimillion-dollar condos. He didn't have a legal leg to stand on, but he sued Fairchild and Montifiore, the builders, just the same."

"I didn't realize Mr. Skinner was fond of old buildings," Bree said.

Liz snorted. "Not him. He was frantic over the lost profit." She smiled reminiscently. "That was Ben all over, though. He was worth close to a billion dollars when he was killed and he got hot under the collar over ten million or so."

"So Montifiore and Fairchild were defendants in the lawsuit," Bree said. "What about John Stubblefield?"

"He'd drawn up the original contract turning the fort over to Fairchild. His firm represents Skinner, or did, until Skinner sued him for incompetent representation. That firm skates on the thin edge of the wedge anyhow. Skinner swore to put Stubblefield, Marwick out of business for good."

"Some significant motives here," Bree observed. "Would you say any of these lawsuits had a legitimate cause of action?"

"Is that a mealymouthed way of asking if these were spite cases? These were spite cases, no question. Part of it was Skinner thought Fairchild had pulled one over on him and part of it was the fact that Fairchild had the pull to get the fort pulled down and Skinner didn't. So he didn't need a legitimate reason, as you call it. Not Skinner. He never was one to lie down and let anybody walk over him, much less a bunch of tight-assed, brainless parasites running through their granddaddies' fortunes." She smiled—a rather mean smile. Bree's family knew the Fairchilds, and she had to admit there was some truth to Liz's malicious assessment.

"Grainger and Jennifer," she said. "I know they aren't on your list of suspects . . ."

"Skinner's list. Not mine."

"Yes," Bree said noncommittally. "Did he get along with his son?"

"Could have been worse. Skinner expected a lot of the kid. I think he was pretty proud of him when he graduated from medical school. Certainly had no objection to footing the bills to get him set up in his practice in Savannah. Now, he didn't lavish tons of money on the boy. Grainger has a trust fund, a modest one, considering Skinner's own net worth. And he won't get a dime more now that Skinner's dead. That was all settled years ago. So I wouldn't say there was any problem on Skinner's side."

"That implies Grainger had a problem with his dad."

"Grainger. Yes. Good old Grainger." Liz squeezed her eyes shut and opened them again. "You know that Skinner pretty much came from nothing. Dirt-poor Georgia farmer, yada, yada. And Grainger married up."

"Jennifer Pendergast that was," Bree said. "Sure. Her family's been in Georgia since Oglethorpe banned all the lawyers."

"I suppose you knew her." Liz smiled that wintry smile. "You debs stick together, huh? Well, Miss Jennifer didn't quite approve of dear old dad's country ways. Especially when she discovered Grainger had inherited all he was going to get, and there wasn't any more where that came from."

"So she may have had a grudge."

"*May* have. Ha! I'll tell you one thing, that young lady was doing her damndest to get Skinner to change his mind about the Skinner Foundation."

"I've heard of the Skinner Foundation," Bree said. "It subsidizes all those PBS programs."

"That's the one. And a lot more besides that. Anyhow, that's what benefits from Skinner's death. Miss Jennifer wanted to change all that."

"Did she?"

Liz shrugged. "Maybe. Why don't you ask her?"

"I just might."

Liz rose, yawned, and stretched her arms over her head. "That's it. God, I'm beat." She sat down abruptly and ran one hand over her face. "So is your curiosity satisfied? You're going to get on with finding out who murdered Skinner? Cianquino assured me that you'd get results. Are you going to get results? I'm not real impressed with what you and your firm have accomplished so far."

Bree tucked her yellow pad back into her briefcase. There was, after all, a limit to how much a lawyer had to indulge a client. She kept her tone as polite as she knew how. "May I ask you something? About this idea Mr. Skinner was murdered?"

Liz scowled.

"Mr. Skinner was on board the *Sea Mew* when he had his heart attack and fell into the ocean. The only two people on board were his son and his daughter-in-law. I know what ... um, Mr. Skinner told you. But what about you? Do you think they killed him and lied to the police? Do you think the two of them are innocent, and that he died of a slow-acting poison somebody slipped into his drink at the country club?" Bree allowed herself a hint of exasperation. "Was somebody else on board invisible to his son and his wife? Not aliens, I hope."

"He didn't drown in the sea," Liz said, after a long minute.

"He didn't?" Bree said.

"He didn't drown in the sea." Liz shivered, although the heat of the sun was winning the battle with the air-conditioning and the sunroom was warming to an uncomfortable temperature. Her eyes widened until the whites surrounding the pupils were visible. Her voice was barely above a whisper, and for the third time, like an incantation:

"Skinner didn't die in the sea."

Eleven

How often have I said to you that when you have elimi-
nated the impossible, whatever remains, *however im-
probable*, must be the truth?

–*The Sign of the Four*, Arthur Conan Doyle

"He drowned in the sea alright," Ron said cheerfully. He
placed the autopsy report faceup on Bree's desk and settled himself cozily on the corner, the edge of his buttocks
smack on top of her file folders. "Seawater in the lungs,
or what was left of them, anyway."

"What was *left* of them?" Bree said.

Ron waved a large manila envelope in the air. "I got
the autopsy pictures, too. It's amazing how fast Chatham
County can move when the dear departed is hugely *im-
portante.*"

Bree looked at him. It was amazing, as a matter of fact.
She decided she didn't want to inquire too closely about
Ron's methods. She extended her hand for the envelope.
Ron held it just out of reach. "Trust me. You don't want to
see them."

"I'm not squeamish," Bree said impatiently.

"Well, *I* am, dearie, and when I got a load of these, I
almost tossed my cookies. Somehow, the poor old guy

got tangled up with the boat motor after he fell into the water and splooey. Big mess."

"Splooey?" Bree echoed. She was creeped out. She eyed the manila envelope. Large spiders made her feel creeped out, too. And she could force herself to deal with them. She grabbed the envelope and slid the photos onto her desk. Very ugly. Very. And in full color, too. "Ugh. But they were still able to claim he drowned? There was enough of the body left to ... um ... check on?"

"Oh, yeah. No question about the cause of death at all. Take all that stuff home. It'll make very nice bedtime reading." He smacked a second report on top of the photos, for which Bree was thankful. "Police interviews with the son and his wife."

"I'm impressed," Bree said. "How did you get those out of the police department?"

"This stuff will be a matter of public record after the case is officially closed, so why not?" He wriggled his eyebrows. "Of course, it was a lot easier with the help of the famous Parchese charm."

Bree picked up the police report. It'd been signed by a Lieutenant Hunter. The transcribed interviews with Skinner's son, Grainger, and Grainger's wife, Jennifer, were clipped to the back.

"I can give you a summary, if you want," Ron said chattily. "Even if you don't want. It'll save you the reading time. Skinner was in the bow of the boat, where he usually sat. They were becalmed and they were headed back to the dock under power. Now, according to doctor boy ..."

Bree raised an eyebrow. "Doctor boy?"

"The son, Grainger. He's a doctor. Anyhow, according

to Grainger, Dad's sipping a diet drink, clutches his chest, and topples into the sea. Doc yells at his wife to bring the boat about and runs to get the grappling hook. He's fishing for Dad while Mrs. Doc ..."

"Jennifer," Bree said, as she leafed through the report.

"Our Jennifer," Ron agreed happily, "runs over the poor soul with the motor, accidentally, of course. So she gets hysterical, Grainger manages to drag the body on board—that's these hook marks in the back in this photo here." He flipped through the photos until he came to the relevant one. Bree wanted to close her eyes, but didn't. "Anyhow, Grainger SOS's the Coast Guard, which shows up in about two seconds flat. Everybody's screaming and crying and carrying on except, of course, our victim, who is unable to, and there you are."

"Wow." Bree took a deep breath and then a long sip of coffee.

By the time she'd gotten back to the office, it was late afternoon. Petru was out at the library. Lavinia was somewhere about upstairs, with Sasha. She hoped the dog didn't like the taste of lemur. Ron had bounced to his feet in gleeful welcome when she'd come through the front door and into the reception room. He had fresh coffee waiting, too. The place was already beginning to feel like home.

Bree paged through the photos again, and rubbed the back of her neck. "I just can't see it," she said finally. "Let's assume that our client's right. Skinner was murdered. The obvious, in fact, the *only* suspects are Skinner's son, Grainger, and his wife. How do we even begin to prove it? They alibi each other."

The front door opened, then shut. A familiar shuffle-*thump* sounded in the living room. Ron hopped off the desk, stuck his head out, and caroled, "Yoo-hoo! We're in here!"

Bree rose to her feet automatically as he came in. Petru was older, lame, and it seemed not only rude but arrogant to sit while he was standing. The one leather chair was obviously too deep and slippery for him. Ron dragged a straight-back chair into her office, set it by her desk for Petru, then surveyed the small space with his hands on his hips. "If you don't mind my saying so, your taste in used furniture is pitiful. Just pitiful."

Bree looked up. She was reading the transcription of Jennifer Skinner's interview with Lieutenant Hunter. A small, tattered, worn Oriental carpet sat on the floor. The brown leather reading chair was so worn in places that the hide of the leather showed through. The floor lamp's glass green shade was scratched with a weird set of parallel lines, as if somebody had drawn their fingernails along it. "My uncle did make a point of telling me NOT to use his office furniture in his will," she admitted. "But I'm on a budget. I can either pay your salary, Ronald dear, or go shopping at Roche-Bobois. So I had them brought over. You pick."

"That was not a matter of good taste, perhaps," Petru said apologetically. "But more of a wish that you might avoid the legacy."

"What legacy?" Bree asked sharply.

Ron went "tsk" and shook his head.

"His law practice, you mean?"

Petru looked at her over the rim of his spectacles. "The legacy of the cormorant."

"If," Bree said, with more patience than she thought she had, "I ask you for details, what are you going to say to me?" She held her hand up in a peremptory gesture.

"Nope. Wait. I've got it. There's some people that run, some people that hide, and some people that jump right in when the times get tough. Is that it?"

"That is it," Petru said.

"Well, you can just bring that old legacy right along," Bree said tartly, "because I can tell you right here, right now, Beauforts don't run from anybody."

"Ha-ha," Petru said with a glum air.

"Ha-ha?" Bree said. "What does *that* mean?"

"It means you know nothing of the sort about yourself until you know much more than you know right now. That is what 'ha-ha' means."

Bree felt herself getting very Southern, which as Payton the Rat knew to his cost, was a very bad sign. "As I live and breathe . . ." she began ominously.

Ron clapped his hands together. "People, people!" Then he added in a diplomatic tone, "I expect we'll *all* know when it's time, so let's not let the fur and feathers fly. Now let's get back to the point here, Bree. This room needs a bit of livening up. As a matter of fact, you *and* the room need a bit of livening up. The braids were a stroke of genius, did I tell you that? But there is much, much more to be accomplished."

Bree got a tight rein on her temper and held on. "If you don't mind my pointing it out, one of the things to be accomplished here is the successful conclusion of this case."

"Too true," Ron said unabashed. "I guess we can set aside the decorating thing for a while."

"I guess we can. Because that's what we're here for, right? Our clients. We're advocates. Champions. Because one of the *other* things Beauforts do is win for our clients.

In as courteous, just, mannerly, and smart a way as is humanly possible."

"Humanly," Petru echoed. "Very good." He set his stick on his knees and applauded.

"So let's take a look at where we are with the Overshaw case, shall we?"

"You were saying that the only two people who could have murdered Mr. Skinner were his son and his daughter-in-law, but that there's no way to prove it," Ron said promptly. "Which looks like a big loss as far as Ms. Overshaw's concerned."

"Do you believe her?" Petru asked abruptly.

"Do I ..." Bree stopped herself in mid-sentence. "Do I?"

"Because, if you do not believe her, you must return that check," Petru said firmly, "and turn her case over to someone who does believe." For a moment, he looked as stern as Professor Cianquino had, when Bree expressed those same doubts about Liz Overshaw's sanity. He cleared his throat apologetically. "I do not think we need to make a judgment on whether or not this is murder. I do think we owe Ms. Overshaw the professional courtesy to believe in her cause."

Bree stared at him for a moment, then said slowly, "Because if we believe in her cause, we'll be able to act in her best interests. You're absolutely right, Petru. And I've been very wrong. I've let the fact that I don't like the woman get in the way of looking at this case with her eyes." She let the silence in the room elapse. "Okay," she said finally, "here's what we're going to do. Ron? I want you to find Mr. Skinner's personal secretary and interview her."

Ron frowned. "You mean that incredibly tacky blonde who lives on the top floor of the Skinner building?"

"No, no, no. That's Chastity Mc-whosis."

"McFarland," Petru said punctiliously.

"Yes. I mean his actual secretary who kept his daily schedule. Liz Overshaw should be able to tell you where to find her—that'd be a blessing and a half. I'd like to set up an hour by hour ... no! A minute by minute calendar of his last two days on this earth."

She looked down at the mass of data Ron and Petru had collected. "Next thing we do is go through all this stuff with a fine-tooth comb. We look for discrepancies, for unexplained facts, items, actions. Petru, if you can make up a chart, or a time line, or something that can give us a snapshot of Skinner's life, it'd be terrific."

"And what are you up to, then?" Ron asked.

"Interviewing the suspects, one by one. I'll start with Grainger."

"Do you think they'll let you waltz in and interrogate him, just like that?" Ron said in admiration. "Oh, Bree. That *is* nervy."

"Jennifer was a few years ahead of me at Miss Choate's in New York. And I know her little brother. If I fudge the reasons a little bit, I think I can get in to see her. I'll schedule that for tomorrow afternoon, if I can. And first thing in the morning, I'm going to track down Carlton Montifiore at one of his construction sites."

"Excellent," Ron said, "but set *both* those meetings up for the afternoon. If you do, we'll have time to do a little shopping in the morning."

Bree slapped her hands flat on her desk. "Ron! What's all this hoo-rah about the way I'm dressing?"

"You are *not* showing yourself to the best advantage."

He narrowed his eyes in what he probably believed was a tough-guy way. "I just want to ask you one thing: Do you have anything other than black and white in your closet? Just one leetle teeny bit of color?"

"Jeans," Bree said promptly, "and a blue and white Duke University tee."

Ron flung his hands up in a "see what I mean" gesture. "Silly me. Just the thing to wear to court, of course. Sweetie, you're about to take on some of the most powerful families in Savannah with this Overshaw case. Now there's two ways to dress to impress. One way is to wear tennis shoes, T-shirts, and tattered jeans to the White House. You can get away with that if you're say, Steve Jobs. The other is to dress like you're the president of a small South American republic. With confidence. With authority. You need a *presence*."

Bree looked down at herself. She'd been busy all her adult life; busy in law school, busy at the family firm, even busier now that she was setting up her own practice. And every time she picked up a copy of *Vogue* or *Oprah* in the dentist's office, she was thoroughly cowed by the kinds of decisions a person had to make to look totally cool. Looking elegant and sophisticated was a full-time job. She'd decided the fewer choices the better. Her closet had five expensive Armani pantsuits in gray, black, and steel, and two dozen Eileen Fisher silk tees in various shades of white. This made it very easy to get dressed for work. And boring.

She looked at Ron and asked sweetly, "Which South American republic would you suggest?"

"You're pissed off at me," he said instantly. "Oh, God. I was just trying to help."

"I am not pissed off at you. I appreciate it. The sentiment, that is, if not the way you expressed it. I'll put it on the It's-Saturday-With-Nothing-to-Do list."

"It'd better be this Saturday," Ron said promptly. "You can't make your debut at the Mansion dressed like a mortician."

"I don't look anything like a mortician!"

"And your mother agrees with me."

Bree stopped in mid-yell. "You've talked to my mother?" She clutched her head. "And my mother thinks I dress like a mortician?"

"Of course I've talked to your mother. You don't think this open house of yours is going to arrange itself, do you?" He resettled himself on the corner of her desk. "What a peach your mamma is, Bree. And she agrees with me. About getting you tarted up. First thing is to find a sensational dress for the party. Do you have any idea who's going to be there?"

"No," Bree said. "I don't. And how did you get hold of my mother? And how do you know who's coming to the party?"

"I found your sister wandering around outside and I asked for your mother's phone number. The rest was easy."

"How did you know she was my sister? We don't look a thing alike. Never mind," Bree interrupted herself. "What did Antonia think of the office? Did she come in?"

"No," Ron said.

"I believe not," Petru said.

"Well, she'll have to wait until the day of the party, then. Maybe I can talk her into staying here to be host. I don't know how many of the guests will want to see the place, but I expect there'll be a few."

"I don't think we have to worry about that," Ron said.

"I will be ke-vite happy to stay here myself, in case of visitors," Petru said. He exchanged a look with Ron, and then shrugged. "You never know, do you? Some of the new clients will be able to find it, of course."

"If they're on the list," Ron said, "which I really doubt, Petru. I should think you of all people would know better."

"Who *is* on the list?" Bree asked with mild interest. "Did my mother send it along?" She smiled slightly. "Anyone from Stubblefield, Marwick, for example? It'd be even better if Douglas Fairchild showed up."

"I haven't had a chance to really study it yet," Ron said briskly, "but there have been quite a few acceptances already." He leaned past Bree and flipped the pages of the desk calendar. "It's Thursday already. We'll just have this weekend."

"Maybe, maybe not. I'm not going to be able to pay your wages, much less buy a new dress, if we don't get back to work." Bree looked at her watch, conscience-stricken. "It's way after five. I've got to let you guys get home. We'll start again on this stuff tomorrow."

Petru placed his cane on the floor and hoisted himself off the chair. "I will take the files home with me tonight and read them thoroughly."

"There's no need to do that," Bree said. The first day on the job, and she was already working them to death. "I'm not paying either of you enough to work full time, much less time and a half. I can't ask you to put in extra hours. I'll take this stuff home with me and read it through myself." She stopped halfway through putting the documents into a neat stack. "Just one more thing, Petru. Did you find anything out about Skinner that I should know right away?"

"He found out about them Pendergasts." Lavinia stood at the open door. Sasha nudged his way past her knees and hobbled over to Bree.

Bree looked at Petru inquiringly. He nodded, "This is true. Mrs. Skinner, Mrs. Grainger Skinner, that is, is a Pendergast."

"I knew that already." Bree looked at her staff. They looked backed expectantly. She sat down with a resigned sigh. "Okay. This is it. Jennifer Skinner's great-great-great-what, grandfather? Anyhow, Josiah Pendergast seems to be buried in our murderer's cemetery. So? I don't want to be rude, guys, but what does this have to do with the price of bananas in Brazil?"

"Bad blood in those Pendergasts," Lavinia said stubbornly. "You want to watch out for them."

"There does seem to be some cause for concern," Petru said. "The Pendergasts have ke-vite an evil history."

"Does this evil history have any live Pendergasts interacting with Benjamin Skinner? Other than Jennifer herself?" Bree demanded. "Any lawsuits? Any motives for murder?"

"Not live Pendergasts, no," Petru admitted. "But we cannot discount the possibility of the influence of Josiah himself. This Jennifer is a direct descendant."

Bree made a face. She was almost afraid to hear the answer from her lunatic employees. "You don't honestly think Josiah crawled out of the grave and pushed Mr. Skinner into the sea?"

"No, no. Naturally not!" Lavinia said reprovingly. "The dead don't take the living down with them. I've never heard of such a thing."

"Or that he possessed my old school pal Jennifer and got her to kill her father-in-law?"

"A malign influence," Petru said, "is more than possible, however. When the dead whisper, there are those that listen."

"I'm getting a headache," Bree said. "No kidding. Let's put that kind of stuff in a miscellaneous file, okay? We'll drag it out when we need to," which will be as soon as the moon turns into a lump of Camembert, she added to herself. "Otherwise, I'd prefer it if we could concentrate on the living, and leave the dead peacefully alone."

"Some of the dead," Ron said, "aren't in the least little bit peaceful. You want to remember that."

"I came down here for another reason," Lavinia said. "Y'all are talking so much I almost put it out of mind. You got a phone call while you were out with that Liz, Bree." She dug into her apron pocket and emerged with a pink While You Were Out slip. "From this Payton?"

Bree made a face.

"On behalf of his boss," she said, "Mr. John Stubblefield. He wants you to meet 'em both at Molly McPherson's 'long about six."

Bree smiled. "Excellent. Call them back to confirm, will you, Ron? Stubblefield is at the top of Liz Overshaw's suspect list. This ought to get things off to a very good start."

Twelve

The graves stood tenantless, and the sheeted dead
Did squeak and gibber in the Roman streets.
—*Hamlet*, Shakespeare

The wind whipped up as Bree closed the office door behind her and stepped into Angelus Street. There was weather blowing in from somewhere—October was the peak of hurricane season, and they'd lucked out this year, at least so far. There had been one tropical storm in mid-September, and then all was quiet.

Bree looked up. The sun was westering, and the horizon was shot through with orange and red. A spray of white, feathery clouds hugged the southeast corner of the sky.

"What do you think, Sasha? Are we in for a mighty rain?"

The dog looked up at her anxiously and whined. He didn't need to be carried to the car any longer—he was hopping along remarkably well on his cast—so it must be something else.

"You can't be hungry," she said. "Lavinia's stuffed you full of chicken and rice."

Sasha snarled at the graves in the cemetery, his eyes

closed to mere yellow slits. Then he threw back his head and howled. Bree's skin prickled at the sound.

Come by here.

Bree whirled. The voice, if voice it was, came from under the live oak.

Ahhh, Bree. Come by here.

She squinted into the dying light. A tall, dark pillar of shadow moved among the strands of Spanish moss. The form spun, shifted, turned, like smoke from a smoldering fire.

It moved against the wind, as smoke never could. The darkness was a sullen riot of bruised purple, fetid green, and oily black. Bree knew whose grave lay beneath the tree. Josiah Pendergast. She took a step forward and nearly stumbled over Sasha. He pressed against her knees, lips drawn over his eyeteeth in a silent snarl.

Two fiery eyes appeared in the upper part of the column—as suddenly as if something wakened. The dreadful, smutty colors compressed. Then a thin cylinder of the stuff raised itself from the columnar mass and beckoned to her.

Bree. Come by here.

Bree pushed Sasha aside. She took another step forward, and another.

And she saw herself at the top of a mountain. A glory of clouds rolled beneath her feet. And she knew, knew with every fiber of her spirit, that what she wanted most in the world was just beyond her reach. If she leaned farther, farther, she would leave the peak and leap into space, to be caught up in the rush of the cormorant's wings. Into absolute, utter belief. No questions. Ever again.

The wind rose and whipped the treetops with a sudden roar. With a rumbling crack, the door to the little frame house crashed open, and Ron stepped into the dying light. The wind eddied around him in a vast rush of sound and for a brief, world-tilting moment, Bree thought the wind came from his outstretched palms. "You still here, Bree?"

The wind rushed, calmed, and died away. The column under the oak trembled, shivered, and drifted into nothing.

Bree took a huge gulp of air. Ron bounced down the steps to the fence and unlocked his bicycle. "I'd offer you a ride," he said, "but I couldn't take Sasha, too. Oh, drat."

Bree steadied herself, one hand on Sasha's neck. "Nobody says 'drat' anymore, Ronald." Her voice was steady. Her palms were wet, and her heart beat uncomfortably in her chest, but at least her voice was calm. "What's the matter?"

"Flat tire." He detached the bicycle pump from its storage spot on the frame, set it up, and pumped briskly. "Are you going to be late to your meeting?"

Bree stared at her watch in dismay. "Yikes. Almost. I'm driving and Molly McPherson's at the City Market, isn't it?"

"Just off of Montgomery at Broughton."

"Then I can just make it, as long as I can find a place to park." She bundled Sasha into the back, and settled herself in the driver's seat. Ron flagged her urgently. She rolled down her window and he leaned in. His breath was fragrant with a spice she couldn't identify. "Hey," he said. "They really can't do much to the living, you know. But you absolutely do not want to 'come by here.' If it happens again, you stay right where you are. Trust me. You don't want to jump off that mountain. Got that?" He slapped the window frame and stepped back. "You give Payton the Rat what for!"

She watched him bicycle off, long legs pumping up and down, his fair hair tumbled around his ears. She took a long, shaky breath, and started the car.

She found a parking spot on Congress, which bordered the south side of the marketplace. The whole of City Market was dog-friendly, and Molly McPherson's had an outdoor seating area a short distance from the fountain in the middle of the square. Bree was glad to take Sasha with her. The dog had a uniquely comforting presence. "And," she said, as he hobble-skipped at her side on the lead, "I wouldn't mind at all if you happened to pee on Payton's shoes."

Sasha grinned up at her, his pink tongue lolling.

"He'll be the one with the day-old beard and the look of Total Cool. And Sasha," she gave the lead a short, firm tug. "I didn't mean it about Payton's shoes."

Bree would have recognized John Stubblefield even if Payton hadn't been sitting next to him in a state of worshipful attention. For one thing, he made the news regularly, in stories featuring record jury awards in personal injury cases. For another, he was the star of the obnoxious infomercials on late night television, soliciting plaintiffs for class action lawsuits against large, rich corporations. He didn't bother suing any company with a net worth of less than a billion, no matter how sorry a state a victim might be in. When he was dead and buried, most of Savannah agreed his tombstone would read "Show me the money."

Stubblefield looked as slick as his ads. His white hair was carefully cut, gelled, and sprayed. His cheeks were smooth-shaven. He wore a sapphire-studded Rolex on his left arm and a thick gold bracelet with his initials on his right. He sat at ease at one of the round aluminum tables near the fountain. One leg was crossed over the other, revealing black silk socks that didn't show an inch of skin.

Payton got up as Bree neared the table. Stubblefield stayed put.

"Hey," Payton said, rather nervously. "Glad you could make it." He pulled out a chair. Bree sat down. Sasha folded himself onto the pavement at her side, his head up, his ears forward, and his eyes on Payton's face. "Bree, I'd like you to meet John Stubblefield." His voice was so reverent, Bree had to quell an impish desire to cross herself.

"Miss Beaufort." His voice was resonant. Bree knew enough about voice training from Antonia to realize that Stubblefield had studied with a voice coach. "I understand that you've been retained by a former associate of Bennie Skinner's."

"That I have," Bree said equably. She raised her hand to attract a waiter's attention.

"Of course, you'd like some refreshment." Stubblefield's smile didn't reach his eyes. "I beg your pardon. What would you like to drink?"

"An iced latte would suit me just fine."

He snapped his fingers. "Payton? See to the lady's needs." He smirked, "He's been quite successful at that in the past, wouldn't you say, Miss Beaufort?"

Payton jumped up, his teeth flashing in an ingratiating grin. Sheer rage washed over her like a hot red blanket. Bree stuck her foot out just in time to catch him at the ankle. He fell forward and recovered himself with a tremendous jerk.

"I do apologize," Bree said, with precisely Stubblefield's inflection. "You'll make that a skinny latte, won't you, Payton? And a lemon peel." She turned her attention back to Payton's boss. With luck, she'd get a chance to trip him, too. "Yes, I'm representing Ms. Overshaw. And in the interests of fairness, John, I should tell you that she has grave questions about your role in Benjamin Skinner's murder."

As she'd hoped, this direct attack took the lawyer by surprise. He was far too old a hand to lose his temper, but he did drop the phony geniality. "What kind of evidence does your client have that it is murder?" His eyes narrowed. "And why the hell should she suspect me?"

"Mr. Skinner had a lot of questions about the way you practice law, John. Uncomfortable questions. I'd like to know just how close to the bone he came with you and your firm."

Stubblefield leaned back in his chair and stretched his legs along the pavement. He took a sip of his drink—a julep, from what Bree could tell—and said reflectively, "That's always been the trouble with a bitch in business."

"I beg your pardon?" At the ice in her voice, Sasha sat up abruptly and growled.

"Women." He sighed with a mock sorrow that put Bree's teeth on edge. "Women don't have the least idea how the game is played, Ms. Beaufort. Liz Overshaw has mistaken some friendly jousting for an all-out war." He put his hand over hers. "Call it a guy thing. The bitch's old, ugly, and if you'll excuse the expression, a royal pain in the butt."

Bree didn't trust herself to speak for a moment. The wind picked up and stirred the paper trash in the square.

"Is she, now?" Bree said politely. "If you don't remove your hand this second, John, I'll ask my dog to bite you in that self-same butt." She rose to her feet and leaned forward, so that her eyes were inches from his. "And if you use that word in front of me again, it's not your ass, but your manhood you're going to have to worry about. Trust me on that one."

She was so mad she could feel the hair on her scalp rise. The wind slammed against the square, spraying the water from the fountain across the flagstones. *And then... She felt herself connect to the wind. If she flung her hands to the sky, she could draw down the clouds and pitch lightning. She rose to her feet, hands outstretched, her body taut with rage. She drew breath...*

"Bree!" Payton's panicked voice cut through her fog of rage.

Some fifty feet behind John Stubblefield was Gabe Striker. His eyes shone like silver coins in the twilight. She stared at Striker. He shook his head, slowly.

"Bree!" Payton's urgency increased to a painful pitch.

There was a stillness in Striker. A calm. It brushed her face, curled around the nape of her neck, gave her breath back. She stiffened and the dangerous moment was over.

Striker turned and melted into the shadows.

She turned to the men. Payton stood with a large glass of iced coffee in his hand and a petrified expression on his face. "Y'all have a problem?" she asked pleasantly.

"Ah. No. Of course not. I've got your coffee." He hesitated, and then set it gently on the table in front of her. He shot a nervous look in Stubblefield's direction then said airily, "Everything okay here?"

Stubblefield frowned, glanced at the empty square over his shoulder, and turned to face Bree. He shook his head a little, as if to rid himself of flies. Then he looked at Payton, surprise and annoyance in his face.

"Can I get you another drink, sir?" Payton asked eagerly.

"No. No. What you can do is get your ass back to the office. I want that Wal-Mart subpoena out before eight tomorrow morning."

"But . . ."

"Run along, Payton," Bree said.

"Yeah. Go on. Beat it." Stubblefield's tone was absentminded. "The week's not over yet. You've got time to get in a few more billable hours."

Payton slunk off with such a wounded air, Bree was almost sorry for him. Almost. It was going to be a long time before she forgave either one of them the crack about meeting her needs or for Stubblefield's remark about Liz.

"Now," Bree said, "we were about to discuss the nature of the dispute between you and Mr. Skinner."

"Tempest in a teapot. He was pis—that is, upset over Fairchild's deal with the county."

"The Island Dream condo project?"

"Ah, yes." Stubblefield took a handkerchief from his pocket and mopped his forehead. "If Fairchild tried to screw him on that one, which was by no means clear, I have to say he succeeded. Douglas made no representation in the contract or anywhere else about what he intended to do with the property. Or if he did, it wasn't in any form that was verifiable. I told Skinner that Douglas really had meant to convert the fort, discovered that it wasn't feasible from an engineering standpoint, and adjusted his plans accordingly. It was just one of those things. For some reason, Skinner got a real bee in his bonnet about it."

"And he sued you for incompetence, failure to perform, and malfeasance."

"He did. Initially, Fairchild thought it'd be cheaper and keep down the negative PR if he and Bennie negotiated some. Fairchild offered him the penthouse, for his personal use, and the opportunity to buy it at a reduced price when the building was sold out." Stubblefield smiled a little. "Bennie grabbed onto that at first. He liked to sue people, Bennie did. One of the things that made him such a good client for us. But he was in the middle of a complex dispute with Carlton Montifiore over a performance bond and he didn't want to get too far embroiled in court cases. So he accepted use of the condo. Put that little chippy of his in there, as a matter of fact. But you probably already know that." He frowned. "Then all of a sudden, he got his knickers in a twist about the penthouse. Wanted out of the whole thing and Fairchild's hide to boot. So he plastered downtown Savannah with summonses, including a couple directed at me. There was no basis for the suit at all." Stubblefield said this in a matter-of-fact way that was quite convincing. "I'll be happy to send the contract in question over to your office. Are you an expert on contract law?"

"Corporate tax law. My father's the best there is on contracts."

"Well, give it to your father, then. He'll tell you Skinner didn't have a leg to stand on. It wasn't worrying me."

"Your position is, you didn't have a motive to kill Skinner?"

"Motive? My motive was to keep him sending me as much business as he sent me last year. Skinner's a huge client of ours."

"Or was. He may have retained another law firm to handle his business."

"He could have, but he didn't. We're probating the will and administering the trust. Still attorneys of record."

"Maybe the only way to retain Skinner Worldwide, Inc. as a client was to knock Skinner off?" Bree knew this was a futile stab before she finished the sentence. Stubblefield merely grinned at her. She tried a different angle. "What about your own interest in Island Dream?"

His sharp little eyes flickered to the left and back. "What about it? It's a hell of a good deal. And I didn't invest a dime until well after Fairchild closed the deal with Skinner." The words "and you can't prove otherwise" hung in the air. Stubblefield had recovered almost all of his self-confidence. He grinned. "You're looking at one person who preferred Benjamin Skinner alive, well, and sending us his checks." He drew a wad of cash from his pocket, slapped it down on the counter, and rose to his feet. He stared down at her for a long moment. Bree stared back. He nodded to himself, gave her a cocky salute, and turned to go.

Bree watched him swagger off. "I'm not writing him off as a suspect just yet, Sash." She looked down at the dog. "If only because he is so *loathsome*!" She shuddered. "Ugh! You know, I almost . . ." She bit her lip. Almost what? She'd been angry, that was for sure. As angry as she'd been at Payton the day before yesterday. If it hadn't been for Striker and that weird sense of calm he'd given her, what would have happened? It'd flowed out of him like light.

Sasha sat up and pawed eagerly at her knee. "You're right. It's time we went home." She gathered her briefcase and stood up. She searched the crowd with her eyes, but Gabriel Striker was gone.

Thirteen

"Ron said some of the dead aren't the least little bit peaceful?" Antonia speared the last chunk of crab from her dinner salad and chuckled to herself. "You've had some first day, haven't you? He's a peach, Ron is, isn't he? From the sounds of it, you've collected quite a staff. Lavinia sounds like a real sweetie, for example. I'd like to meet her."

"You could have, if you'd come into the office." Bree hadn't known whether she'd find Antonia home or not when she got back from the meeting with Stubblefield, but she'd brought a double helping of crab salad and sourdough bread for dinner with her, just in case. She was still too upset by the encounter to fill Antonia in, so she stuck to talking about the lighter parts of her day over dinner.

She had half of her mind on the conversation; the other half was going over and over the appearances and disappearances of the elusive Gabe Striker.

"I couldn't find it," Antonia complained. "If it hadn't been for Ron running into me with his bicycle, I would have wandered up and down Houston for hours, like a little Flying Dutchman. Where did you say it was again?"

"Angelus, a block beyond East Bay, one over from Houston. It's five blocks from here, for Pete's sake." Bree buttered the last of the sourdough with exasperated swipes of her dinner knife. "What were you doing looking for me, anyway? I thought you were job hunting today." Bree bit into the bread and said thickly, "Or maybe thinking about going back to school."

"I haven't heard from Savannah Rep yet," Antonia said with an air of long-suffering. "Good grief, Bree. Is my working or not working any of your business?"

Bree took another bite of bread while she thought about this. "Probably not," she admitted. "But you're putting me into a bit of a bind with Mamma and Daddy. For one thing, where are you planning on staying when they come into town next week for the party? We've only got the two bedrooms. And I was here first. For another, when are you going to tell them you dropped out of school?"

Antonia made a face. "I don't have to tell them yet, do I?"

"And when they want to know why you're here instead of in Charleston?"

"I'm here to help you with your party, of course," Antonia said promptly. "I can set up some wine and cheese in your office—and handle all the new clients who want to see where you work. If the office exists anywhere but your imagination, of course."

Bree froze for a moment. Then, a little huskily, she said, "Oh, the office is real enough." She shoved her kitchen chair back from the table and stretched her legs out on the tile floor. "It's this case that's unreal. I wish I knew why Liz Overshaw thinks Skinner's ghost is haunting her. I wonder if we should do a background check on her. See if there's any history of this kind of thinking in her past."

"You want to find out if she's been in the booby hatch?"

"I guess," Bree said dryly. "Although I wouldn't put it quite that way, myself. I was thinking more about something like post-traumatic stress syndrome. Maybe she's under a lot of pressure from somewhere and this is how she's dealing with it." She got up and began to carry plates to the sink. "I'll have to think about it some."

"Why don't you think about it while we walk on down to Savannah Sweets?"

"Now there's a plan I like," Bree said. "I could use a good praline and a cup of coffee. Besides," she added, "I want to check out how the repairs are going down at Huey's. I feel so guilty about that, it makes me itch. Do you think I should send them some money anonymously?"

Antonia, already halfway out the front door, turned and looked at her. "Why in the world do you want to send money to Huey's? Are you thinking we should maybe do a little charity fund-raising? They don't have insurance?"

"Well, it pretty much was my fault, wasn't it?"

"This little windstorm out of nowhere was *your* fault?"

Bree didn't say anything. She picked up her purse and slung it over her shoulder. Sasha nudged her knee with an anxious whine. She fondled his ears, and then gave him a regretful pat. Flights of stairs were placed at intervals down Factor's Walk. All led to the bottom of the wharfs and the shops and restaurants that lined River Road. And all of them were steep. "Those stairs are no place for the handicapped, Sasha. Sorry."

She followed Antonia out the door, and across the little bridge that spanned the road below. The closest stairway to River Road was right at the end of the town house, an almost vertical plunge of wrought iron with narrow treads.

"People in olden times must have had little feet," Antonia said. She walked sideways down the stairs, balancing herself lightly with one hand. "There's no way my size-eight shoes fit these stairs."

"I believe they did have little feet," Bree said. "Just look at the little teeny shoes in the clothing museums. They were short, too." She took a breath. "Tonia?"

"What?" She waited until Bree joined her at the foot of the stairs.

"What did you see at Huey's when it happened? I thought you blamed the whole mess on me."

"What did I see at Huey's? You mean when the place got wrecked? You were at your feminine best, of course. Payton pushed it too far, and you reached over the table and grabbed him by the ears. You would have slugged him a good one, I bet, but all of a sudden ..." she trailed off. Then she put her fingers to her temples and gave them a furious rub.

"All of a sudden, what?"

"I don't quite recall!" she said with some surprise. "Maybe the air pressure dropped or something, the way it does before a tornado. Anyhow, next thing we all knew, the wind came through and tossed us all rearend over tea-kettle. You told me you were going back up to the town house and I hung around for a bit."

"*I* told you I was leaving?"

"Well, it sure wasn't SpongeBob SquarePants," she said sarcastically.

"Are you sure it wasn't somebody else who told you that'd I'd gone? Some guy, maybe? Very good looking. Really built. Kind of odd-looking eyes. I mean, things were a little confused."

"You think I'd forget a really built, good-looking guy even in the middle of a mini-hurricane? Are you crazy? Why? Did you meet somebody that cool? Did you get his phone number? I've told you this before, the absolute only way to get over Payton the Rat is to find somebody else."

Bree felt like sticking her fingers in her ears and screaming. Instead, she said, "You're sure?"

"You know," Antonia said confidingly, "I am *this close* to telling you to shut up. No, I didn't see anybody like that, and yes, you told me you were going home and if you ask me one more time I'm going to pull your hair out by the roots!" She took a breath and said equably, "So. Are we going to get pralines or what?"

Bree made her mind up. She wanted Striker off her case. Literally and figuratively. "Or what," she said absently. "I've got to go."

"Go? Go where?"

"I forgot about something." She turned and started back up the steps. "I'm taking the car. Don't wait up for me. And make sure you walk Sasha one more time before you go to bed."

"Bree!"

Antonia's frustrated wail followed her to the car, and as she pulled out onto Bay, she imagined she could still hear it. Nothing aggravated her sister more than being outside the action. Bree drove down to Montgomery and tuned into the Chatham County Courthouse lot. She parked under the sodium lights. Professor Cianquino had given her Gabriel Striker's card. She was pretty sure she'd tucked it into her wallet. She was right. She'd stuck it between her driver's license and an expired gym membership card.

GABRIEL STRIKER
PRIVATE INVESTIGATIONS
140 TAYLOR, CHATHAM SQUARE

No phone and no e-mail address. But Chatham Square was just off Forsyth Park and the address should be easy to find. Historic Savannah had twenty-four village squares, laid out by the city's founder, James W. Oglethorpe, almost three centuries ago. Bree wasn't sure how she felt about James W. Oglethorpe. On the one hand, he laid the foundation for one of the most beautiful cities in the United States. On the other, he banned lawyers, Spaniards, and spirituous liquor from the new colony. Bree figured that for the first fifteen years of the colony's life, Savannah suffered from a huge number of unrighted wrongs, chief among them the lack of the comforting solace of a good stiff drink and paella. Things got a lot better after Oglethorpe sailed back to England.

The squares were beautiful. Most were landscaped parks with statues, fountains, and tons of flowers. Houses, churches, schools, and a boutique business or two surrounded them all. Savannah had burned at least three times in her tumultuous history, and each time they re-built the city, a new architectural style joined the survi-vors. So the district was a heartbreakingly lovely mix of Georgian, Federal, and Regency. Colonial, Victorian, and an occasional Art Nouveau. Bree wondered what kind of office Gabriel Striker occupied. You could learn a lot about somebody from the way they chose to live.

She drove around Chatham Square twice before she found 140. The house was a converted three-plex. Origi-nally a center entrance Georgian design, a flight of matching steps was built on either side of the raised front porch. The steps led to 136 and 138 on the second level. Apartment 140 was located in the basement. The entrance was tucked back from the street, at right angles to the square, almost hidden by a live oak draped with Spanish moss. As Bree approached, she could see that the build-ing backed onto a garden surrounded by a wrought-iron fence. The steps leading to the front door were brick; she paused in the middle, and leaned over to run her hand over the fence panels. It was hard to see in the dim light from the sconce, but she would have known that pattern anywhere: spheres so elegantly cast that they seemed to have a life of their own.

The front door was painted a dark, heavy red. There was no bell or buzzer. There was a doorknocker, though. It was a design she'd seen before, too; a pair of justice scales cupped by heavy bronze wings.

Striker didn't keep her waiting long. He opened the door and stepped back to let her in. Bree gestured at the scales of justice. "I see," she said, "that I am expected."

The first thing Bree noticed about Gabriel Striker's of-fice was the swords. Five of them hung one on top of the other on the wall behind his desk, with the longest at the bottom, and the shortest at the top. They were very old. Bree didn't know why she was so sure they were antiques. They were polished to a dull sheen. The blades were straight and true, with a blue tinge to the steel. Maybe it was the jewels set into the hilts; none was faceted in the way artisans cut jewels within the last two hundred years or so, but instead were rounded lumps of red, blue, and green. The bottom sword was at least six feet long; the top less than twelve inches.

"Pretty impressive," she said. "But who would be tall enough to dink around with the one at the bottom? They're ceremonial, I suppose?"

"Quite the contrary," he said. "Please sit down." He waved at the wooden chair in front of his desk. Bree took a cautious look around before she actually sat. The floor was of scuffed and untended pine. A worn carpet remnant of an indeterminate color covered about a third of it. The fireplace on the end wall was bricked up and a wooden box of old newspapers sat on the tiled apron. A reading chair and a standing lamp sat in the far corner, and that was it. A cheap plastic blind covered the window facing the street. There was a half-open door to the right of the fireplace; Bree saw the edge of a stove and the top of a refrigerator. He worked here; she wondered if he lived here, too.

Gabriel was dressed in a pair of worn jeans, some kind of a dark pullover, and tennis shoes. His desk was bare except for a mug filled with pens and pencils. He sat behind it and propped his feet up on the top. "Well," he said. "Here you are."

"Here I am." Bree leaned back in her chair and crossed her legs. "I'd like the answers to a couple of questions about the Skinner case."

He nodded.

"I can trust you to tell me the truth?"

He looked a little surprised at that. "Of course. It's an odd question under the circumstances. Have you been lied to recently?"

"Have I been lied to?" Bree asked indignantly. She uncrossed her legs and sat up. "I most certainly have!"

"By whom?"

Bree noted the "whom." For all his scruffy appearance, Mr. Striker was an educated private eye, if nothing else. She also didn't have an answer; no one connected to the Skinner case had lied to her. Everyone had answered her questions. It was the answers that didn't make any sense.

"As far as I know, Bree, no one connected with Bennie Skinner's death has misled you or tried to obscure the truth."

"Then what's going on?"

He smiled a little. "You'll have to be a little more specific. I don't have true answers to open-ended questions. None of us do."

Here at least was a question that should have a definitive answer. "Who is 'us'?" She scowled at the amused look on his face. No open-ended questions, he'd said. This was a lot like the Techniques of Cross-Examination elective she'd taken her third year in law school. "All right. Let me phrase it this way. What's the one thing that you, Professor Cianquino, Petru Luchet, Ronald Parchese, and Lavinia Mather have in common?"

"At one time, we were all citizens of the Celestial Sphere."

A cult. Bree was surprised at the depth of her dismay. She raised her eyebrow and said dryly, "You said at one time? You aren't anymore?"

"No," he said. Then, so quickly that she almost missed it, a spasm of intense sorrow passed across his face. "Not anymore."

"Has it been disbanded? This Celestial Sphere? I don't recall reading anything about it."

"It exists."

The quiet certainty in his voice rattled her.

"Is there someone in charge of the whole thing? A founder?"

"Not in the sense you mean, no." He hesitated, not, she felt, to conceal anything, but to make sure that he could find the right words. "It exists. It has always existed. It always will exist. There are those of us who pass in and pass out according to the purpose. Petru, Cianquino, Lavinia, Ron, Sasha—we're those who have passed out."

"And my little dog, too?" Bree said flippantly. This was feeling very much like Oz. Then, since Gabriel Striker looked like the sanest man she'd ever met, even though he was talking absolute nonsense, genuine perplexity temporarily overcame her annoyance. "Passed out? For a purpose? What purpose?"

"To form the Company. Your company. The Company that's been created to defend Skinner and others like him."

She took a few minutes to think about her next question. "You're saying all of you have some common purpose in the Skinner case?"

"Yes." He smiled, then sat back in his chair and folded his hands behind his head. "We do. So do you."

"What is it? It can't be to find out who murdered him. There's a big question about whether he's been murdered at all."

"Somebody killed him. Took him out of this life well before his time."

Bree was getting very tired of this. "I'm glad you're so certain. I suppose he's been haunting you, too? I'll tell you something. I'd be a little less skeptical if maybe Mr. Skinner could tell me himself. No reason why he shouldn't, right?"

"No reason at all. Ultimately, he is our client of course." His expression didn't change, but the gray of his eyes looked ever more silvery in the dim light. "It's Skinner, and those like him, that we're here to defend."

Bree felt her temper slipping. She held on to it with a mighty effort. "There's more clients like Skinner? Cordially loathed by everybody while they're alive? Demanding some kind of justice when they're dead?"

"Exactly," Gabriel said. He looked very pleased. "Skinner's soul has been sentenced to purgatory. He's filed an appeal. He claims his actions have been either misinterpreted or that they were legal to begin with."

"What," asked Bree, fascinated despite herself, "has he been convicted of?"

"Greed."

"Greed," Bree said pleasantly, "of course. Naturally. You bet."

"One of the Seven Felonies, as you know."

"There're only seven?" She smacked the palm of her hand against her forehead and answered herself. "D'uh. Sure there are. What could be more screamingly obvious? Pride, Wrath, Envy, Gluttony, Lust, Greed, and the Damn Lazy. And his defense?"

Gabriel grinned at her. He had a perfectly charming smile, and Bree, to her annoyance, found herself smiling back. "He claims mitigating circumstances. That he has, in fact, acted more than once out of disinterested charity and compassion and that the scales of justice will tip in his favor if these actions are taken into account. But the proof lies in the temporal. Therefore, he requires a temporal defense team. The Company."

"And that would be all of you," Bree said. "Of course. All this is screamingly obvious. I don't know why I didn't cotton on to this before."

The sarcasm bounced off him like water off a duck's back. "We each have a role, as any good defense team must. Mine is to protect you from physical harm." The infectious grin lit his face again. "Harm that you'd do to others, as well as the harm others would do to you."

Bree felt herself blush. "Thanks," she said tightly. "But I'm perfectly capable of taking care of myself. Which is part of the reason for my visit tonight. I haven't hired you, Mr. Striker. I haven't recruited you. And I'm pretty sure I don't want you hanging around my cases. In short, I'd appreciate it if you'd butt out."

Gabriel clasped his hands behind his head and leaned back in his chair. "Ah. You're planning on interviewing Carlton Montifiore tomorrow?"

Bree decided not to answer that. She also decided she'd had it with Mr. Striker's despotic and condescending attitude. And why was she trying to deal with a crazy man, anyway?

"It'd be a good idea to let me accompany you."

"I thought I was pretty clear about this, Mr. Striker. I've got enough on my plate without having to worry about you showing up unannounced. So please take me off your client list."

"All right."

"All right?" For some reason, Bree thought she would have more of an argument on her hands. "Just like that? All right?"

He spread his hands in a "there it is" sort of gesture. "It's your call."

"Well." Bree got to her feet and stood in front of him uncertainly. "Well, okay, then." She slung her purse over her shoulder and turned to go.

"You're going to need me, you know," he said with an even bigger grin.

Bree gritted her teeth. "I doubt that, Mr. Striker."

"All you have to do is call."

"Got it right here." She picked his business card out of her jacket pocket and waved it at him, then remembered there was no phone listed. Annoyed, she stuck it back in her pocket and stalked to the front door.

She'd had it. Enough. The inmates were on the streets and running the asylum. She put her hand on the door, then turned back to gauge the effect of her exit.

He was gone. And the swords on the wall were gone, too.

<hr />

Bree slammed home, ignored Antonia's plaintive questions about where she'd been, and went to bed for the best night's sleep she'd had in a week. She woke refreshed, focused, and ready to shove the bewildering events of the past few days into the mental category: Stress of Setting Up Shop All by Herself.

<hr />

Carlton Montifiore's pleasant, efficient secretary directed her to the Pyramid Office Building renovation on Liberty, where Montifiore himself had stopped to check on the project's progress. "The very spot," she said after she introduced herself to him, "where I'll be moving in a couple of months."

Montifiore looked pleased. "That's right. You have the judge's old office on the third floor."

The television interview after Skinner's death hadn't done justice to him. Relaxed, and clearly glad to be in the middle of the crowd of stone masons, carpenters, electricians, and plumbers who scurried around the building site, Montifiore seemed affably open to Bree's questions, and to have all the time in the world.

"I won't take up too much of your time," she said a little apologetically. "I can see that you're busier than a one-armed paperhanger." She made a face; her father's genial clichés seemed to pounce on her when she least expected them.

"No trouble at all. I've got some of the best crews in the business. There's not much for me to do other than sign the payroll checks at the end of the week. Would you like me to show you around?"

"I surely would, Mr. Montifiore."

He smiled and shook his head. "It's quite a mouthful, isn't it? Why don't you call me Carlo?"

Bree looked at him inquiringly. "It's my wife," he said in an amused whisper. "She's a little sensitive about the Italian thing. My mamma named me Carlo, and that's what I am to my friends." His eyes darkened momentarily. "It's the outsiders that call me Carlton. Like those goddamn media parasites." He ran one hand through his thick, dark hair. "Forget that. Let's take a look at your uncle's office."

The Pyramid was built of cobblestone badly in need of repainting after two hundred years of Savannah's semi-tropical weather. The huge oak beams that formed the building's skeleton had been rotted away due to a combination of damp and that scourge of Southern architecture, the termite. Carlo led her up a broad marble staircase that reached from the ground floor to the fifth and highest floor of the building.

"We had to strip off the whole face of the building, re-place the wood framing with beams, and put the cobble-stones piece by piece in the original pattern." He stopped in the third-floor stairwell and opened the door to the hallway for her. "After you."

Bree stepped into the hallway. The terrazzo floors had been sandblasted clean. The pecan paneling had been stripped, sanded down, and refinished to a glossy sheen. The air smelled pleasantly of raw wood, fresh paint, and some piney astringent. Carlo led the way down the hall past thick old office doors topped with rippled glass. He came to a halt in front of number 7. "Here it is. Now this looks pretty good, but we're not going to get a C of O for another couple of months. So you'll be in your temporary office space for some little time yet." He stepped back, to allow her to open the door herself. "You knew there'd been a fire in your uncle's office? That he died here before he could be rescued."

Bree paused, her hand on the heavy bronze doorknob. "Yes," she said briefly.

Carlo drew his eyebrows together in a slight frown. "Very odd, it was. Intense. Killed him instantly."

Bree shook her head. "We never did hear how it started."

He shrugged. "Fire department couldn't get a handle on it. Nobody seemed to know. Kept itself to this room, thank God."

Bree hesitated a moment, and continued on inside. It may have been her imagination, but a faint smell of ash and rotten eggs hung on the air. An aftermath of the fire? The room was small—no more than fifteen by fifteen. A single, double-sashed window looked out over Liberty Street. His desk was gone, of course, and so were the glass-fronted barrister's bookcases that lined the far wall. Bree lost herself in thought. She remembered the office well. She could almost see her uncle's stooped and kindly figure, sitting behind the heavy oak desk in his old red leather chair.

And now, as she stood in the middle of the office, she felt something else: desolation, betrayal, an overwhelming fear. Then, with a sudden, horrifying blow, she felt the pitch and sway of her nightmare ship beneath her feet. The percussion of deadly wings beat above her head. The screams of the dying filled her head. She clapped her hands over her ears and bit her lip to keep from screaming.

A battle had been fought here.

And Franklin had lost.

Carlo touched her arm. "You okay there, Bree?"

She pinched her nose to keep the tears from falling, then took a steadying breath. "I miss him," she admitted. "He was very old, you know, and past his time, Mamma said." She breathed in with a sort of hiccup. "But what's that mean? His time. Past his time. I wished he'd lived forever." Tears welled up and rolled down her cheeks.

"Well." Carlo cleared his throat and looked at his feet. She'd embarrassed him. She put the backs of her hands under her eyes and took another deep breath. She was losing it. And in front of one of the most influential men in the city. "Sorry. Now, about Ben Skinner . . ."

"I know Liz is convinced that someone did the old guy in," Carlo said wryly. "The sooner that's cleared up the better. What is it that you need to know?"

Bree took him through her list of prepared questions. Yes, Skinner had hit the roof over the change in the design plans for the Tybee Island site and yes, his rage had been directed at the innocent and guilty alike. He'd threatened to pull all his project business from Montifiore Construction, and yes, that would have put a significant hole in Carlo's business. "We took care of most of his projects here in Georgia," Carlo admitted, "and the old bastard had a way of getting under my skin, no question about it." He guided Bree out the office door and down the marble staircase that led to the bottom floor. "But the Island Dream project had the right kind of financing behind it and the project itself wasn't in jeopardy."

"There was enough money to stay afloat, even if Skinner insisted on pulling his cash out?"

Carlo shrugged. "No problems there. Always plenty of cash around. Besides, my guess was that it was all going to blow over in a month or two."

"Guess?" Bree let her dubiety show.

"Well, 'hope' is a better word, I suppose." He followed as Bree walked through the magnificent old front doors and onto the pavement outside. She faced him. "Where were you the morning Mr. Skinner passed on?"

"Here." Carlo turned and looked up at the cobblestone wall towering above them both. "Right here. There's a good twenty people that were here along with me."

Fourteen

How sharper than a serpent's tooth it is
To have a thankless child!
–*King Lear*, Shakespeare

"Of course we're truly sorry he's gone," Jennifer Skinner said. "He really was a bit of an old pet."

"I suppose his mother said that about King Kong," Grainger Skinner said under his breath. He added another two inches of Tanqueray to his gin and tonic and smiled at Bree. "Can I freshen that for you?"

Bree looked down at her own gin and tonic. She'd forgotten how much she liked gin and tonics, especially when the afternoon was warm and the sun was bright. "No, thank you." She shifted restlessly on the stone garden seat. It was damp, hard, and uncomfortable. Jennifer's garden was spectacular, though. Many of the mansions in the Historic District had enclosed gardens at the back or side, and the Skinners had one of the loveliest. The entire quarter acre was surrounded by a wrought-iron fence (paneled with a design, Bree was relieved to see, of perfectly normal acanthus and ivy leaves) and paved with brick cobblestones. A large live oak shaded the northern half of the garden, drooping protectively over five-foot-wide hostas, huge freesia bushes, and waist-high plantings of Canterbury bells. The southern half of the garden held azaleas and rhododendrons. Bree wished she had seen the garden in the spring, when these flowering bushes were at their best. Roses and hydrangeas were planted in between; the last of their summer blooms were faded now, an echo of former glory. A new, and to Bree, rather garish outdoor kitchen had been added on to the rear of the house. A stainless steel outdoor grill held pride of place in the center of the brick U that formed the kitchen itself. A counter-high refrigerator and a big double sink made of Italian tile flanked the grill. Grainger and Jennifer sat at the large outdoor dining table; Bree had retreated to the stone bench at the edge of the little fountain, where a replica of Niobe dripped tears into the stone pool.

"Grainger, darling," Jennifer said plaintively. "He hasn't even been buried yet."

"The funeral's tomorrow?" Bree asked.

"Yes. We thought we'd wait until everyone who wanted to attend could get here . . ."

"All three of them," Grainger interrupted. "And *they're* just coming to make sure he's safely underground."

Bree choked a little.

"Too much gin for you?" Grainger asked sympathetically. "I tend to make drinks a little stiffer when I'm not on call at the hospital."

"It's just fine, thank you," Bree said.

"We wouldn't want Bree to think we're glad Dad's gone," Jennifer said. "Maybe you are making those drinks a little too strong, darlin'."

"I *am* glad the old bastard's gone," Grainger said. Then, with a rather vicious twist to his voice, "*darlin'*."

Jennifer rolled her eyes at Bree in a "these men!" gesture.

Jennifer hadn't been a beauty when she and Bree were at school together, but she had a slim and elegant presence then and an even more high-fashion look now. Her dark hair was drawn back in a sleek bob. For these Saturday afternoon cocktails ("Drinks in the garden, Bree. About four o'clock? Don't worry about dressing up."), she wore cream loose linen trousers, an extremely flattering matching linen shirt unbuttoned to show a tank top in sepia brown, and a robin's egg blue scarf around her waist. Bree didn't know where the turquoise and silver jewelry at her ears and throat came from, but the total effect was spectacular.

Bree wore her best pair of jeans. At least her white shirt was silk.

"From all accounts, he must have been a difficult man to be around in business," Bree said. "But you must have been on pretty good terms. You said y'all went out sailing at least once a week, barring the weather?"

Jennifer gave her a sharp look. "I didn't say that," she said coolly. "Who told you that? But yes, we did our best to make time for him. Poor pet, it was almost the only relaxation he had. He just didn't take any personal time for himself, you know what I mean. Personal time," she repeated, rather vaguely. She poured herself another glass of white wine from the bottle on the table. It was now about five o'clock in the afternoon. In the last forty-five minutes, Jennifer had been through a large whiskey julep and two glasses of wine. This made the third. Bree got dizzy just thinking about drinking that amount of liquor in so short a time.

Grainger Skinner caught her observing his wife and lifted his eyebrow with a knowing sort of smirk. Bree felt her cheeks turn pink.

"I understand you're opening a practice here in Savannah?" he asked genially. He didn't look much like his father; Benjamin Skinner had been a short, wiry man with a big nose and, in later years, a bald head. Grainger Skinner was tall, with a thick head of light brown hair and a slight paunch. "Finding our city to your liking?"

"It's very beautiful," Bree said. "The family spent a few summers here when I was little. When my uncle Franklin died and left me his practice, I was glad to think I'd spend time here again."

Grainger snapped his fingers. "That's right! You're kin to the judge. I'd forgotten all about that."

"You've forgotten all about the fact that Bree was the one who called you the day Daddy died, too," Jennifer said suddenly. She smiled, spitefully, and sipped at her wine.

Grainger blinked at her through the haze of gin. "That was you? Ambulance-chasing?"

"A mistake," Bree said hastily. "I do beg your pardon for that. It was a thoughtless joke on... somebody's part."

"But it's not a mistake that you're representing that crazy Liz," Jennifer said coldly. "She's telling anybody who'll listen that Daddy was murdered."

"He wasn't *your* Daddy," Grainger said. "I wish you'd stop calling him that."

"And, of course, since we were the last ones to see him alive—since we were there when the poor man fell overboard and into the ocean—since you think Grainger benefits from the will, it's *us* you're accusing of murder, isn't it?!" Jennifer lowered her head, got to her feet, and walked toward Bree. Her face was flushed. Her voice rose to a squall. "What I want to know is, where you get off spreading this kind of shit around town."

It'd been too easy. The phone call to Jennifer, the glad cries of renewed friendship, the instant offer of a pleasant afternoon in the garden. Bree could have kicked herself. She was a sap. She'd walked right into a trap to make her give up the investigation.

For the first time since the whole peculiar business began, Bree began to believe Benjamin Skinner really had been murdered.

"You're absolutely right," she said in a matter-of-fact way. "So maybe you could help clear a few things up."

"You're out of your mind," Jennifer said. She sat back down at the table, almost missing the seat. She adjusted herself with a flounce. "Why the hell should we help you?"

"If you're guilty, you're absolutely right. You should ask me to leave right now." Bree set her glass on the stone bench with an air of finality. "On the other hand, if you're innocent, why not help me? Savannah's a small town. I'm not the only one with questions about Mr. Skinner's death." This, Bree reflected, was probably true. "You don't want to end up with tour busses going up and down in front of your house, like they do at Mercer House."

This reference to the Billy Hanson case, Savannah's most notorious modern murder, sent Jennifer rigid with rage. Grainger Skinner, on the other hand, threw his head back and began to laugh. It was genuine, spontaneous laughter.

"Shut up!" Jennifer threw her wineglass at him. It shattered on the brick paving.

"Ah, darlin'." Grainger sighed. He looked at the shards of glass. He bent down and picked them up carefully, one by one. When he had a handful, he flung the pieces into the fountain pool and began all over again. "Thing is, *Ms.* Beaufort, there's a witness."

"A witness? To Mr. Skinner falling off the *Sea Mew*?"

He straightened up, his face flushed. "Dougie Fairchild was out in his boat and saw the whole thing."

"There!" Jennifer shrieked. "You see?"

"Mr. Fairchild saw the whole thing?" Bree looked thoughtfully at them. Jennifer had the triumphant look of the vindicated. Grainger merely looked shifty. "That wasn't reported at all, was it?"

"Not initially, no." Grainger tossed a few cubes of ice into his gin and tonic and replenished the gin. "Why would he? The only person who's had a question about Dad's death was Liz, and the police brushed her off. That is," he added malevolently, "until your people started poking around."

"And that bimbo girlfriend of his, of course," Jennifer added.

"Chastity," Bree said.

Jennifer snorted derisively. "That little whore. Can you believe it? She's refusing to move out of the penthouse at Island Dream. Claims Dad left it to her. A million and a half dollars' worth of property." Jennifer rolled her eyes. "We're going to have to get the sheriff's office down there to evict her. Stupid little bitch."

"I hear you got hold of the autopsy report and the police investigation? Sure like to know how you accomplished that," Grainger added.

For that matter, so would she, although she certainly wasn't about to say that to Grainger. "The quickest way to satisfy my client's concerns about your father's death is to offer her as complete an account as possible of the circumstances surrounding it." The patio was growing colder. She began to wish she'd brought some kind of hoodie. Jennifer and Grainger, both pickled in the warmth of the alcohol, didn't seem to notice. "Can I ask you a couple of questions about that Tuesday?"

Husband and wife exchanged a look. "Depends," Grainger said shortly. "What do you want to know?"

"When did you decide to go sailing?"

"A lot depends on the weather," Jennifer said condescendingly. "You can't plan for sure all that far ahead. Especially in October. And a lot depended on Daddy's schedule, too. I guess we got the phone call about . . ." she hesitated.

"About nine Tuesday morning," Grainger said. "I'm four days on, three days off at the hospital. Tuesday's an off day. It was fair and calm, so Jenny and I"—at this point, he reached across the table and covered Jennifer's hand with his own. She looked at it in surprise—"Jenny and I decided to take the boat out for a little spin. Just the two of us."

The sunlight darkened and a slight breeze began to rise, rattling the hostas in the north corner of the garden. Bree looked around with a frown.

"Mr. Skinner called you?"

"Yes," Grainger said.

"No," Jennifer said.

The air grew colder. Bree shivered and hugged herself, then rubbed her hands together.

"It was Doug Fairchild, as a matter of fact," Grainger said smoothly. "He and Dad were in a meeting about the conversion of the Trident building into office space. They finished up early. Doug called to tell us Dad was headed on down to the marina. He wanted us to wait up. So we did."

"Why didn't Mr. Skinner call you himself?"

Grainger shrugged. "Who knows? He was in a hurry to get to the marina before we cast off, I suppose."

"I'm freezing out here," Jennifer said petulantly. "I'm so cold I can't stand it. I've got to go inside."

"Just hang on a minute," Grainger said. "You're about through with this, aren't you, Bree?"

"What time did Mr. Skinner get to the marina?"

"Oh," Grainger shrugged. "Just before we cast off. I remember he jumped on board from dockside, as we'd already drawn up the walk."

"Grainger!" Jennifer said. She stared over Bree's shoulder at the azaleas, a vulpine smile on her lips. "I've got to get inside. I'll leave Bree to it."

"Go on in, then," Grainger said impatiently. "What's the matter with you, anyway?"

Bree turned around and looked into the depths of the garden. Something low on the ground disturbed the dank leaves; a cat perhaps, except Bree got the sense it was bigger than a cat. Jennifer jumped up. Her wineglass fell to the ground and shattered. If this was typical of the Skinners' afternoon cocktail hour, Bree thought, they must go through a lot of glasses. Jennifer half-ran to the patio doors, paused, looked back at Bree with a triumphant smile, and disappeared inside the house.

"It is a little chilly out here," Grainger frowned. "What the hell's up with this weather?"

Bree got up and moved to the chair Jennifer had just vacated. This gave her a full view of the north end of the

garden. The leaves were still, but she was certain something lay there, peering out at them.

Was it blue-eyed, whatever horror lay there?

"You were about to tell me what time Mr. Skinner got
to the *Sea Mew*."

Grainger brushed his hand over his face. "About ten, I
think. Must have been."

No wind stirred. The brush was silent.

"And you raised sail and set off."

"Yeah."

Bree ran her mind over the transcript of the police in-
terrogation. Lieutenant Hunter's interview began as the
Sea Mew set sail. If Grainger was lying about the events
leading up to his father's arrival at the boat—and Bree
was sure he was—he'd lie about the rest of it. And those
lies were already recorded. She didn't need to hear them
again.

She turned and looked at Grainger Skinner. "Did you
kill your father?"

"No," he said. "No, I did not."

Bree knew, with a sudden, cold certainty, that Jennifer
left them alone in the garden for a reason. *Them Pendergasts!* Lavinia's voice whispered. *Evil in them Pendergasts!*

The scent of decayed corpses mingled with the dying
roses. Grainger sat back in his chair, his eyes closed, lost
in a stupor of gin. Bree got up casually and set her glass
on the table. "I'll just see myself out."

Grainger didn't move.

A dark, fetid cloud of oily smoke took slow shape in
the brush behind him. Bree forced herself to walk calmly
to the wrought-iron gate. She fumbled with the latch,
slipped outside to the welcome heat of the sidewalk, and

leaned against the fence, trembling. Nervously, she cast a look backward, over her shoulder. Grainger opened his eyes and grinned at her.

Whatever had lain in the garden behind him was gone.

Fifteen

When th' Arch-felon saw,
Due entrance he disdain'd and, in contempt,
At one single bound high overleap'd all bound
Of hill or highest wall ...
—*Paradise Lost*, John Milton

"I'll tell you what I think," Bree said to Ronald. "I think Mr. Skinner was dead before he got to the boat." She was halfway in and halfway out of a little black dress Ronald had brought to her town house on approval. "And that creepy Jennifer had something to do with it."

"His lungs were filled with seawater," Ronald said. He twitched the bodice into place, and stepped back to look at her. "He drowned. And it's no use thinking that they bribed the coroner or anything, because the body's still around, and after he's buried tomorrow, they can dig him up again if they have to. So that," he said, as he spun her around and zipped her up, "is that. Why would they drown him in one place and move him to another?"

"Nah," Antonia said. "It's skimpy in the wrong places. The dress," she said in response to Bree's lifted eyebrow, "not your theory of the crime. If there was a crime."

"There was a crime all right," Bree said grimly. "And

Jennifer's connected with it somehow. I'm convinced of it."

"You're right," Ronald said to Antonia. "She doesn't look chic. She looks cheap." He unzipped the dress. Bree stepped out of it, and stood there in bra and panties. He tossed it on top of the heap of others on the couch and dived back into the shopping bags that littered the floor. Sasha poked his nose into the tissue paper, and Ron shooed him gently away.

"Well, at least Miss Overshaw has been moved from the loony tune to sober citizen," Antonia said. "Why did you decide she's right after all?"

Bree didn't know why, but she was certain. It had everything to do with the presence in the garden, and Jennifer's malicious pleasure in the cold. But she couldn't tell Antonia that. What she could say, to Antonia or anyone else, is that for a whole bunch of more practical reasons— Jennifer's obvious unease, the couple's inconsistencies, their schizophrenic reaction to Benjamin Skinner himself, not to mention the eerie sensation she'd had of being stalked—she was convinced somebody had indeed, as Striker put it, "taken Benjamin Skinner out of this life before his time."

Ron pulled a red outfit from the bag labeled GoFish and shook it out. It was a brilliant cardinal red. She'd seen the color somewhere recently. "What do you think?"

Bree looked at it doubtfully. "It's awfully bright, isn't it?"

"I think the color would suit you like anything," Antonia said. "Try it on this minute. I wish," she added enviously, "that Ron would shop for me."

"I would if you had any money to spend, ducky," Ron said. "You can't even qualify for unemployment."

Antonia giggled. "Too true."

Ron clucked his tongue. "Any word on the job yet?"

Bree marveled a little at how well Ron and Antonia had hit it off. Her sister would have shaved Bree bald if she'd said half the things to her that Ron got away with. He was, Antonia had said with a grin, the big brother she never had and never wanted.

"Nope. I called today. The tech job's down to me and this guy with a degree in stage design from some drama school in the Midwest, if you can believe it." She shook her head in disgust.

"Gee," Ron said. His eyebrows rose. "Why in the world would they pick somebody with a college degree over you, with your vast experience? I ask you."

"Shut up," Antonia said unperturbed. "The director loves me. And why would he choose some geek with a degree who can't act over a person who can learn the job perfectly well and *can* act?"

"Oh, I don't know. Maybe because he wants to get the job done?"

"Hey, you guys," Bree said. "What do you think?" She smoothed the red dress over her hips and twirled around.

Antonia shrieked, "Yes!"

"Do I know what I'm doing or what?" Ronald said complacently.

Bree looked down at herself. The material was a light, silky velvet with the sheen of sunlight on water. The gown was tea length. At mid-calf, the skirt flared out in soft ripples. The neckline draped at the throat.

"Fabulous," Antonia said. "Just fabulous."

Bree stood on tiptoe to see herself in the mirror that

hung over the mantel. She did look fabulous, if a little imperious.

"Just the thing to face down the power of the Skinner clan." Ronald smiled at her; it was a joyous, confiding smile, and Bree smiled right back.

"Thanks," she said. "You're right."

"*De nada*, as we say south of Montgomery. Way south, of course. And I'm *always* right about clothes."

"Doorbell," Antonia said as the chimes ran through the house. "I'll get it. And whoever it is," she threw over her shoulder, "make it short. I'm starving to death."

She was back in a few moments, a powerfully built, saturnine-looking man in her wake.

He was a cop. He had to be. Bree could see the outline of his shoulder holster under his cheap sports coat, and he had that guarded, self-aware look that characterizes most veterans of the force. Bree was conscious of an intense flare of attraction. His eyes were hazel. His brief glance at her was detached, but thorough. Bree could almost see the information as he stored it up: *White female, late twenties, five feet nine, white blonde, 125 pounds, green eyes, no distinguishing marks.*

"This," Antonia said unnecessarily, "is the police." She waved a business card and handed it over to Bree. "Lieutenant Hunter, Chatham County detective first class, or something like that. Lieutenant, this is my sister, Queen Bree." She shot an impudent glance at him. "So I suppose this'll take as long as it takes? Just to let you know, we haven't eaten yet."

Bree, suddenly very conscious of the dress, and the clothes and shopping bags strewn around the floor, felt at a considerable disadvantage. She scowled at Antonia, and then nodded at the detective coolly. "I'm Brianna Beaufort. I'm glad to see you here, Lieutenant. I had intended to come and talk to you Monday morning. I'm flattered that you've anticipated me. And on a weekend, too."

"More of a courtesy visit," Hunter said shortly. His voice matched his face; rough, experienced, and rather cynical. "It shouldn't keep you from your dinner."

Ron grabbed Antonia's elbow. "Tell you what, ducky. Let's you and me go down to the shrimp place and bring something back for Miss Bree."

"But ..." Antonia said.

"No buts. Back in a tick, Bree."

Sasha followed them to the front door, and then scrambled stiff-legged back to the living room, where he flopped on the floor with a grunt. Bree had come to depend on his reactions to people. He seemed indifferent to the detective.

"May I sit down for a moment?" He indicated the cluttered couch with a sweep of his hand.

"Of course." Bree stacked the clothes onto the coffee table with as little fluster as possible. She sat in the chintz chair at a right angle to the couch; Hunter followed suit at the opposite end of the couch. Her father had taught her early on that silence was sometimes the best offense in unfamiliar situations; she sat with her hands in her lap and waited for him to speak.

"Your client, Ms. Overshaw, has been rattling a good few cages around town."

He said "Ms." without the self-conscious twist most middle-aged white males gave to it. Although, looking at him more closely, he was probably in his midthirties. It was his expression that made him seem older. "Yes," Bree said composedly, "she has."

"You haven't been in Savannah very long, Ms. Beaufort."

"No." Then, with some surprise because it seemed like a lifetime by now, "A little over a week."

He smiled, which lightened his face. She was right. He wasn't too much older than she was. "And you practiced in North Carolina for several years with your father's firm. Corporate tax law? Is that right? Winston-Beaufort, Montgomery."

"Your information's good, Lieutenant."

"So you're new to the criminal investigation business."

Now, *that* was condescending. Bree's temper stirred. She gave it a mental whack and said, "Yep. That's right."

"But you are familiar with the requirements of your profession ..."

So he *was* capable of sneering, too; she knew that most cops didn't care for lawyers, but still ...

"... which are quite clear, Ms. Beaufort; any information you turn up in the course of an investigation of a crime should be turned over to us."

"By 'us' do you mean the Chatham County Police Department? Or the folks who get together for whiskey juleps after work?" This reference to the powers behind the throne was a calculated one; if the Skinners had sent him and meant to intimidate her, they had another think coming.

Anger flashed across his face so quickly she wasn't sure she'd seen it. But had she enraged him because the establishment sent him? Or because he thought she *was* the establishment? Winston-Beaufort, Montgomery had been around since well before the War Between the

States; if he'd gone as far as looking up her work history, he would have known that, too.

"Why don't you just flat out tell me what you want, Lieutenant? We can save ourselves a lot of time."

He rubbed his hand across his mouth with a weary gesture. Bree felt a stab of compunction. No city paid its policemen and women enough. It was hard work, among hard people, and she had more sympathy than she cared to admit for the force.

"Let me get you a cup of coffee before we get down to it. And do you have a first name other than Lieutenant?"

There was that faint smile. "Sam. And a cup of coffee would be welcome."

"Will you come on into the kitchen, then? I won't have to worry about slopping coffee all over those clothes Ronald brought home for me."

His eyes ran over her body, coolly appraising. "You're looking for something to shine down the opposition at your open house? That ought to do it."

Bree looked down at the red dress, embarrassed. She glanced at him; there was a faint smile in his eyes. She smiled back, and for a long moment, the air held promise.

Bree turned on her heel and went to the sink. She ground coffee beans, put them into the automated coffeemaker, and filled the tank with water. By the time she'd accomplished these small, familiar tasks, her embarrassment receded. She sat down at the kitchen table across from him, composed and guarded.

"I got a call today from someone in the mayor's office. You seem to be conducting your own investigation into Benjamin Skinner's death, Miss Beaufort."

"Please call me Bree," she said with just the right

amount of friendly distance. "Are you warning me off talking to Grainger and Jennifer Skinner again?"

His eyebrows went up. "Am I warning you off? No. Would the ..." he hesitated, then said, "individual who called me from the mayor's office like me to warn you off? Sure. But doesn't matter to me who you harass during this digging expedition. Although, I'll tell you this; if you keep poking around, it's going to affect the quality of your practice here in Savannah. That's no concern of mine and you look like a smart woman to me, so you probably already know that. If you find anything out that's relevant to this case, *that* concerns me a great deal."

"It doesn't matter to you who I harass, as you so tactfully put it?" Bree said. She was nettled. "Are you that sure of your job? Much less any future promotions in the hands of your superiors in the force? I've only been practicing law for a few years, Lieutenant, but I already know how things work. Guys who refuse to play ball at crucial times don't get back in the game."

He shrugged. "Why is this a concern of yours?"

"Because I'm representing the interests of my client," she snapped. "If the police investigation is compromised in any way ..." The look on his face, dangerously angry, made her stop in mid-sentence. "I'm sorry," she said immediately. "I didn't mean to imply anything crooked."

"Sounded as if you were headed that way." He folded his arms across his chest and looked at her, as if weighing her worth to him as an ally. "You saw Grainger and Jennifer Skinner this afternoon."

"I did," she said, although he hadn't made it a question. "And Carlton Montifiore this morning."

"I'd like you to repeat the gist of the conversation."

She did, and quite well, too, even if she did think so herself. Her summary was accurate, focused, and accomplished with just enough skepticism to let Hunter know she didn't believe a word of the Skinners' story. She left out the part about the cold and the watcher in the garden.

"They claim there was a witness to the accident?"

Bree set a cup of coffee in front of him, put the sugar and creamer at hand, and sat down at the table. "Douglas Fairchild, yes. They didn't offer any explanation as to why he hasn't come forward until now. My guess is, they heard Liz had retained me to look into the murder and they cooked this up among themselves to verify their story." She traced invisible circles on the tabletop with an impatient fingertip. "Can I ask you something, Lieutenant? Do you think Benjamin Skinner was murdered?"

"Chief Hartman is closing the case. Accidental death."

"But you don't believe it."

He looked at her impassively.

"Oh, come on," Bree said. "Why else are you here? Unless it's to shove me around so that I'll drop my client and the investigation along with it." His eyes, she noticed, became flat amber brown when he was angry. "I'll be absolutely straight with you. I'm convinced Benjamin Skinner was murdered. Not only that, I'm almost sure he was dead before he ever got on that boat. I mean, before somebody put him on the boat."

Hunter eyed her narrowly. "That's quite a set of assumptions. Anything to back it up? Other than intuition?"

"Nothing that would make any sense to you," Bree admitted. "And I know it flies in the face of the facts. You're sure no one got at the coroner?"

"Bribed Doc Bishop, you mean?" He was obviously

taken aback. "Do you know how many witnesses there are at an autopsy? I was there myself."

"You were? Did you walk away from it with any unanswered questions? Was there anything at all about the condition of the body that didn't add up?"

He looked at her for a long moment, as if deciding how much to let her into his confidence. Then he said, slowly, "His daughter-in-law backed the boat over the body. Pretty convenient to have the corpse chewed up like that. It makes it possible to hide a number of problems, especially since they had time to haul the body into the boat, make sure any signs of assault had been chewed up by the props, and dump it over the side before the Coast Guard got there."

Bree made a face.

"Do you sail, Miss Beaufort? You do. Then you know how difficult it is to maneuver a boat like the *Sea Mew*. I'd be surprised if either one of them was sailor enough to do that on purpose."

"Maybe they didn't drive the boat over the body. Maybe they just dropped him into the motor." She shook her head violently. "Ugh. I wish that hadn't occurred to me. I'm not going to be able to get that picture out of my head for a long time."

He winced. "Quite an image."

"But you agree with me? You think there's something suspicious about this death."

"I'm not entirely satisfied, no."

"You don't look like the kind of man to operate on intuition, Lieutenant. Quite the opposite, in fact. So what's convinced you this is murder?"

He drained his cup, then rose and put it in the sink. "Thanks for the coffee. You'll let me know if anything else comes up? You have my card?"

"Wait just a second." Bree looked up at him, her voice steely. "The only reason to keep information from me is if it's going to impede the murder investigation. You made it pretty clear that the department's ready to—what was the expression y'all use? Close the book on this one. Officially, it's accidental death. And if it's officially an accidental death, anything to the contrary that you tell is unofficial, isn't it? So? Spill it."

He laughed.

"Sit down, please." Bree patted the seat of the kitchen chair invitingly. "Let me get you another cup of coffee. If you wait just a little bit longer, they'll be back with the shrimp."

"Who's 'they'? If you're meeting some of your friends . . ."

"Antonia and Ron. My secretary."

"Your sister works as your secretary?"

"No," Bree said, exasperated, "the guy who was with her just now. The one who was helping me dress. Ron Parchese."

"You and your sister were alone when I came in." His gaze was dark and shuttered.

She stared at him. He looked back at her with an appraising, assessing air that chilled her. A cop look. "You know," she said uncertainly, "I guess Ron was here earlier and left before you got here. Sorry. It's been a long day. I didn't mean to . . ." She put as much energy as she could into her smile. "Hey. You've eaten at the Shrimp Factory, haven't you? I shouldn't wonder if it isn't the best food in Georgia, practically. Antonia always brings more than a battalion can eat."

He sat down. Reluctantly, but at least he sat down. This

made her guess at a number of things. He didn't wear a wedding ring. It was Saturday night. He was off duty. No wife or girlfriend, and maybe not many friends, either. He was a Yankee, probably from the Northeast; that flat, clipped accent was unmistakable. And he carried himself like a soldier.

The fact that he hadn't seen her highly visible, even flamboyant secretary was something that she didn't want to think about. Not right now.

"You aren't from Georgia originally, is my guess," she said as she poured the coffee, "and maybe not from anywhere in the South?"

"Not too hard to guess. I don't have the accent," he said.

"*We* don't have an accent. You folks from up north do, though. But it's not just that." She smiled sunnily at him. "You take your coffee black. All true Southerners take it regular, which means cream and sugar." She held the cream pitcher up in the air. "You sure?"

He shook his head, and then commented, "Yours seems to come and go."

Bree raised her eyebrows inquiringly.

"Your Southern accent."

If Antonia was here, she'd tell Sam Hunter to keep his guard up when Bree went Southern, but she wasn't, thank goodness. Bree occupied herself with cream and sugar, and watched him out of the corner of her eye. "How long have you been down south?"

"A couple of years. I joined the Marines after undergraduate school and served two tours."

"That's long enough to soften those Yankee vowels, if not get rid of them altogether."

He tipped his chair back, long legs stretched out. He looked amused. More important, he looked relaxed. "Are you trying to flirt with me, Miss Beaufort?"

"I surely am, Sam. My intent, a fell intent, to be sure, is to charm all of the information out of you that I can about the Skinner case. Did you ever meet him? Up close and personal, I mean?"

"As a matter of fact, I did. He has a project over on Liberty."

"The Pyramid Office Building," Bree said promptly. "Nearly completed, isn't it? My uncle's office space is over there."

"It almost wasn't completed ... There was a real disagreement over whether or not to tear the building down or keep the façade and rebuild where necessary."

"I heard about that." A cold breeze curled through the kitchen. Bree got up and shut the windows over the sink halfway.

"Fairchild prevailed, over Skinner's strong objections. And when they began excavating the basement to reset the footers, they dug up a body."

"A body?"

"A white male, as it turned out, with a hole the size of Topeka in the skull. As I understand it, there was a period in Savannah's history when people were buried in the most convenient spot—not necessarily a cemetery."

"That's true. It was mostly the pirates, I think."

"Be that as it may, construction was halted until we determined specifics."

"It was an old body?"

"A very old body. Mid-eighteenth century, as near as the anthropologists at UNC could figure out." The lines around Sam's mouth deepened into a grin. "There was some speculation that it was the body of an errant lawyer, who'd managed to sneak into the city despite Governor Oglethorpe's ban."

"Huh," Bree said indignantly. "I suppose you all thought that was pretty funny."

"Everybody but the lawyers," Sam admitted. "It was Skinner's joke, believe it or not."

"From all I heard, he didn't have much of a sense of humor."

"Not as a rule, no. He was a thoroughly unpleasant guy, as a matter of fact. Didn't seem to give a hang that the holdup might bankrupt his partners."

"If a lousy personality were a motive, we'd quadruple the current murder rate," Bree said. The kitchen was getting cold. She rubbed her hands up and down her arms, and thought about excusing herself to get a sweater. "How long ago was this?"

Sam shrugged. "Eight, nine months. Very early in the project."

"And it's still not finished. And then there's the Island Dream condo project. Although I think one of Mr. Skinner's very close friends lives there already?"

"The surgically enhanced Miss Chastity McFarland. Yes, she does. She agrees with you, by the way. She thinks Skinner was murdered."

"Does she know anything we don't know?"

"Ms. McFarland's interest appears to be limited to the state of Mr. Skinner's personal finances. I talked to John Stubblefield, who's the executor of his estate. Skinner didn't leave her a thing. Ms. McFarland had every reason to keep Skinner alive."

"Oh," Bree said, disappointed. "So she didn't bump him off so she could inherit. Does anything at all change

for Grainger and his wife because Skinner's dead?" Bree
asked, already knowing the answer.

"That's a good question. And the answer is that it
doesn't appear to."

"Does anything change for *anybody* now?"

"He has a charitable trust. Most of the revenues subsi-
dize public television programs."

"'Brought to you by the good offices of the Benjamin C. Skinner Foundation,'" Bree muttered. "Oh, dear."
She looked around the kitchen a little crossly. "Is there
another window open? Aren't you getting cold? I can
count the number of times I've had to have the heat on
during our winters on one hand. And it's never been in
October."

Mildly surprised, Sam said, "No, I'm not cold." He
had his back to the archway leading to the living room.
Sasha limped into view. His ears lay flat against his skull.
He drew his upper lip over his teeth in a silent snarl. Beyond him, Bree saw a finger of the pus-yellow curl of water.

Sam leaned over the table and looked intently into her
face. "Is anything wrong?"

Bree put her hand up to her forehead. "I ... no. I mean,
yes, there is. To tell you the truth, I'm feeling a little bit
under the weather. I'm sorry; it just came and hit me all of
a sudden."

He got to his feet. "You really don't look well at all.
What can I do for you?"

"Actually, my sister will be back in a bit. But if we
could continue our talk at another time ... God!"

The yellow stream curled around Sasha's feet, swelled,
and grew into a cloud of evil brilliance. The dog's eyes
glowed with a sudden, demonic red. He opened his jaws

in a terrible grin. His eyeteeth were stained with something dark. He turned, awkward with the cast on his leg, and disappeared around the corner.

"Look, maybe I'd better go down and find your sister. She's at the Shrimp Factory?"

"No! No. I just think I'm going to be sick. If you could come back tomorrow . . ."

The vicious light was waist-high now, a horror-filled ball of glowing water. It pulsed with the beat of some terrible heart.

"Of course." Hunter turned and headed to the living room, where he had come in. He stopped in front of it. He didn't see it. She knew he didn't see it.

"NO! Out the back door, please!" She grabbed his arm, pulled him across the tile, and almost pushed him out the kitchen door.

She threw the dead bolt and stood there, her back to it all.

And then she turned around.

Sixteen

I form the light, and create Darkness; I make peace, and create evil; I the LORD do all these things.

—Isaiah 45:7

A river of hellish light poured from the mirror. Sasha, snarling, kept her at bay. She couldn't get too close—the dog behaved as if possessed—but she faced it. Her heart pounded so hard that she trembled with the beat. But she faced it.

And she didn't know what to do. It didn't seem fair, somehow, to curse her with these visions, these people, this mysterious task Gabriel Striker had laid before her, with no guidance at all.

The dog's snarls rose to a shriek, and then stopped. Sasha threw himself down, cowering, and began to crawl toward her, every muscle in his body quivering.

In the mirror, *through* the mirror, a pair of giant wings rose and fell once, twice, three times, with the sound of a giant scythe.

Bree's fear almost suffocated her. Like Sasha, she fell down before the terror of the wings. She put her hands over her ears; the dog reached her, crawled into her lap, and shoved his head under her chin, whimpering. She knew with a sickening certainty that this thing, this being, this force, had done things to Sasha she hadn't even seen.

Suddenly, she was swept with rage. She scrambled to her knees, her dog in her arms. If she had one of the swords from Gabriel's wall, could she fight it? The sickly light was shoulder-high now, and moving toward her with the deliberate, inexorable power of an ocean tide.

She backed up.

The light followed.

She backed through the kitchen to the bolted door, and fumbling with one hand behind her, the other clutching the uncomplaining, terrified dog, she tried to throw the dead bolt.

Behind her, the dreadful light spun, and began to coalesce. Bree glimpsed the shape of a huge, horned figure.

Call for me, Bree!

A huge and dread-filled weight pressed on her heart.

Call for me, Bree!

She drew in a great, shuddering breath.

NOW!

"STRIKER!" Bree cried. "STRIKE-E-E-E-R!

A thunderclap split the air like a huge bronze hammer.

She got the door opened and stumbled into the coolness of the night. A narrow planked path led from the kitchen door to the wooden patio in front. Bree got halfway down it, and then sank to her knees. Sasha wriggled out of her arms, and stood up. He licked her face with frantic swipes of his tongue. Bree sat down, her back against the handrail, and stared up at the evening sky. The stars wheeled overhead, their brightness dwarfed by the light and clamor of the shops on River Road forty feet below.

"There you are, ducky!" Ronald crossed the small

bridge that connected Factor's Walk to her house—and
he was real, wasn't he? With those feathery curls combed
forward to hide the fact that his hairline was receding, his
elegant loafers, and his crisp striped shirt. Antonia trailed
behind him, a large paper bag in one hand. She was looking down at River Road, calling to someone below with
cheerful impudence.

"Oh my, oh my," Ron said softly. He bent down and
gathered her in his arms. He smelled of soap and starch.
"We did have a bad time, didn't we? I shouldn't have left
you so long, but with that hunky lieutenant, I thought
you'd be safe."

Bree realized, with some dismay, that she was sob-
bing. Ron set her gently on her feet. Then he turned, his
tall body concealing her from Antonia's sight. "Tonia
dear. We forgot the praline ice cream."

"No, we didn't. You said it was too fattening."

"Well, a girl can change her mind, can't she? Scoot
off and get it now, there's a pet. And leave the shrimp
with me."

"Is that you, Bree? What are you doing outside?"

"She's got Sasha out for a pee, of course. Tonia, the
sooner you get the ice cream, the sooner we can eat it. I'm
starving."

"Okay, okay. But," she tossed over her shoulder,
"there's not going to be a dime left of that money you
gave me, sis!"

He waited until Antonia bounced back across the
bridge, and then said, "Here we go. Upsa-daisy."

"I don't want to go back in the house," Bree whispered.

"Of course you do," Ron said robustly. "I'll just go

ahead and check things out, okay? You sit right there with Sasha."

"But Ron . . . you don't . . ."

The streetlights left pools of shadow around the town house; Ron stood in the warm darkness, tall, his fair hair glowing softly, his eyes kind. Bree was so rattled she thought she imagined it; he was half-enveloped by a pair of feathery wings that swept from the top of his head to his feet. "I know," he said quietly. "I know what came to plague you." He clasped his hands in front of him, and then brought them to his lips. "What I don't know is *why*." He stood for a moment, quite quietly, and then he said, "Stay here."

He wasn't gone long. By the time he returned, Bree had collected herself. She shoved the remnants of fear aside like so much garbage. Sasha was subdued, but physically fine. He was starting to bear weight on the broken leg, and the sores on his flanks and chest were scabbed over with a healthy pink.

"All's well on the home front," Ron said cheerily. "But I've called for reinforcements. If you don't mind, we'll head on over to Professor Cianquino's after dinner." He bent down and ruffled Sasha's ears. "Sorry about all of this, Sash. There are changes ahead." He sighed. "I'm telling you, it's always something."

This view of her experience seemed somewhat cavalier. "Something," she said tartly, "doesn't even begin to describe it."

"Oh, I know, ducky, I know." He smiled at her, with that rising-sun, joyous grin that was irresistible. "But you ain't seen nothing yet."

The living room was the same as always. The mirror

hung clear and unclouded over the fireplace. The air was clean. Sasha took up his accustomed place by the couch and settled down. Antonia came back with a half gallon of praline ice cream from Savannah Sweets. Bree was astonished to learn it was only eight o'clock; she felt as if days had passed since she shoved Sam Hunter out the back door.

"So," Antonia said, "what happened with the sexy lieutenant? He's hot, Bree."

"He had to leave." Bree turned her shrimp salad over with her fork. It looked delicious. She couldn't imagine stuffing it down her throat. Restlessly, she got up, turned on the television mounted under the kitchen cabinet, and sat back down again.

"Don't tell me you let him go without getting his phone number?"

Bree laughed a little. "I have his card, idiot."

Antonia paused, her Po' Boy shrimp sandwich halfway to her mouth. "You okay?"

"I'm fine," she said testily.

"You don't look fine. You look," Antonia paused, her forehead furrowed. "I don't know. Shocky."

"Leave her alone, Tonia," Ron said. "Here, have an onion ring. I can't believe I actually let you talk me into buying these. Fat, fat, fat."

"You're trying to distract me," Antonia said wisely. "Come on, what's going on, Bree?" She frowned. "Hunter didn't harass you or anything like that."

"Nothing like that. Will you shut up, Tonia? The news is on."

"So?" She looked incuriously at the screen. The TV was mounted underneath the cabinets built over the peninsula. "It's just local stuff."

"It's not just local stuff. It's Doug Fairchild."

"So?"

"So, he's Skinner junior's alibi," Ron said. "He claims he saw Skinner senior clutch his Diet Coke can to his bosom and fall over the side like a lead sinker. Didn't you pay attention to your sister this afternoon, ducky?"

"I was too busy looking at those dresses you picked out for Bree. Did you decide to buy the one you're wearing, sis?" She leaned forward, her sandwich dripping mayonnaise onto the tabletop. "What the heck have you been doing in that thing? It looks like you've been wrestling with a bear!"

"Will you please shut up? I want to hear this."

"...my good friend and longtime partner, Bennie Skinner," Doug Fairchild said to the perky anchor. "He was the real force behind the construction of Island Dream, one of the most innovative residential projects in Georgia today." He stood in front of a ten-story condominium that looked like all the other new condominiums built in the Southeast in the past five years; pastel clapboard façade with porch-style balconies. "And I can't tell you how much I miss that man today, as we dedicate the opening of one of Tybee Island's finest structures yet."

"It's the dedication of the new building, which was this afternoon," Ron whispered. "It's a slow news day apparently. They ran it at six o'clock, too."

"Who's that muscle-bound guy behind him?" Antonia squinted at the screen. Carlo, wearing an orange hard hat, stood with folded arms, just at the edge of the camera range.

"Carlton Montifiore," Ron said.

"Do you know him?"

"No. But it says Montifiore Construction on his T-shirt."

Bree snorted.

"... one of the most traumatic events of my adult life," Doug Fairchild said earnestly. He was a beefy, red-faced man. He'd slung his blue blazer over his shoulder, and his rep tie was askew. "I saw my best friend die."

"The TV people just asked Fairchild about Skinner's accident," Ron informed her. "Look at Fairchild's face. Do you believe that face?"

"He does look pretty shifty," Bree agreed.

The camera cut away to the perky anchor at her newsroom desk. "And that's Mr. Douglas Fairchild, developer of Savannah's newest combined office and residential building now available for rent." She turned to the equally perky male anchor at her side. "That's some office space, Frank."

"And now for the weather... That's some tropical storm that's headed our way, Sheila ..."

"Bleah." Bree clicked the TV off and tugged at her lower lip. "Shifty expression or not, Fairchild sounds pretty believable, doesn't he?"

"Sure does," Antonia said. "Are you positive that this is really a murder? I mean, if the police, and Skinner's own son, and now a witness all present the same kind of info, don't you think that maybe, just maybe, you're barking up the wrong tree?"

"I'm right," Bree said quietly, "and I'm not going to quit."

Ron smiled and touched her shoulder. "There's a couple of people who need to hear you say that, Bree. Tonia? We're going out. Don't wait up."

"To which," Ron said an hour later, "I say 'bravo!'" He smiled joyously at the assembled group. "I'm just incredibly impressed. I don't believe I could have survived the encounter half so well, especially since we didn't prepare the poor girl at all. And she refuses to quit."

They sat at the round table in Professor Cianquino's office: Gabriel Striker, Lavinia Mather, Petru Lucheta, Professor Cianquino, Ronald, and Bree herself. Sasha sat at her feet. The bird Archie stamped restlessly on its perch. For the first time since she faced the thing in the mist, she was free of fear. The people in the room didn't scare her, or the animals, either. Although, by most rational standards she ought to be afraid of them, too. But if they were lunatics, they were harmless lunatics. And they seemed to be on her side.

Whatever that side was.

There was an odd, almost inaudible thrumming in the room as though they were near a source of great electrical power. The air shimmered, as if someone had thrown a giant handful of fine glitter into the air. Bree felt half-hypnotized.

"I'd like to know what's going on," Bree said. She glanced at Gabriel Striker. He sat with bent head and his arms folded across his chest. There was a slight frown on his face. "According to Mr. Striker, you all belong to some secret society? He made some mention of Celestial Spheres? What do they stand for?"

"They don't stand for anything," Lavinia said. "They just are."

Bree had had a long day, and she'd been badly frightened. She roused herself from the semi-trance the room's atmosphere had induced. "Okay," she said a little snappishly. "Fine. I asked the wrong question. Too open-ended. What did you say, Gabriel? That it's impossible to give a truthful answer to an open-ended question? I'll try to be less ambiguous. More specific. So you can feel as if you're telling me the truth. What is a Celestial Sphere?"

"The universe is ranked," Professor Cianquino said, "and it is made of Spheres upon Spheres. God is at the center of the Sphere within; the Adversary is at the center of the Sphere without. All life, all being, all creation radiates out from the center of the Sphere within. That is the Celestial Sphere and it is the only one of its kind."

Bree shook her head, "I can't believe this. You, of all people, a creationist?"

Professor Cianquino smiled slightly. "No. God created Darwin, too. Who else set the train of evolution in motion but the Divine? And all the other marvels of the worlds of science?"

The throbbing hum was so soothing that this not only made sense to her, it sounded true. Bree looked around the table. "And you all believe this? Does the sect have a particular purpose?"

"I would object, I think, to the term 'sect'. We are guardians," Petru said. "We are several among many. Guardians have many purposes. Those of us here are members of your new and hopeful law firm. We are here to plead justices for lost souls. There are other guardians fulfilling other tasks elsewhere."

"My great-uncle Franklin," Bree said slowly. "Was he a member of this ..." She paused, searching for the right word, but nothing came to her. "Whatever," she said.

"Company," Petru supplied, with a rather condescending air. "He was not *of* us, but he was *with* us, you understand."

"I don't understand a thing." Bree tugged angrily at her lower lip.

"You are resisting," the professor said.

"And no wonder." Lavinia shook her head in sympathy. "After what happened to poor Frank, why should the chile want to know any more than she knows already?" She leaned over and patted Bree's hand.

"What *did* happen to my uncle?"

"Died in that fire, didn't he," Lavinia said. "Metatron's fire."

Metatron.

Silence settled on the room like a heavy hand. Bree went cold.

Petru cleared his throat.

Gabriel smiled at her. It was a brief smile, but it warmed her. "And your first case is poor murdered Mr. Skinner."

"It *was* murder," Bree said. The humming in the air made her feel a little drunk. "I believe that absolutely. And it sounds like a fine thing to save his soul from whatever basement it's wandering around in, but how do I do it? I mean, say I find the murderer. And say I bring him"— she thought of the two-faced Jennifer and amended herself—"or her to temporal justice." She bowed her head and thought about this. It sounded like a fine thing, temporal justice, so she said it aloud one more time. "Temporal justice. How does that help Mr. Skinner?"

"We cannot forecast, we cannot ordain, we cannot defend until all the facts are brought to light," Petru said.

"He means we'll know when we get there," Ronald said. "Like any case for the defense, we have to get all the facts together."

"He's accused of Greed?"

"One of the seven . . ." Lavinia said.

"Deadly Felonies. I know." Bree rubbed her temples. It was hard to think clearly through the humming and the light. "So maybe the defense lies in the reason he was murdered?"

Professor Cianquino nodded approvingly.

"So if we find out why, we can defend him from the charge of Greed. That's a start." She was beginning to feel her way now. "There's a problem, though. Shouldn't I interview him? I hope," she said a little uneasily, "that I don't have to go to wherever he is now."

"You have to go to the place he died," Lavinia said. "And see if he comes to you."

The boat. That was easy enough. If he had, in fact, died on the boat. But it was a start. Bree took a deep breath. "Okay. So. What happened in my living room this afternoon?"

"That," Professor Cianquino said, "is actually why we are here. We are quite concerned."

There was a murmur of agreement from everyone at the table. Sasha thrust his cold nose in her hand and whined.

"Everyone has a temporal destiny," Professor Cianquino continued. "Each of us discovers it alone, and in our own time. You were on your way to accepting yours. And then this." He raised one frail hand and held it, palm out. "Nothing less than an attack. And you had no weapons to respond with other than your courage. It's quite puzzling."

The bird marched up and down the length of its perch. "Avarice! Wrath! Envy!"

Professor Cianquino nodded thoughtfully. "In a general way, that's true, Archie. The Adversary and those who follow him are driven by those evils and more besides. But there was a specific reason behind this breach of the balance between the Spheres. I'd like to find out what it is."

"Maybe it was just to scare her off," Lavinia said. "She bound for glory, this one. On'y one in a century that could even think about taking on them Pendergasts."

"You think so, Lavinia?" Professor Cianquino asked. "That is quite interesting. An advocate of sufficient strength to do that hasn't been seen for some time. And yes, he would be determined in his desire to see her task aborted. We may be faced with many such intrusions as she experienced tonight."

Bree shuddered.

"I would not be counting chickens too soon," Petru said. "She is untried, untested. Who knows what she will be able to do? Perhaps nothing." His kind eyes twinkled at Bree. "You understand, my dear, that I am seeming ke-vite rude, without intention."

"Well, she didn't fold when the cormorant went after her," Ron said tartly. "That's a whole pile of healthy chickens in my book."

Bree disliked being a subject of a conversation in which she had no part, especially when she was being misrepresented. So she said frankly, "I certainly did fold. When that thing came out of the mirror, I've never been so scared in all my life." She glanced at Striker and then away again.

"Pst!" Lavinia said. "You grabbed the dog and shut the door in the cormorant's face. And you ain't even a probationary guardian yet. Me? That happen to me when I was no more than a green girl, I would have thrown myself into the Pit and gladly."

Ronald snorted. "None of us believe that, Lavinia. We've all seen you in action." He turned to Bree and patted her hand soothingly. "But we don't want to lose you, Bree, and the next time the cormorant flies, you had better be prepared." He looked at all of them in turn. "What just gets me is that she had *nothing* to defend herself with. No faith. No belief. Just her own gutsy self. So I say 'Bravo!' again, Bree."

"I take it you have a solution to keeping her safe?" Gabe asked dryly.

"She needs her name," Ronald said promptly.

Professor Cianquino shook his head. "You're far too impetuous, Ronald. It wouldn't work. It's not time for that yet."

"Then what if we give her *our* names?"

There was a short silence. "It could work," Petru said doubtfully.

"You could call us then, you see," Ron said, "when you needed help. It's a bit unusual, doing things this way, but this isn't a usual situation."

Bree wanted to point out that she'd known Professor Cianquino's name, at least, for most of her twenty-nine years, but she didn't.

"We're agreed, then?" Striker said.

"I agree," Petru said. "But under protest. It is always dangerous to walk outside the correct path."

"You're such a stick in the mud, Petru," Ronald complained.

"She's goin' to need all the help we can give her," Lavinia said. "Them Pendergasts is vengeful folk. So hush, Petru."

"Close your eyes, ducky," Ronald said comfortably, "and try not to think of anything at all." He reached across the table and took her hands in his. Bree closed her eyes halfway, and watched them from underneath her eyelashes. The humming, crackling energy in the room increased, bit by bit. The shimmer in the air thickened to a golden mist that veiled them all, and when it lifted, Bree stood in a meadow thick with velvet green grass and starred with flowers. The silence was absolute. A light breeze touched her cheeks. The scent of some unknown, indescribably fragrant flowers drifted past. There was a sound of wind chimes, an infinite number of crystal bells stirring with the breeze.

A winged, glowing column took shape before her, a furled and spinning rainbow, and radiant with all the colors of the stars.

"Tabris." The voice was Cianquino's, and not Cianquino's.

And a second spun into being next to the first. The light was the color of the moon.

"Matriel," Lavinia said.

Then the others:

"Dara," said the Petru shape.

"Rashiel." That hint of laughter was Ron and Ron's alone.

"Sensiel." Sasha's was the voice of a boy.

"Gabriel." The word was deep, soft, and vast as the oceans.

"You're one of us," they said. "The Company."

The crystal radiance swept her, surrounded her.

"Bree, you're one of us." And then, with a shout that seemed to reach the heavens, "The Company!"

———⟨∞⟩———

She woke up in bed, in her room at home, to the sound of rain and the howling of a rising wind.

She was sure she was going crazy.

Seventeen

Unbelief is blind.
—*Comus: A Mask*, John Milton

"Why does it always rain on Sunday?" Antonia stabbed at her yogurt with a spoon. "And I can't believe I ate all that crap last night. Why didn't you stop me?"

Bree sat at the kitchen table and looked out at the river. The Savannah was less than a quarter mile across here, and she could see the green of the opposite shore through the rain. The Atlantic was a few miles downriver to the west; to the east were the warehouses, cranes, and piers of the Savannah docks. Normal. It was a normal view on a normal Sunday, and she was as mad as a hatter. She didn't know what to do. Who to call. Maybe she should check herself into a clinic somewhere.

"Don't you want your yogurt?" Antonia raised her voice. "Hello! Hello! Earth to Bree!"

"Keep it down to a dull roar, will you?"

"Dad always says that," Antonia said. "And if you aren't going to eat your yogurt, can I have it?"

Bree pushed it across the table.

"You're quiet this morning." Her sister tore the metal foil off the top of the yogurt cup. "Yuck. Raspberry, I hate raspberry."

"You could have found that out without opening it up."
Bree got up, grabbed it out of Antonia's hands, and found
a spoon. "I'll eat it myself. There's cherry in the fridge."

"Let's go down to Huey's for sugar doughnuts."

"You just finished shrieking about how much junk
food you ate last night and you want more? Besides, I
have to go out to Tybee Island this morning. I want to take
a look at Skinner's boat."

"It's miserable out there!"

"It's not cold," Bree said. "And I'll take an umbrella."

"Bet they won't let you on it," Antonia said wisely. "I
mean, it's a crime scene and all."

"Officially it's an accident. And besides, how hard can
it be to duck under that yellow crime scene tape?" Bree
swallowed the last of the raspberry yogurt, and went to
collect her rain gear. Sasha, lying quietly on the kitchen
floor, raised his head in protest as she walked by. "You'll
take care of Sasha this morning?"

"I was going to go down to the theater and see if there's
any movement on the job front."

"On Sunday?"

"There's a matinee and a show tonight, stupid. It's
Mondays that theaters are dark."

Bree ignored the rudeness. "Mom and Dad are coming
in around noon tomorrow," she said sympathetically. "Is
there anything I can do?"

"I hope you realize I'm facing outraged floods of pa-
rental disapproval, if not outright disinheritment."

"I don't think 'disinheritment' is a real word."

"The effect will be real enough," Antonia said glumly.

Bree draped her raincoat on the kitchen counter and
sat next to her sister. "Listen. Why don't we talk to them

about sending you away to a real drama school? Maybe something in New York?"

"I'm supposed to major in something that'll get me a 'real' job. Like yours."

The bitterness in her voice shocked Bree. "I don't think they want you to be a lawyer."

"I'm not smart enough to be a lawyer."

Bree made a real effort to control her exasperation. "You don't have to be particularly smart to be a lawyer. You just have to study hard."

Antonia drew her knees up to her chin and wrapped her arms around her legs. "Did you ever wonder if we were really sisters?"

"What!"

"I'm serious. We don't look alike. We don't think alike. You were the gorgeous brain and I was the dumb-ass clown. I think," she said woefully, "that I'm adopted."

Bree had to bite her lip to keep from laughing. "Well, you aren't. I remember Mamma being pregnant with you, and I remember when she brought you home from the hospital and I threw away all my Barbies because I figured I had this cool new doll to play with."

"Then maybe *you're* adopted. Ever think of that?"

Bree stared at her.

Antonia went pale and jumped to her feet. "Hey!" she said. "Hey! I was just kidding. Are you all right?"

"Fine," Bree said through stiff lips. "I'm fine." She got up mechanically and gathered her rain gear. "So you can't take Sasha with you today?"

"I will if you want. Sure."

Sasha, as if to demonstrate how well his leg was healing, sprang to his feet and wagged his tail frantically. His gaze clearly said: I want to go with *you*. His eagerness and his big doggy grin lifted her spirits.

"Okay, so somebody thinks I'm good normal company," Bree said to him, "but you stay in the car while I take a look at the boat. I don't want you falling overboard like Mr. Skinner."

It was a forty-minute drive to Tybee Island in good weather. The rain-slick roads slowed traffic down. Bree found herself muttering at the Sunday drivers who figured the best defense against falling off the road was to straddle both lanes. It was more than an hour later when she took Highway 80 to the exit, and rolled along the coastal road to the marina. The rain had stopped. The wind was stiff. The weather had kept most of the smaller motorized craft, and almost all of the sailboats, at the docks. The parking lot to the clubhouse was full. Bree saw Grainger and Jennifer's powder blue Mercedes among the Acuras, Jaguars, and BMWs, but the piers were vacant. Everybody with a boat seemed to be inside the marina drinking Bloody Marys or mimosas.

A quarter mile or so beyond the marina stood Skinner Tower. Red, white, and blue bunting flapped from the penthouse, torn loose by the gusting wind. A huge banner printed with NOW RENTING blew awkwardly against the fourth-story balconies. Bree wondered what the old building had looked like before Fairchild tore it down. Made of cobblestone, most likely, or perhaps red brick.

She parked in the "reserved for regatta master" spot, under the assumption that Force 2 winds and a heavy chop precluded the usual Sunday regatta, and wrapped herself in her raincoat against the chill of the air. She cranked the car windows down, to leave air for Sasha, and got out of the car. The halyards chimed wildly. She drew her hood over her hair and started her search for Slip 42, the *Sea Mew*'s berth.

She found it at the end of the pier farthest from the clubhouse, with Sam Hunter standing at the helm.

She stood for a moment, squinting up at him. He had a Windbreaker on, open to the weather, and a NYPD billed hat on his head. He regarded her for a long moment, then moved to the bulkhead and extended his hand. The boat pitched against her lines, and Bree waited for a downswing before she grabbed his hand and scrambled aboard. She fell against him as the ship yawed up, and then regained her feet, conscious of the hard muscling of his chest.

"Are you feeling any better?"

"What!"

He drew her toward the cabin and opened the door. Once inside, the noise of the wind dropped almost completely. The *Sea Mew* was a well-made boat.

"I asked if you were feeling any better. You don't look well, if you don't mind my being frank."

Reflexively, Bree put her hand on her forehead. "I don't?"

He touched her cheek gently. "Looks as if you haven't had a great deal of sleep."

She stepped back and his hand fell away. "Looks like we both had the same idea." She shot a glance at him. "Unless this is official?"

"No, it's not official."

She moved about the small cabin, looking out through the rain-lashed windows at the deck. She wasn't sure what she was looking for—or what she was waiting for. Her aunt Cissy had an expression that summed up what she felt; she was as nervous as a long-tailed cat in a room full of rocking chairs.

Sam stood behind her. His breath whispered by her ear. "Skinner senior sat in the prow with his back to the sea. Jennifer stood at the helm. Grainger said he was in here, getting a bottle of water from the refrigerator when he saw his father clutch his chest and go over the side."

"And then he rushed outside, yelling at his wife to come about, et cetera, et cetera," Bree said.

"You've read the police report. I'd sure like to know how you got hold of it before the investigation closed."

She leaned back a little and looked up at him. "We lawyers have our ways."

For a long moment, his coin-colored eyes looked into hers. "Yes," he said, "well." He stepped back, and the moment passed—if it had been a moment, and not her hopeful imagination. "See anything we might have over-looked?"

Bree shook her head and then said, "Wait a second. What's that at the base of the deck?"

"The wall, you mean?"

She brushed past him and out into the wind. "Here!" she shouted. "These clips set into the deck! They don't have any sailing purpose that I've ever seen."

"For the fishing lines?"

She rolled her eyes, then knelt down and examined the clips more closely. They were brackets, actually, two inches high, about an inch deep, and bolted onto the deck at two-foot intervals. They led from the helm to the bench seat at the prow. Above the bench, two galvanized steel rings were bolted on either side of the ship's wall just as it came to the vee. Bree had been in this class of yachts before. She put her hand on the cushioned seat.

Nothing.

She closed her eyes. Feeling like sixteen kinds of a fool, she tried to imagine Skinner's face as she had seen it in the *Forbes* magazine article.

Not a peep. If Skinner's ghost truly lingered at the spot where he died, he hadn't died here. She opened her eyes and turned to Hunter. "I know how they did it."

"How they did what?"

"Disposed of the body. You see these rings? They tied him to the bench. And at the right moment, probably when they were sure they had a witness, they jerked on the lines and sent the body overboard." She shaded her eyes and looked over Sam's shoulder to the concrete towers of the Skinner building. "And he didn't die here."

He snorted. Bree scowled and said, as icily as she could while still keeping her balance on the deck, "Did I say something funny?"

"Guesswork isn't admissible."

"Then we should look for some hard evidence, don't you think?"

"*Now* I get it."

"Get what?"

"You're more Southern when your temper's up."

Bree smiled sweetly. "Do tell, Lieutenant. What about searching for some evidence?"

He ran his hand over his face. A spatter of rain swept across the deck. He looked up at the sky, which was gloomier than ever. "Let's get out of the rain and talk."

"Like where?" She gestured at their surroundings. "The nearest place is the country club. And I'm not a member."

"My car."

"*My* car. I want to check on my dog."

Sasha watched their approach with his nose pressed against the driver's door, his tail thumping wildly. Bree edged him carefully into the passenger's seat. Hunter got into the back.

"I don't know how he managed to scoot over the top and up into here," she said. "You wouldn't think he had a broken leg at all."

"You never heard anything about who did that to him?"

"You know about that?" Bree said in surprise.

"I did a little checking on everyone concerned with the Skinner case. Your complaint's on record."

She smoothed Sasha's ears, and then turned so that she could face him, her back pressed uncomfortably into the steering wheel. "Did you check on Skinner's girlfriend?"

"The nurse at Chatham General? She was out of town at a medical conference all last week."

Bree blinked at him. "That poor blonde's a nurse?"

"What poor blonde—oh!" He laughed at that. Although it wasn't really a laugh, Bree thought. More of an amused rumble. Sam Hunter didn't look like a man who laughed very often. "You mean Skinner senior's girl-friend. Chastity McFarland. We put some routine questions to her, yes."

"*Grainger* Skinner has a girlfriend?" Startled, Bree sat back and bumped against the steering wheel. "Holy crow. Hm. That goes some way toward explaining Jennifer's cranky attitude, I suppose. How long has that been going on?"

"I have no idea. Why should I care? I don't see its relevance to Skinner's death."

"Maybe he wanted to divorce Jennifer and marry this girlfriend and his daddy didn't approve?"

"It's possible," Hunter said, "but not very probable. If that's so, why is Jennifer backing his story up?"

Bree made a face. "Good point."

"And it's a pretty slim motive for murder, if you ask me."

"Oh, I don't know. Savannah society's a lot different from where you come from up north. Sometimes these things matter a lot." She gestured at his NYPD hat. "You were a New York City cop before you came down here?"

"Yes," he said shortly.

He couldn't have been clearer that this was a no-go zone if he'd put up a sign. Bree stared at him, wondering what kind of story lay behind the stony eyes and weary mouth.

"Something wrong?" he asked testily.

"No! Sorry. I was thinking about something else."

"Fine." He put his hand on the door handle. "If that's about it, I'll be getting back to my Sunday."

"Hang on a minute. What about those clamps?"

He drew his brows together in a frown. "Miss Beaufort ..."

"And I thought we'd gotten things on a first name basis."

"Bree, then. You've got quite an imagination. What makes you think Skinner didn't fall off the boat and drown? I don't have to remind you that the autopsy report—"

"I've been on boats like the *Sea Mew* before. Those clamps running alongside the deck and the rings over the seat weren't put there for any sailing purpose I know of. I've never seen such a thing. The least you can do is ask Grainger what in the heck they're for. And if I were you,

I'd get some of your forensic guys to go over the boat with a fine-tooth comb."

Hunter took his hat off, ran his hand over his hair, and jammed the hat back on again.

"Doug Fairchild said that he and Skinner were partners in Island Dream?" Bree nodded in the direction of the building. "Those towers right there. But he sued John Stubblefield because he screwed up the contracts. And he sued Doug Fairchild to get out of the deal. Why? Something doesn't add up. I'm going over to check it out, if I can. And I'm going to have a talk with Chastity McFarland and maybe ask her some nonroutine questions."

"Suit yourself." This time he got all the way out of the car. He bent down and said through the open door, "If you come up with anything relevant, remember what I told you. If it's a police matter, I want to know about it."

Bree didn't know if she was relieved or annoyed that he didn't offer to come with her. She watched him walk to his car—an anonymous Chevy of the kind ubiquitous to law enforcement everywhere—and decided she was relieved. "The man," she said aloud to Sasha, "has what you might call a disturbing presence. And I've been disturbed enough lately, don't you think?"

She put the car in gear, and headed toward Island Dream.

Eighteen

Truth will come to light; murder cannot be hid long.
—The Merchant of Venice, Shakespeare

Georgia hurricane codes required all new beachfront construction to be built at least fifteen feet off the ground, and a quarter mile from the water. This would protect the buildings from storm surges up to twenty-five feet high. Island Dream followed the code, but Bree bet the front drive was exactly a quarter mile to the inch.

The pastel pink building seemed to embrace the water. It was wing-shaped, and only wide enough to allow one condominium per floor. She drove around the back of the building once before she parked. Two white vans with MONTIFIORE CONSTRUCTION signs on the side sat parked at the rear of the garages. There weren't any workers in sight. The condos had balconies front and rear. The end unit balconies stretched around the side of the building, so that an owner could walk out the French doors in the back and walk all the way around to the living room. The landscaping was new, and not overly generous. Squares of sod made up the lawn, and a few plantings of magnolias and small live oaks grew around the building at random. The swimming pool at the back was lavish, though, with cabanas, an outdoor tiki hut, and an elaborate out-

door kitchen. She wasn't surprised at this. Builders usually put the common areas in first, to nudge buyers into
faster decisions.

She drove back around to the front. A bright green
Lincoln Continental was the only car occupying the guest
spaces. Bree parked next to it, apologized to Sasha for
leaving him once again, and headed toward the front
door.

It opened as she ran up the walk and a male voice
called heartily, "Come in, come in! It's wet out there."

A salesman. She should have guessed. Bree entered
the lobby and shook the rain from her hair.

"Calvin Tiptree at your service, ma'am. I'm as happy
as can be to welcome you to Island Dream. And you
are?"

Calvin extended his right hand. He was youngish,
maybe early thirties, with an expensive haircut and an
even more expensive smile. Those teeth must have set
him back a considerable sum. She smiled. "I'm just here
to visit a friend, Mr. Tiptree. Miss McFarland? In the
penthouse?"

His overly white smile got a little rigid. "You aren't a
reporter or anything, are you? She didn't say anything
about any more interviews today. And you don't look like
any friend of hers I've ever met."

Bree thought about the hostility under Calvin's cheery
manner. Big empty condos were usually sold by people
who encouraged visitors, lots of them.

"Actually, I'm an attorney," she said. "I've come on
behalf of the family."

Calvin rolled his eyes. "Oh, God. Of course. She's on
the top floor, but then you already know that. No luck in

getting her out of there? Come on. I'll show you the elevators."

Bree followed him across the terrazzo tile floor to the sleek bronze elevators on the far wall. These expensive new buildings were starting to look all the same; she bet the kitchens were stuffed with granite countertops, stainless steel Viking stovetops, and Wolf ovens, and that the bathrooms were tiled in travertine marble.

"Here we go." Calvin pressed the "up" button. "Any luck in getting her to move?" he asked in a confidential tone. "I mean, if you ask me, it's going to take a SWAT team to get her out of there."

"We're working on it," Bree said. The doors swooshed open and she stepped inside, pressed "P" for penthouse, and smiled good-bye to Calvin. The elevator clanked and swayed on its way to the top and stopped with a jerk.

Bree stepped out into a hallway that smelled of fresh paint and new carpet. The entry to the penthouse suite was directly across from the elevators. The double doors were Brazilian hardwood. Two ceramic planters stood on either side. The sago palms were dry and shriveled. Bree wasn't much of a gardener, but she knew it was pretty hard to kill a sago palm. Before she could press the door chime, Chastity opened the door a crack and peered out. "I heard the elevator," she said. "Who are you?"

"I'm Bree Beaufort. Liz Overshaw hired me to find out who murdered Mr. Skinner."

Chastity flung the door wide. "I was *wondering* when you'd get around to me!" Her voice was high-pitched and girlish. Bree didn't peg her accent as Georgian; more Texas, or maybe Arkansas. "What took you so long?"

"Sorry," Bree said without a blink. "I came as soon as

my schedule permitted." She stepped inside. The huge living room, with the panoramic view of the Atlantic, was an amazing mix of Condo Modern and McFarland Kitsch. The ochre Tuscan tile floors were no surprise, nor were the elegant stainless steel light fixtures, the coffered ceilings, and the crown moldings. The lava lamps, fuzzy pink pillows, and brightly dyed sheepskin rugs added a raffish charm. One wall held an étagère with the complete set of ceramic characters from *Gone with the Wind*. Bree picked up the Rhett Butler and put it down again.

"That has to be my all-time favorite movie," Chastity said. "Isn't that little Melanie sweet? And I just love the Scarlett." She picked up the Scarlett O'Hara character and set it next to Rhett Butler. "I should have lived in those days instead of these modern times, you know?"

"They didn't treat women very well," Bree observed, "or African Americans, or Yankees, or anybody who wasn't white, male, and over twenty-one. I think you would have hated it."

"You do?"

"I do." Bree didn't wait for an invitation, but settled herself on the overstuffed sofa. It was white leather, and surprisingly comfortable.

"That was where Bennie used to sit." Chastity perched on the arm of a matching leather chair. She wore tight Guess jeans and a cropped T-shirt that barely contained those astonishing breasts. Bree wondered if having a bosom that large was as uncomfortable as it looked.

"They're real," Chastity said without the slightest embarrassment. "Everybody wonders, so I just up and say so."

"I didn't mean to stare," Bree said apologetically. But she did wonder about the lie. She was no expert, but

Chastity's bosom was definitely fake. Was she generally untruthful? She hesitated, trying to decide on the best approach. Did Chastity believe, like Liz, that Benjamin Skinner was haunting her? Or had she overheard an actual threat?

"I know you believe that Mr. Skinner was murdered," Bree said. "Ms. Overshaw believes it, too. I was hoping that you might give me some reasons why you feel this way?"

"He always said they'd get him in the end, you know." Chastity curled up in the chair and brooded over a fingernail. "And sure enough, they did."

"Who's 'they'?"

"You know, all those people who were out to get him, and that." Chastity looked at her hopefully. "A lot of people hated his guts."

"Did you?"

"Me? No, I didn't hate his guts. He gave me a chance."

"A chance?"

"Sure. I'm finishing up my GED."

"You are?" Bree said.

"Look here." She crossed over to the armoire that held the wide-screen TV and scrabbled among the pile of paper there. "See? Homework. Bennie said you don't get anywhere without an education. If I passed my high school exam, he was going to help me go on for a two-year degree."

"Was there something in particular you wanted to study?"

"I thought maybe I'd work with animals, and that. At a vet's maybe. But then, I checked out how much they get paid." She frowned. "Didn't sound so hot. And of course now, it doesn't matter, because the sons of bitches got him, like he always said they would."

"Did he have anyone specific in mind?"

"Well, it wouldn't knock me ass over teacup if it turned out to be that Jennifer. Spiteful bitch. You know, she's the one trying to get me kicked out of here." Chastity's face flushed pink. "I embarrass her, that's what I do. Stuck-up snob. If you could pin it on her, it wouldn't make *me* lose any sleep."

"Do you have a deed to the condo here?" Bree asked gently.

"Well, no. That's kind of a problem, see." She uncurled her legs and leaned forward confidingly. "It belongs to the partners. Bennie was trying to get out of this deal, and *supposedly* was in the middle of signing his share over to the other guys."

This didn't make a lot of sense to Bree. "And this unit was part of his share?"

"I guess." Chastity threw her arms wide. "Basically, he didn't want a thing to do with this place. So the stuff that he owned, he was trying to get rid of."

"Are you saying that he had a partnership agreement with Doug Fairchild and he wanted to get out of it?"

"Yeah," Chastity nodded. "But he hadn't done it yet, and so Miss Priss Face and that geek husband of hers have to pay, like, all my utilities and the management fee. That stuff."

"I see," Bree said. She coughed a little to hide her grin. No, Jennifer wouldn't like keeping her father-in-law's girlfriend in luxury one little bit. Aside from the social humiliation, the management fees alone had to be astronomical. And they were prorated by ownership. If Chastity was the only occupant of the building, and the legal ownership was in dispute, the younger Skinners would be facing a hefty charge every month. "You don't know why, um ... Bennie wanted to get rid of his share?" She looked out the windows at the incredible view of the ocean. Places like this were gold under the mattress, no matter what state the real estate market was in.

Chastity shrugged, unconsciously echoing Bree's thoughts. "Me, I think it's fabulous. You know how much this place would go for on the open market? Couple of million, easy."

"Did Mr. Skinner—Bennie—receive any direct threats to his life?"

"You mean, like, 'I'll kill you, bastard!' sort of stuff?" She smiled like a gleeful kid. "Just from me, once in a while." She nibbled her lower lip and added, "We didn't go out much. And when we did, it wasn't with any of the people he knew."

"I see," Bree said. It was a sad life this girl had chosen for herself. "And to the best of your recollection, he didn't give you any specifics."

"Just that they were going to get him one of these days." She twiddled her hair evasively.

Bree leaned forward a little. "Chastity, what you're telling me doesn't sound like a murder plot. It sounds like a fairly aggressive businessman complaining about his universe."

"Just sort of general bellyaching, you mean."

"Exactly."

She sighed heavily. "So, listen. It's like this. His death's ruled an accident, then the case is closed, and the will is, you know, probated."

"Yes."

"And then I'm outta here." She looked at the opulence surrounding her with a wistful air.

"Probably," Bree said kindly.

Suddenly, she got up and clasped her hands tightly together. "Can I ask you something?"

"Sure?"

"It's this friend of mine." She stopped, and chewed on her lower lip.

Bree made her voice calm. "If you have something to tell me that might be incriminating, give me a dollar."

"Huh?"

Bree held her hand out. "If you give me a dollar, anything you tell me—short of a confession that you murdered Mr. Skinner yourself—is privileged information."

"You mean you don't have to tell the cops."

"Did you kill Mr. Skinner?"

"No!"

"Then I won't have to tell the cops. Do you have a dollar?"

"I got more than that." She went to the fireplace mantel and took a wad of bills from the cloisonné jar that stood there. She handed them to Bree, who extracted a dollar bill and returned the rest to her. "Good. You're now officially my client. You didn't kill Mr. Skinner. But you know who did?"

"Maybe." Then she burst out, "How much time does a person have to do if they lie to the police?"

"That depends a whole lot on the consequences of the lie. And why you lied in the first place. Why don't you tell me about it?"

Chastity flung herself on the couch. "I'll tell you something not very nice."

"Okay," Bree said equably.

"They said I could have this place free and clear, see?"

"The condo."

"Right."

"If I told this lie. Now, they're saying they'll send me to jail for lying if I don't move outta here." She flushed beet red. "It's kind of justice, if you know what I mean. I lied to maybe get Bennie's killer off, and I end up getting shafted. Not," she added bitterly, "that I don't deserve it." She took a deep breath, calmed down, and said briskly, "He was here that morning."

Bree sat up. "With you?"

"Yep. Just before he went to the marina. He was going sailing with his son and that bit . . ." she saw Bree's minatory look and amended lamely, "that wife of his. He was going to tell them about us getting married."

Bree wanted to jump up and dance around the living room, but she said, "Okay."

"We'd already told Mamma. We called her and Denny about nine o'clock . . ."

"From here? That morning?"

She nodded. Bree bit back a shout. Independent verification to boot!

"And she was happy as a tick in a pen of puppies. The last I saw of Bennie, he was headed down to the parking garage to get his car and drive to the marina." She pushed her hair back. "I should have said something earlier. But I didn't really think it was murder. Not then. I thought it was like that Fairchild said, that he had a heart attack and that it wouldn't make any difference what I said. And they promised me the condo."

"Who promised you the condo?"

"That asshole Fairchild. I mean, at first Bennie did, but then he wanted to take the condo back." She frowned a little. "He's never been an Indian giver before."

Bree took a few moments to sort this out. "Ben … I mean, Mr. Skinner, changed his mind about wanting you to have the condo?"

"Bennie wanted to dump the whole building, I guess. He dumped that jerk Stubblefield and was getting himself a whole new slew of lawyers from Atlanta."

So Stubblefield had lied to her about still representing Skinner. What a surprise.

Chastity's gaze shifted away from Bree, a sure sign of a fib to come, in Bree's opinion. "But he wanted me to live here, even if he did want to shove the whole project up Fairchild's behind. At least until he found me somewhere else to live."

"But then he died," Bree said. "And you lied to the police about not being with him that morning so Fairchild wouldn't throw you out. And Fairchild went back on his word about letting you stay here?"

Chastity's sigh seemed to come from the bottom of her heart. "Mr. Fairchild said that stuck-up bitch Jennifer wouldn't go for it. And that I'll go to jail for making a false statement to the police. Will I?"

Bree didn't hesitate. "No. You won't. Not if I can help it, anyway. These people put a lot of undue pressure on you."

"Not to mention screwing me out of my house."

"No kidding." Bree looked at her with compassion. "If it's any comfort, you've done the right thing."

"Yeah, well. I was feeling pretty bad about Bennie. So it's just as well."

"Is there anywhere you can go after this is all over, Chastity? Back to your mamma down home, maybe?"

"Nah. She was happy enough when I was going to marry a billionaire. She's not going to be so happy if I come back without a nickel to my name. I'll be just another mouth to feed. I'll go back to Life's a Beach, I guess."

"Excuse me?"

"Strip joint down in Altoona. It's where I met Bennie. Say!" Her eyes lit up. Without the foot-long eyelashes and the forty pounds of makeup, she was a pretty girl. "You're my lawyer now. Maybe you could help me keep this place after this is all over?"

"Did anyone hear Mr. Skinner promise the penthouse to you?"

Her gaze shifted away and fastened on the replica of Tara sitting at the top of the étagère. "You mean, like, an outside witness."

"Exactly, like an outside witness."

"I've got this girlfriend back at Life's a Beach. She mighta heard him say it. As a matter of fact, I think she did." The gleeful little-kid look was back.

Bree bit her lip to hide her grin. "Well, if you can find a good solid witness that heard Mr. Skinner promise this to you, then you might be able to"—she couldn't say "threaten," that would be crossing the line for sure—"make a very strong case to Grainger and Jennifer Skinner."

"You couldn't take it on for me?"

"I'm afraid not."

She looked around the living room again, at the cobblestone fireplace on the far side and the elegantly painted walls. She sighed. Then, in a very practical way, she said, "Thanks, anyhow. You gave me a couple of things to think about, anyways. I'll tell you what, though. I'm not leaving here until the sheriff shows up to throw me out. What d'ya think about that?" Suddenly, she became very much the chatelaine. "Shall I see you out?"

"Thank you," Bree said politely. She followed Chastity to the double doors. "Good luck. And you'll think about finishing up that GED?"

"Hey!" she said cheerfully. "I'll think about it. Tell you what. In this life, you make your own luck."

Nineteen

There are more things in heaven and earth, Horatio,
Than are dreamt of in your philosophy.
—*Hamlet*, Shakespeare

Bree punched the "parking" button on the panel in the
elevator. She'd avoid the obnoxiously hearty Calvin by
sneaking out that way. She'd go into the Angelus office,
track down Hunter, and feel him out about protecting
Chastity before she dropped her bomb. And Liz Overshaw! There was another phone call she couldn't wait to
make.

The car clattered down and bumped to a stop.

She stepped out into the garage. The breeze was gusting stronger now. The rain was back. The parking area
was below grade, and ribbons of rainwater ran onto the
asphalt and curled into puddles where the surface wasn't
completely even. She hugged herself and shivered; it was
getting cooler. Her raincoat didn't give her a lot of protection against the cold.

A curbed lane led from the elevator to the ramp that
led outside, and she picked her way along it past a large
pile of construction debris. The choice parking spots were
located here. The spaces nearest the elevator bore "reserved for" signs. There was one for D. Fairchild, one for

E. C. Tiptree—and what kind of first name did Calvin
have that he preferred Calvin?—and one for B. Skinner.
As she walked past, she reached out and traced his name
with her forefinger.

Something bit her upper arm. Puzzled, she ran her
hand over her sleeve—

And the pain was like a booted foot in her chest. She
staggered, gasping for breath. Her throat squeezed shut.
She fell and shouted for help. Her/his voice was a hoarse
and raspy whisper.

Footsteps. Then two hands on her/his shoulders. Bree
lost herself in the Other's body. A voice in his ear. He
sagged back into somebody's arms. A sharp, tearing pain
in his throat, a bitter taste, and a terrible, squeezing pain
in his chest.

He was drowning. The seawater flooded his mouth,
his eyes, his lungs. He fought his way upward out of the
dark, choking, gasping for air. Then the light whirled
toward him, white light, bright light . . .

Bree staggered up the ramp out into the open air, fight-
ing to stay on her feet. The possession left her as suddenly
as it had come. She turned, shakily, and looked down the
ramp to the shadows below.

Go back to the place where he died, they'd said.

And she had.

⸺∞⸺

Bree ran up the ramp and stood in the lee of the parking
garage at Island Dream with the rain dripping from her
nose and her back to the parking space with Benjamin
Skinner's name on it. He'd been murdered in there. She
was sure of it, although the how and the why remained a

mystery. She took a deep breath, turned around, and went back into the shadowy garage.

The sign didn't look any different from the others. It was about twenty-four inches square, of white PVC plastic, with letters etched in dark green. It was attached to the concrete block wall with Phillips head screws.

She walked up and down the sidewalk between the asphalt and the wall, turning over the piles of Sheetrock, discarded insulation, metal boxes, and wastepaper with her toe. She peered intently at the concrete walkway, and then walked carefully around the parking spot itself. She wasn't sure what she was looking for, but nothing seemed out of the ordinary.

She stopped in front of the sign and hesitated. Then with a mental "what the hell," she lightly tapped Skinner's name.

She wasn't sure what to expect; moans, a pale and ghostly apparition, a sudden wave of cold, or eerie lights. What did happen was weird enough. A few minutes passed and then a barely recognizable Benjamin Skinner took shape in front of her. His shade was exactly that: shades of transparent gray and white. The image rippled and fragmented.

Except for the eyes. The eyes were ice blue, piercing, and horribly human.

It was as if she saw him on an ancient piece of movie film. His voice came through a strange-echoed static, in fits and starts so that she only caught a repeated phrase or two.

Drowned ... drowned ... drowned ... murdered me ... murdered me.

Bree took a moment to catch her breath. She was afraid

to blink, afraid to move, in case the fragile image shattered and disappeared. "Do you know ..." she began in a croaky whisper. She cleared her throat several times, and said in a dismayingly small voice, "Do you know who killed you, Mr. Skinner?"

A hideous shriek echoed around the parking garage. Bree clapped her hands to her ears, and stepped back into the heap of construction debris piled next to the elevator. A short piece of white plastic pipe rolled free and came to rest on her shoe.

Save her ... save her ... save me ... please ... save ...

The image winked out, as if a door had slammed shut.

Bree stared as hard as she could at the spot on the wall where Skinner had begged her to save him, but the image didn't return. She shoved aside the piece of pipe, tapped the sign, and then placed the flat of her hand against it.

Nothing.

Did she only get one interview with her client? And why hadn't he saved her a pile of time and trouble and told her who the murderer was? How could he drown when the ocean was almost a half a mile away? How come the finger-tapping trick didn't work anymore? This business of communicating with ghosts was quite frustrating.

The pipe rolled against her shoe again as if someone had kicked it. It was about an inch wide and perhaps two feet long. It was scrap, probably from a plumbing installation. Bree picked it up. That bright white light flashed through her like a sudden yell. She shuddered. Someone had used this on Benjamin Skinner.

Trembling a little, she put it into the pocket of her raincoat, and knelt by the pile of trash: bits and pieces of

Sheetrock, insulation, more pieces of pipe. Gently, she moved the stuff aside.

She uncovered an air compressor.

Bree sat back on her heels, her mind racing. It looked undamaged, and perfectly operable. The flexible rubber hose that shot air into whatever air needed shooting into was neatly coiled and looped over the top.

With a sense of dread, she reached out and touched the hose.

NO!

A bitter taste flooded her mouth. Her heart beat frantically, as if a bird were trapped in her chest.

She jerked back, as if stung.

Seawater? Had the killer forced seawater down Skinner's throat?

She had a small tool kit in her car with a Phillips head screwdriver. Maybe she should remove the sign, pack up the coiled hose and the half-inch pipe, and take it all home with her. On the other hand, maybe she shouldn't touch any of it. An unbroken chain of evidence was vitally important in any criminal case; she knew that as well she knew her own name. But she didn't have to guess what Hunter's reaction would be if she told him why she wanted the sign and the pipe and the rubber hose tested for fingerprints and maybe even blood. And how definitive would the evidence be, anyway?

It took her only a few moments to run to the car and come back with the tool kit. She started with the sign. She knelt down to get a better angle on the bottom screws.

Then everything went black.

❈

"How many fingers do you see?"

Calvin Tiptree's voice was naturally high-pitched; anxiety raised it to a squeak. Bree blinked at him. She sat in a comfortable armchair in an unfamiliar office. Sasha whined at her feet. Calvin hovered on the outer range of her vision. He clutched a damp towel in his left hand. He held his right up in the air and wiggled two fingers.

Bree put her hand to the back of her head and winced. "Ouch."

"I *told* Mr. Fairchild that we needed gutters on the outside of that parking garage," Calvin fussed. "Now look what's happened. You slipped in all that water and banged yourself on the noggin." He bent closer and peered into her eyes. "It's one heck of a lump. Do you I think I should call the EMTs?"

Bree looked down at her knees. Her jeans were dry. Her feet were dry, too. A dusting of concrete covered both knees. "The sign?" she said.

"What sign?"

"Mr. Skinner's parking sign. Is it still on the wall?"

Calvin threw his hands in the air. "For heaven's sake. I have no idea."

"My raincoat?"

"You're wearing it," Calvin said worriedly. "Can't you tell?"

She patted her pockets. The pipe was still there. She took a long breath. Then she eased herself to her feet. Her head hurt like billy-be-damned. But the rest of her seemed to be in working order. "I don't need an ambulance. But I do want the police."

"The police!" Calvin turned pale. "Oh, my God. You're a lawyer, aren't you? We're going to be sued. Oh, my God. Look, forget what I said about the gutters, will you?"

"I didn't fall down," Bree said patiently, "and I'm not a litigious person, Calvin. Somebody hit me over the head."

"Nonsense," Calvin said briskly.

Sasha pawed gently at her knee.

She patted him. "I'm just fine, boy. But I'd sure like to know what happened to me."

"Well, it was your dog that raised the alarm." Calvin folded the towel and draped it over the back of his desk chair. "I was waiting in the foyer to see if any buyers might be showing up and he started to howl. And I mean *howl*. I ran out to your car and he was pawing at the window so I opened the door and let him out. I thought maybe he had to wee, you know? I have two dogs of my own, and they'd rather die than mess where they aren't supposed to. As soon as I let him out, he took off across the parking lot like a banshee was after him, broken leg and all."

Bree took Sasha's head in her hands and looked deep into his golden eyes. "Did you see who hit me, Sash?"

Men. There were two men.

"Two men," she said aloud.

"I just don't believe it," Calvin said. "Oh! Of course, I believe you. I mean I just don't believe it could happen here! I mean, this is an island, for goodness sake. Where would they go? Did you actually see them? Do you think you can identify them?"

"No," Bree said. "I haven't a clue about what they look like." She remembered the Montifiore Construction vans in the back of the building. "You had workmen here today?"

"Yes, we did. Do you think that they . . . ? No. I can't believe it. They were here to redo some of the Sheetrock in the condos just under the penthouse. A bit of a leak. Nothing serious. They skedaddled out of here way before I heard the elevator come down from the penthouse."

"Are you sure?"

"Very sure," Calvin nodded. He tugged nervously at his earlobe. "So do you want me to call the Tybee sheriff's office? The state troopers?"

Bree thought a minute, then went through her purse. Everything seemed to be there.

"Has anything been taken?" Calvin asked. "This is just terrible. An assault and robbery right in our parking garage. If word of this gets out, it's not going to be good for business." He groped for his cell phone. "Do you think I should give Mr. Fairchild a call? I'm sure we can handle this without calling the police."

"I'd like to speak to Mr. Fairchild, yes." She'd tucked Hunter's card behind her Neiman-Marcus charge card. "And I'll call the police." She squinted at the number— her vision was a bit blurry—and tapped it into her cell phone. He picked up on the third ring. It didn't take long to bring Sam into the picture. He suggested an ambulance; she turned it down in no uncertain terms.

"You're sure?" The concern in his voice warmed her. "Concussion can be tricky."

"Positive." She blinked the room into focus. The walls and the hunter green carpeting were a little blurry around the edges, but the ache in her head ebbed a bit and she felt more clearheaded by the minute. "It's just a bump. But whoever hit me on the head was after something specific. I want to show you where it was."

"*Where* it was, and not *what* it was?"

"It was the place Benjamin Skinner died."

There was a long pause. Then he said, "Give me twenty minutes."

Bree clicked off and put her cell phone back into her purse.

"Mr. Fairchild's on his way. He won't be more than a few minutes. I caught him at the clubhouse marina." Calvin walked up and down the carpeting, wringing his hands. "He has Sunday brunch there, most weekends, when he's not out of town on business."

Fairchild. She had more than a few questions for the man. "Good," Bree said grimly. Calvin made a small whimpering sound. The last thing she needed right now was a hysterical male. She interrupted him briskly. "Could we have some coffee, do you think?"

Calvin looked around the office in a bewildered way. Bree pointed at the Mr. Coffee sitting on the credenza behind the desk. "Right," Calvin said. "Right."

"I'm sure Doug Fairchild would like a cup," she added for encouragement.

"Water," Calvin said. "I'll just pop into the bathroom for it, shall I?" He picked up the carafe and wandered out the door. As soon as he disappeared into the lobby, Bree got up, went to the desk, and opened the drawers one by one. The upper drawer contained a lot of glossy brochures, a thick stack of sales contracts, and some bills from a waste management company for Dumpster rentals. The bills were marked "Past Due." Bree noted the initial invoice date was almost eight months ago. Quite a long time to let a relatively small amount remain unpaid. She made a mental note to have either Ron or Petru check out the company's credit-worthiness. She leafed through the brochures, and paused at the description of the swimming pool. *"Completely free of chlorine and other chemicals, the lodge's Olympic-size saltwater swimming pool demonstrates our commitment to an eco-friendly environment."*

"Well, well," she said. "The picture's becoming a little clearer, Sash."

Sasha lifted his head, stared at the office door, and growled a warning at the sound of voices in the hall. Bree slipped back into her chair and folded her hands in her lap.

"You let her call the cops?" somebody snapped. "You goddamn fool."

Her parents knew the Fairchilds, but Bree herself had never met Douglas. He walked into the office with his hand held out in welcome, and a big smile on his face. Sasha got up, sniffed the cuffs of his trousers without interest, and lay down at Bree's feet again. Bree frowned at the dog. She had a half-formed theory of the crime in her head, and Douglas Fairchild featured prominently in it. "Well, here's the little lady," he said heartily. "I hear you had a small accident in my parking garage."

"Somebody hit me over the head," Bree said bluntly. "It wasn't an accident. It was an attack."

He clasped her two hands between his own. He was a large man with scant brown hair and a soft, round belly that strained the cloth of his short-sleeved Izod shirt. He smelled like gin. "I'm truly sorry to hear that, Bree." His smile widened. "You don't mind if I presume on an old family acquaintance and call you Bree? Your daddy and I go way back. As a matter of fact, I'm looking forward to seeing him and your lovely mother at your open house tomorrow night. They were kind enough to send me an invitation. Now, little lady." He released her hands, pulled a chair away from the wall, and sat down next to her. "Tell me what happened."

Bree looked at her watch. Sam would be here in less than five minutes, if he was as good as his word. She didn't trust Fairchild as far as she could throw him. "I'd like to show you where it happened, if I may. I think I may have discovered something relevant to Benjamin Skinner's death."

Doug Fairchild's smile stiffened. "Okey-dokey. Anything for an old family friend." Keeping his eyes locked on hers, he barked at Calvin, "Get hold of John Stubblefield, Tiptree." He patted Bree's knee a little too hard. "If she's half the lawyer her daddy is, I might just need a little legal advice myself."

"Gotcha, Mr. Fairchild." Calvin began a flurried search of the credenza.

"What the hell are you doing, Tiptree? If there's no goddamn phone book call the goddamn operator." He turned his attention to Bree and switched his smile back on. "We'll take the elevator. You look a bit woozy." He put his hand under her elbow. Short of kicking him loose, Bree couldn't see a way to disengage, so she allowed herself to be directed. Sasha followed them with the same unconcern he'd shown before.

The elevator bumped to a halt at the parking level. Bree flinched from the sudden stabbing pain in her head.

"You might think about having that bump checked out, Bree. You're looking a bit pasty, if you don't mind my saying so."

Bree took a long step out of the elevator and Fairchild finally freed her arm. "What were you poking around here for, anyway?" he asked genially. "You thinking maybe of buying one of the units? We could probably come up with a pretty fair price, seeing as how you're an old ..."

"I'm sure neither one of us would want to presume on friendship," Bree said tartly, "as real or imagined as it might be. I was taking a look at the wall here, when somebody—actually I believe there was more than one— came up from behind and slammed me over the head." Bree walked over to Skinner's parking space and stopped short. The sign was still there. So was the air compressor. So whoever had hit her hadn't been after the evidence. She closed her eyes against another attack of dizziness.

She could be absolutely wrong.

"Did you actually see these guys?" Fairchild stood well away from her and from the spot where Skinner's ghost still lurked, for all that Bree knew. "Did they snatch your purse? Go through your wallet? Take your credit cards and such?" He ran his eyes over her raincoat, T-shirt, and jeans, and asked doubtfully, "Did they take any jewelry?"

"It wasn't a robbery." Bree frowned at the sign. Somebody—she suspected Fairchild himself, who had only been five minutes away at the marina—had hit her over the head to keep her from collecting the evidence. And yet here it all was.

"You're looking a bit peaked, Bree." Sam Hunter strolled down the ramp. Rain glistened in his hair. He walked with the easy confidence of a man who knew where he was going and where he had been. He smiled at her. Bree's world tilted a little, and she swayed on her feet. He caught her arm, and in direct contrast to Fairchild's clammy grasp, his hand was warm and strong. He touched her head lightly. "That looks pretty nasty."

"I am absolutely fine." She jerked her arm free of his grasp and stood upright.

"Is that a fact. But as soon as we're through here, I'm taking you in to get checked out. Now. What happened?"

Bree walked to the parking space, then turned and faced them both. "I'm convinced that Benjamin Skinner was killed right here."

"That's insane," Fairchild said. "You're out of your cotton-pickin' mind. I saw Bennie Skinner die." He jerked his chin in Sam's direction. "He'll tell you. I spent this morning giving an eyewitness account to the police. I was out in my boat, not six hundred yards from the *Sea Mew*, and I saw Bennie jerk back and go over the side as clear as daylight."

"You saw Bennie Skinner's corpse fall over the side, if you actually saw anything at all," Bree said stubbornly. "I think he was killed here, and his lungs filled with seawater from your saltwater swimming pool."

"You think somebody drowned him in my swimming pool?" He hawked and spat on the sidewalk. "I've never heard such bull crap in my life."

Bree shook her head. "He had a heart attack. I'm pretty sure it was induced. He fell here"—she stood on the spot where Skinner's ghost had called to her—"and when he was dead, the killer brought a gallon of seawater from the pool, stuck this piece of PVC pipe down his throat, and forced the water into his lungs with that." She pointed to the air compressor. She looked at Sam. "I've got fifty bucks that you find Benjamin Skinner's blood and lung tissue on this pipe, and another fifty that says you find seawater in the compressor hose."

The sharp, searing pain in his throat.
The rhythmic rush of water into his lungs.

Skinner didn't die in the sea.

Hunter's expression was a study. Skepticism, irritation, and a faint, very faint interest warred with each other. The interest won. "That's quite a story."

"I know." She smiled at him. "I wouldn't believe a word I said, if I were you."

He didn't smile back. "You have an eyewitness you aren't telling me about?"

"No, sir."

"Did you kill Skinner?" His tone was urgent, commanding, and angry.

"I did not. I've never met the man. At the time he was killed, I had an appointment with my landlady to rent my current office space. I wasn't anywhere near Island Dream."

Although, if what she was beginning to suspect was true, he wouldn't be able to find her office space, much less interview Lavinia Mather. A stab of irrational fear hit her. She had a brief, horrible vision of herself in handcuffs. "After I saw my landlady, I took my dog Sasha to the vet." She shut up, aware that she was babbling.

Hunter walked carefully around the humped debris that covered the air compressor. Then, to Bree's infinite relief, he took out his cell phone and called for a crime team. He flipped the cell phone shut and shoved it into the pocket of his anorak. "Where did you find the pipe?"

"I came by this way to get to my car. I was in a bit of a hurry, because of the rain, and I sideswiped the pile of junk. That dislodged the pipe. It rolled onto the sidewalk and I picked it up ..." She paused, knowing that she had to leave out her encounter with Skinner's ghost. She cleared her throat. "And I picked it up so somebody else wouldn't trip over it. Then, it just sort of hit me. Chastity said Skinner left her around ten thirty. He parked right here, as he always did, so he must have come down here to his car. I don't think Chastity's lying." Her gaze swept over Fairchild, who was grimly silent. "I know you are, Mr. Fairchild, and I'm pretty sure Jennifer Skinner is, too."

Fairchild opened his mouth to speak. Hunter held his hand up, forestalling him. "You think Mr. Fairchild here killed him?" Hunter asked.

Bree shook her head. "I don't know."

"What you don't know, young lady, is what your future's going to be like here in Savannah." Fairchild was so angry that he only managed a whisper. "We'll run you right back to North Carolina."

"Take it easy, Mr. Fairchild." Hunter's voice was a whiplash. "Miss McFarland's statement directly contradicts yours about Skinner's whereabouts."

"Chastity's a lying little whore," Fairchild said contemptuously.

"She also has independent verification of her story," Bree said mildly.

Fairchild backed up until he hit the garage wall. "That's a lie, too."

Bree shook her head. "'Fraid not. They were both on the phone with her mother in Arkansas. Making plans for their wedding, as a matter of fact. The phone company records will bear out the phone call. And there were two people in on the conversation from the Arkansas end."

"I want a lawyer," Fairchild said. "This is a load of crap."

"Your need for a lawyer depends on what you were doing that morning," Hunter said. He gave Fairchild a reassuring smile. To Bree, who was beginning to know

Hunter pretty well, the smile was as reassuring as the grin of a shark in shallow water. "Were you down here in the parking garage the morning of Mr. Skinner's death?"

Fairchild swallowed, and then muttered, "I was in Savannah. In a meeting with two bankers and a goddamn lawyer. I left the meeting about eleven, and came down to the marina to take my boat out. I was never near this place that day."

Hunter looked at him, his gaze steady and unrelenting. "Did you see Skinner at all that morning?"

"No."

"And the phone call to Grainger Skinner? Was that a lie, too?"

Fairchild tightened his lips. Hunter kept it up, his questions a barrage. "The eyewitness account you gave the police—that you saw Skinner alive in the *Sea Mew* at noon—was that a lie?"

Fairchild took out his handkerchief and patted the sweat from his forehead. "I'm done here, Hunter. You want to talk to me, you talk to John Stubblefield first." He ran his hand nervously over his tie. "You putting me under arrest?"

A clatter of sound outside the parking garage heralded the arrival of the forensics team. Hunter turned to meet them and said over his shoulder. "Not yet, Mr. Fairchild. But you'll make yourself available."

With a final glare in Bree's direction, Fairchild scurried up the ramp. In a few moments, she heard the roar of his Mercedes.

She patted her pocket to make sure the pipe was still there, then leaned against the wall and waited for Hunter to come back to her.

Twenty

Thou art thy mother's glass, and she in thee
Calls back the lovely April of her prime.
—"Sonnet #3," Shakespeare

"I brought some color samples along just in case you wanted to think about repainting," Bree's mother said. Francesca Winston-Beaufort was warm, rounded, and as unlike her oldest daughter as a rose from a lily. Bree's father told and retold the story of how they first met; he caught sight of her red-bronze hair in the dining hall at Duke and fell in love with that before he ever saw her face to face. She had soft gray eyes, a rosy complexion, and charm like a fountain, bubbly, gentle, and constant. "And isn't this clever? Your aunt Cissy did it for us. It's a sketch of the living room and then you put the color transparency over it like this." She laid a sheet of cellophane marked with deep green splotches over the computerized drawing of the living room. The splotches left bare spots for the furniture and the fireplace, so when the sheet was on top of the print, the color fit the walls exactly. She put a sheet with red splotches over that; the walls in the room turned purple.

"She can do a sketch of your office, too, Bree darlin'. I'd love to get a chance to fix that up a little bit for you."

Bree laid the transparency over the drawing and took it away again. The reality of the room was different depending on which layer was on top. She imagined a map of Historic Savannah with the twenty-four squares laid out by Oglethorpe. Then the extra streets where the offices of Gabriel Striker, PI, Beaufort & Company, and Georgia's own all-murderer's cemetery sat laid out by ... whom?

"This nasty case gettin' you down, Bree?" Her father eased into the leather chair next to the couch, and fondled Sasha's ears. "Kind of a rough start to a solo practice."

Bree tucked her feet underneath her. Her parents had arrived too early Monday afternoon, and she had to leave the office to meet them. Ronald was busily setting up the open house. Petru was investigating the financing of Island Dream. Lavinia had made a quick appearance downstairs with a measuring tape, and demanded to know exactly how tall Bree was.

"You can wrap this up now, can't you?" her father continued. "That was your brief, wasn't it? To prove Skinner was murdered?"

Bree nodded. "Sam Hunter called me this morning. The preliminary swabs on the PVC pipe and the air hose show human tissue, blood, and spit." She took a sip of her iced tea. "I'm betting it's Skinner's. So's Lieutenant Hunter."

"You've let the client know?"

Bree smiled. "Oh, yes." She'd hoped to impress Liz Overshaw. Liz had listened, and then grunted in assent when Bree offered to send an accounting of her time against the advance retainer. Then she'd said, "I knew it last night, you know. He's stopped coming around. I had the first good night's sleep since the whole thing started."

Then she'd hung up. Bree spoke aloud. "Liz wasn't wild with gratitude, I'll say that for her."

Francesca patted her hand. "Clients can be incredibly rude. But now you can put the whole nasty thing behind you."

"I don't think I want to do that just yet."

Royal raised his eyebrows.

"The man was murdered," Bree said flatly. "I need to find out who murdered Ben Skinner."

Her mother shook her head, her curls bouncing. "It was that Doug Fairchild, I suspect. I never did like that man. Not one little bit. But I'm surprised to find him a murderer." She sighed. "It's bound to affect how many people attend the open house tonight. Nobody cares too much about the Skinners, but Fairchild's got friends. It's a shame, that's what it is." She looked out the window at the river. A small tropical storm was heading up the Atlantic, and the rain was heavy. "Between that and the weather and the bump on your head, maybe we ought to think about heading back home."

"I'll be just fine," Bree said absently. She looked at Sasha. "Besides, I don't think Fairchild killed Mr. Skinner."

"You think he's covering up for Grainger?" Her father frowned. "Can't think of a reason why he should."

"The police aren't saying much. But Grainger's lawyered up and I know they aren't getting spit out of him."

"Seems hard to think Grainger killed his own father." Royal Beaufort swirled his whiskey in his glass. He wasn't happy. Like her mother, he wanted Bree to wind up the remainder of Uncle Franklin's practice and come home. "I'm not sure what all this has to do with you, though. You've discharged your duty to Ms. Overshaw."

"But not to myself, Daddy. They pulled Skinner back up before they shoveled the first bit of dirt on the coffin. The body's off to Atlanta for a second autopsy. It's more than likely that they'll get enough forensic evidence to cast doubt on the accidental death ruling. They'll hold an inquest this time, for sure. If it comes back murder by person or persons unknown, I can put 'paid' to Liz. But I have to find out who did it." She made a face into her iced tea glass. Her father'd haul her back to Raleigh for sure if she told him she had one more client to satisfy, and that one a ghost.

And Skinner wasn't happy. She had a sinking feeling he'd stopped haunting Liz only to start haunting her. There'd been a bit of red Georgia clay and a rose petal by her bedside this morning. The television news last night had excited coverage of the police as they impounded Skinner's rose-covered coffin. And she had dreamed of drowning.

"You look tired." Francesca peered worriedly at her. "You haven't been getting enough sleep. The case is just wreckin' your complexion, Bree."

"Leave the child alone," Royal said. "She looks fine. A little thin, maybe."

Bree took a deep breath and prayed for patience. Her father—who let very little escape him—grinned engagingly at her. "I know, I know. We'll be out of your hair by tomorrow afternoon. And we'll take Antonia with us."

"Where *is* that sister of yours?" her mother fussed. "You did let her know we were here, didn't you?"

"I left word at the theater," Bree said. "She was in a director's meeting for this new show."

"A stagehand," her mother said despairingly. "I ask

you. What kind of life is that going to be? Hand to mouth. Well." She sighed from the bottom of her toes. "There it is. She seems happy, you think?"

"Very," Bree said. "She was over the moon at getting this job."

"It's gainful employment, Francesca." Royal crossed one knee over the other and took another sip of his drink. He'd given up his pipe years ago, but even without it, he was the picture of a contented man.

"True, true, true," her mother mourned. "And God knows we couldn't compare the two of you. Not, of course," she added hastily, "that we wanted to. But if Antonia just had a little more gumption." Then, with a tragic air, "I suppose it's all from my side of the family."

Bree looked at her dog. Sasha looked back at her with his deep, loving eyes. Family. What family? Whose? It had been on her mind since that eerie, amazing meeting at Professor Cianquino's. The doubt had grown to an insistent, demanding question.

The only way to find out was to ask.

She kept her voice steady, casual, uninflected. "What do you suppose I inherited from my side of the family? As a matter of fact, who was my family?"

Nobody moved. The silence was sudden and profound. Her parents didn't look at each other. After a long moment, Royal demanded, "What in the world are you talking about?" With an impatient twitch of his shoulders, he got up and walked toward the kitchen.

"Don't you take another step, Royal Beaufort," her mother said. "Come back here and sit down. Now!" She shifted her position on the sofa so that she faced Bree. "What is this about? Has somebody been talking here in Savannah?"

Bree found it hard to catch her breath. "About my being adopted?"

"You weren't adopted," her mother said angrily. "You are our very own daughter. I hate that word 'adopted'. What does it mean, anyhow? It sounds like you were left on the church steps somewhere like a little orphan. And if you don't think I'm your mother, and your daddy's your daddy, you have another think coming."

Bree, familiar with her mother's loving—if confusing—illogic, said patiently, "Of course you're my parents. My question is, are you my *parents*?"

"I did not bear you in the same way I carried Antonia, that's true," her mother said. "But you were a gift in the same way that all babies are gifts. You just came to us a different way."

Bree waited.

"What your mother is trying to say ..." Her father stopped, patted his blazer pocket for his long-vanished pipe, and repeated, "What your mother is trying to say is that you are my father's brother's child."

"Great-uncle Franklin?" Somehow, she wasn't surprised. "But he never married, did he? I mean, not that I'd expected to be legitimate ..."

"Bree!" her mother said.

"... but it does seem strange he didn't want to raise me himself."

This time her parents did look at each other.

"Franklin did marry." Francesca's face was solemn. "Very late in life. A very beautiful girl, dear Bree. And very young. He met her in a church, of all places. But she died. And before she died she made him promise to give you up."

"Give me up," Bree repeated. The words had no meaning.

"I don't know if it's because he was so much older—he was seventy when you were born—although he lived to be ninety-eight, wouldn't you just know it? Although if he'd known he was going to live so long, he wouldn't have let us raise you, and then where would we be?" Her mother took a breath. "But she did. Make him promise. And your uncle Franklin never went back on his word."

"And of course he was with you every minute he could be," Royal said.

"So that's it," her mother said airily. "Case closed, end of story, no more to say except that"—she leaned forward and wrapped her arms around Bree—"you *are* half a Beaufort. And if you're not half a Carmichael, by blood . . ."

"Yes, Mamma," Bree said. She and Antonia had grown up with stories about the Carmichaels. Her mother's side of the family was notorious.

". . . you're a Carmichael through ties of my dearest love." She kissed Bree affectionately.

"Do you know much about my mo—my uncle's wife?" Bree asked. "Are there pictures of her? Do you know where she came from?"

"He promised, promised, promised her to leave all that alone," her mother said frantically, "and we agreed. If we hadn't agreed, he wouldn't have let us take you. And we wanted a baby so much, darlin'. Most important, we wanted you. You were such a wise little thing."

Francesca was on the verge of tears. Bree thought she might be on the verge of tears herself.

"So, we'll try to answer any questions you have,

but…" Francesca bit her lip, dashed the heels of her hands against her eyes, and said, "I'll just go to the bathroom and wash my face. I'll be right back."

Royal watched Francesca leave the room. He looked as if he'd give anything to go with her. He'd never been comfortable in the face of emotion. "Let's pretend this is a case," Bree said suddenly.

Royal tightened his hand around his drink, but he said, "Excellent idea. I'll try to be a little more objective." He gave her a lopsided smile. "It's difficult, though."

"For me, too."

"It doesn't change anything," he said stubbornly. "We're your parents. We've been you're parents since you were two days old."

"Nothing could change that," Bree said. "Ever."

The air was heavy with unasked questions.

"Are you regretting we didn't tell you this before?" Royal asked.

This obliqueness was so characteristic of her father's style that Bree had to laugh. "Not regretting exactly, no. But I'm very curious, Daddy."

He covered her hand with his own. "It was a curious situation. Franklin had his reasons, very compelling ones, apparently. And his stipulations—that you not be told unless you asked—weren't legally binding, of course. But he asked for my word, and I gave it." His face softened. "We both loved you from the moment Leah put you into your mother's arms. We would have promised almost anything to keep you."

"That was her name? Leah?"

"Yes."

Neither one of them broke the silence that followed. Her father kept his thoughts to himself. Bree wondered about that young girl, that image of herself, determined to keep her daughter set apart. The question was, set apart from what?

"Why the secrecy?" Bree demanded suddenly. "Why couldn't you tell me?"

"I don't know," her father admitted. "It was the price we paid for making you our own. And to be truthful, until Franklin died and I probated his will, we'd almost forgotten about it. It was nearly thirty years ago. We were happy. We're still happy. There didn't seem to be any need to go ferreting around in the past."

"Until Unc—until Franklin's will?" Bree prompted. "Leaving his practice to me?"

Sasha dropped his head on his paws with a huge sigh and closed his eyes. Bree frowned at him, then leaned down and stroked his nose. He rolled his eyes up at her, licked her cheek, and yawned. "Yes," Bree said. She straightened up and looked at her father. He would always be her father, no matter what the past had been. "About Uncle Franklin's will?"

"I was his executor, as you know. His original will divided his estate among the Beth-el Synagogue, our local mosque, and St. Peter's Church. He left nothing to you. The week before he died he added the codicil that listed his outstanding cases and left his practice here in Savannah to you."

"Do you know what changed his mind? About putting me in his will?"

"I have no idea, Bree. But when I went to get his signature I did ask."

"What did he say?"

Her father shrugged. "He said, 'You can't fight City Hall.'"

Sasha rolled his eyes up at her. Bree started to laugh. It was infectious, and Royal began to laugh, too. "It means something to you?"

"Oh, dear. I'm afraid it does." Bree searched her pocket for a tissue, couldn't find one, and accepted her father's handkerchief. "Oh, well. I do wish I'd known him better before he died. I need some answers to a couple of questions. More than a couple." She closed her eyes briefly, against a rush of sadness. "Most of all, why he didn't want a daughter."

Royal looked at her with such love that Bree leaned over and hugged him. "Of course, it turned out to be the best piece of luck a girl could have."

Her father nodded. He wasn't able to say anything.

"Anyway," Bree continued cheerfully, "it's nothing to bother you, Daddy. His client list, for example. I haven't had a chance to do more than send them all a letter that I'm taking over his practice." A brief, horribly unwelcome thought about the nature of his clients sprang to her mind. She shoved it away with a shudder. Time enough to look at that when the Skinner case was finally over. "I'd like some background on them."

"I'm sure you would."

"So if he left any other papers, anything at all, I'd like to see them, if I may."

"Nothing, I'm afraid. You know there was a fire in his office the day before he died."

"Yes," Bree said. "I knew that."

"Everything he had went up in the fire."

"Not even a picture ..." Bree trailed off uneasily.

"Of Leah? No, not that I recall." Royal thought a moment. "As a matter of fact, I've never seen one. Not while she was alive. Not after she died. Odd, that."

Sasha sat up as if galvanized and began to bark.

"What the devil?" her father said.

Bree looked at Sasha's ears, which flopped eagerly forward. And his bark was a welcoming one. "It's probably Antonia."

The front door slammed. Francesca shrieked, "Antonia! You're home!" Antonia shrieked back. Bree unfolded herself from the sofa. "I've got to get back to the office. I set my paralegal onto the financing for Island Dream. I'm hoping he'll have dug something up by now."

Her father cast a rueful look in the direction of the kitchen. Antonia was talking a mile a minute at the top of her voice. Francesca's voice kept rising as she tried to get a word in edgewise. "I don't suppose ..."

Bree dropped a kiss on the top of his head. "I'll be back in a couple of hours. We'll all go together to the Mansion, shall we?" She paused, and bit her lip. "And I need just a little time alone. To think."

"Bree? You headed out, darlin'?" Francesca called out. She bustled out of the kitchen, an envelope clutched in one hand. Antonia slouched after her. "Wait just a minute. Tonia!" she added, with sudden exasperation, "I want you to go right on into the bedroom and pull out that nice dress I brought for you. We all want to look good for Bree's party. Go on! Go!"

Antonia rolled her eyes dramatically at her sister, kissed her mother, and ambled off to the bedroom.

"There!" Francesca said in a conspiratorial whisper. "Your sister doesn't have to know everything quite yet." She smoothed the envelope between her fingers. "I wanted to show you this. Leah wasn't one for taking pictures, but I did catch her once, when we were all here for a picnic. I've never even told your father. I've kept it in the back of that old junk drawer, along with this."

She held a pendant on a chain. She took Bree's hand in hers, and coiled the necklace into her palm. It was cold and heavy. Bree stared at it. The chain was short, perhaps eighteen inches, and made of fine gold links. The pendant was small, perhaps an inch long and half an inch wide.

It was a talisman. Two wings surrounding the scales of Justice.

"Ah, honey," Francesca said. She smoothed Bree's hair. "And then there's this."

Bree took the envelope and opened it. The photograph was faded to orange and brown. Leah Beaufort sat on the top of the stone wall just outside the town house. Bree would have known her anywhere.

She was the pale-eyed, dark-haired woman from the nightmare, the *Rise of the Cormorant*.

⸺∽⸺

She wasn't angry. Nor was she filled with grief. Something lay ahead of her.

It was time to find out what.

Twenty-one

Tous pour un,
Un pour tous.
—*The Three Musketeers*, Alexandre Dumas

The sky was sullen with clouds, but the rain had stopped. She grabbed her raincoat, left Sasha with her family, and walked to the office, turning her parents' revelation over and over in her mind. She needed to see Professor Cianquino. It was all very well and good to tell her that she would only know her own reality when she had experienced it. She was experiencing it now, and she didn't have a clue as to what she was or why she was here.

She jogged across West Bay, turned onto Houston, and wasn't surprised to find Gabriel Striker at her elbow. "You," she said.

"That it is," he agreed.

She stopped in the middle of the sidewalk. She hadn't really looked at him before. His skin was smooth and tanned, as though he spent a lot of time under a beneficent sun. Here, on Houston, in the middle of this old but very real city, his eyes were a clear, untroubled gray. He moved like a dancer, or maybe a boxer, although what she knew about boxing she could put in a very small bucket. He

was balanced, that was it, despite the heavy muscles of
his chest and arms. Balance was the key to his peculiar
grace, as if he could move instantly in any direction with
the slightest provocation.

He'd sought her out twice; she'd found him once.
"Each time you've come to me," she said, "it's been to
keep me from harm." She thought about that, then added,
"Or to keep me from whacking somebody."

He smiled. "So you know a bit more."

"I know way too little," she retorted. "I knew Uncle
Franklin; at least, I thought I did. And I haven't a clue
about my mo . . ." she stumbled over the word, and said
instead, "Leah."

She'd fastened the talisman pendant around her neck.
It lay against her skin, cold and disproportionately heavy.

He didn't say anything, just continued to walk beside
her with a warrior's ease as they approached the cemetery. They rounded the corner at Angelus. A whirl of magnolia leaves eddied around her feet. The sky darkened
with a furious rise of black storm clouds. The wind gusted
suddenly. Rain fell in a vast rush, as though a giant spigot
had opened in the heavens.

The house stood solidly firm against the wind and the
rain. Bree shaded her eyes with one hand against the rain
and broke into a run. She ran smack into Gabriel's broad
back.

"STAND BEHIND ME."

Gabriel's voice. And not Gabriel's voice. It had grown
to a vast echoless sound that filled her head with nothing
else. The sound of it blocked the wind and the rain. She
put her hands to her ears and shut her eyes for a long moment.

"DON'T MOVE."

"I'm getting awfully wet," Bree protested. She stepped around him and fell back with a shout. A thin, questing stream of pustulelike yellow light poured from the grave beneath the live oak tree. As it had before, the river rose, snakelike, turning this way and that. Bree stared at it, engulfed with a terror that came from outside her own mind and spirit. She choked, "What? What does . . . ?"

"Run now!" Gabriel shoved her hard in the small of the back. She stumbled as he shot past her and faced the yellow light and the great horned figure that slowly rose beyond it, beneath the tree.

Gabriel seemed to grow in size, until his white, shining form blocked the river and its attendant spirit from sight.

"Bree!"

She staggered toward the sound of the voices: Ron, Lavinia, and Petru.

"Bree!"

They called again, and again, and she stumbled past the front door into the safety of the foyer. Ron slammed the door shut behind her.

"You *are* wet," Lavinia clucked. "Come into the bathroom and let me dry you off some, chile."

Gently, Bree pushed Lavinia's hands away and faced the door. Petru stood in front of it, his arms folded. Bree stepped up until his face was inches from her own. "You have to let me pass, Petru."

"Striker's just fine out there," Ron said. "C'mon. Lavinia's right. You can't meet new clients with your face wet all over."

Bree ignored them both. "Petru!"

He cocked his head, as if listening. Then, with a satisfied nod, he opened the door and backed away. Bree sprang to the front porch. The rain was coming down in warm, thick sheets. The hideous river of light was gone. She could barely see the outline of the oak tree through the rain, but no presence lurked there.

Gabriel was gone.

Bree whirled around and went back inside. "What happened out there?" She looked at each of them in turn. "You work for me, don't you? It's Beaufort & Company. It's my name on the door ..."

"My Lord, you're right," Ron murmured. "I forgot all about an address plaque. Somebody remind me about that."

"... so, dammit, report to me!"

"Of course," Petru said, nodding his head. "Of course you want to know. There has been some ..."

"Opposition," Ron supplied.

Petru thumped his cane on the floor approvingly. "Excellent word. That is correct. Opposition to the opening of the law firm."

Bree didn't think she wanted to ask who the opposition was. She had a pretty good idea. "So we're ruffling some feathers?" she said. "Is that good?"

Petru spread his hands wide in a "what do I know?" gesture. "We believe this is why you have been harried more than is usual. That Pendergast, for one. A Tempter, that one, and sly as they come. And the horned one, too. Metatron."

A short, cold silence fell over the company.

Petru, looking inward, sighed and came to himself. "Yes, you have been harried by the Hounds of Hell. That, in Russia, would be alliteration. *Harried*," he repeated with some satisfaction, "is an excellent word."

Bree shuddered. "Not if you're the quarry." She glanced

over her shoulder involuntarily. "Gabe is all right, isn't he? Should we go look for him? Would he have been . . . um . . . injured in some way?"

Petru's broad belly shook with laughter. "Gabriel? Injured by that thing? Not a happenstance."

"He means not likely," Ron said. "You, on the other hand, ducky, are not so invulnerable. You keep an eye out in the future, okay?"

Bree led the way into the reception area. "But why now? Is it to keep me from going to the open house?"

"Open?" Ron said. "Oh! No! Why would they care about that? It's a temporal thing, nothing to do with them. I mean, I care, of course, but purely because I love a party. And," he said after a moment's reflection, "your mother."

"Which one?" Bree said flippantly.

"So they tole you," Lavinia said. "About time. She would have wanted that, Leah would have."

They looked at her, their faces warm and welcoming.

"You knew my mother?" Bree said.

Petru chuckled. "George wrote of her that she had a face that launched a thousand ships. Like yours, Bree."

George? George Gordon, Lord Byron? Petru's casual references to long-dead poets and artists as if he'd met them personally were just a character quirk. Weren't they? He couldn't really have met them all.

"And *brave* like you, too," Lavinia said. "We missed her a good bit, until you came to head us up."

"But why . . ." Bree stopped, and began again. "What is all this? What am I? Who are you, really?"

Petru smiled benignly. "We're a Company of angels, with a temporal leader. The leader is you, now. It was Leah, in the past. And it will be your daughter, in the future."

"Angels," Bree repeated. Then, "My daughter?"

"Assumin' things go as planned," Lavinia said. "You just never know."

"Right," Bree said.

"We got that there to worry about." She jerked her thumb to the outside.

"Right," Bree said.

"There will be time for you to sort this through," Petru said kindly. "As much time as you need. An eternity, if all goes well."

Suddenly, Bree didn't want to hear any more. She'd had enough. She'd learned too much, in too short of a time. It was all she could do to look at the faces of her company, ringed around her as they were.

"Enough!" Ron clapped his hands together, breaking the silence. "We have work to do. Time's a-wasting. We have a client to defend. Now!" Ron said briskly. "Petru's ferreted into the finances behind Island Dream. Our Mr. Fairchild owes money all over south Georgia, and parts of South Carolina, too."

"Really," Bree said, with deep interest. "Did you get a rough figure for me?"

"To the tune of twenty million," Ron said. "It took a bit of digging, but I've got a list of the principal creditors for you. Poor old Mr. Skinner was on the hook as guarantor, by the way."

"Is there any one creditor that stands out?"

"Montifiore, of course. He's owed a ton." Ron wriggled his eyebrows. "There's something else about Montifiore. A couple of his last projects have been shut down temporarily by the building inspectors. I couldn't find out if there was anything in it—but from all accounts, he's in pretty tough shape."

"Now, that is interesting," Bree said thoughtfully. She became aware that Lavinia was tugging at her sleeve. "I do apologize, Lavinia. Did I forget something?"

"Only my poor niece. If y'all don't mind? She's been waiting some time. Yes."

"Golly," Ron said. "I almost forgot about her. She's in your office, Bree."

"Lavinia's niece is in my office?"

"New client." Ron hustled her gently to her office door, opened it, and ushered her in. "Business is picking up!" he beamed. He backed out and left Bree to face a broad black woman with a familiar face. She sat in the worn leather chair, with her purse settled firmly in her lap.

Bree extended her hand. "How do you do? I'm Bree Beaufort, but you probably know that already. And I believe we've met. At Liz Overshaw's? You were giving her a hand with the housekeeping. It's Mrs. Mather, isn't it?"

"Elphine Mather. It's Rebus Kingsley who's kin to me and, through me, kin to Lavinia. I'm Lavinia's niece. That'd be it."

Rebus Kingsley. The name struck a faint bell. Bree frowned thoughtfully and settled herself behind her desk. "How can I help you, Mrs. Mather?"

"It's my husband's boy. My stepson."

Bree nodded. "Rebus Kingsley?"

"You heard about that county building inspector fallin' off the tower and getting killed?"

"I'm afraid I didn't, no." Bree thought a moment. "Wait a second. There was an item on the news, yes. About a county employee who was killed on the job." She looked thoughtfully at Elphine. "That was your stepson? And he was a building inspector for Chatham County?"

"That's him. And he was murdered. Or so he keeps on tellin' me and tellin' me." Elphine heaved a deep, somewhat exasperated sigh. "Now I'm here to tell you that the boy was a thorn in my side when he was alive, and he's an even worse thorn in my side now that he's dead."

Bree swallowed hard. "You mean he's haunting you."

There. It was out. And it didn't feel too weird. It felt almost . . . routine.

"That'd be the case, Ms. Beaufort. Claims he was murdered. Won't rest until there's another just grave in the cemetery out there."

Georgia's only all-murderers' cemetery.

Of course.

Bree felt a little dizzy. She didn't think it was because of the bump on her head yesterday. Her head felt just fine. But her law firm was located right in the middle of murderers' graves. And it wasn't by accident. Of that she was certain.

"Ms. Beaufort?"

"I do apologize, Mrs. Mather. You'd like to retain Beaufort and Company to find the murderer and set your stepson's soul at rest," Bree said.

"I don' know if that alone will do it," Mrs. Mather said. "The boy has a lot of sin to answer for, and perhaps he's hoping that you'll plead his case the way you're going to plead Mr. Skinner's."

Since Bree had absolutely no idea how this was going to be accomplished, she merely said, "Hmm."

"We won't know that until you sit down and talk to him."

"Yes," Bree said. She had to take a moment to swallow, and then she said, "Of course. You'll take me to him, I suppose?"

"Ms. Beaufort, if I never see that boy again, it'll be too soon." Mrs. Mather folded her lips in a grim expression. "I expect you'll find him on your own, the way you did Mr. Skinner. All I want is a good night's sleep."

"Yes," Bree said. "That's been a common problem for our clients. An unfortunate consequence of the hauntings. We will do what we can."

"I can write you a retainer check right here." Mrs. Mather dug into her purse, rustled around, and brought out a checkbook. "If you'll suggest an amount?"

"There is some professional courtesy here," Bree said. "Lavinia, I mean, your aunt, is a member of our company. I'm not even sure I should ..."

"Elphine!" Lavinia's voice came through the office door loud and clear. "You write that girl a check for five hundred dollars. Don't you even think about takin' advantage."

Elphine wrote the check. Bree accepted it with thanks. "We'll do the best we can, Mrs. Mather." She looked at her watch. Half an hour to the open house. "If you can tell me where your stepson died? I'll be out there to inter ... um ... that is, I'll be out there first thing in the morning."

"That's no secret, Miss Beaufort. It was out at those condos of Mr. Skinner's. The place they call Island Dream."

Twenty-two

The play's the thing
Wherein I'll catch the conscience of the King.
—*Hamlet*, Shakespeare

"Now, who would have thought with all this weather there'd be such a wonderful turnout!" Francesca was in her element. Dressed in a softly elegant suit of blue silk shantung, the family pearls at her throat, she hummed with pleasure. She twinkled up at Bree. "And that shimmery red velvet dress, honey. You look like a queen. As for the food—the chef deserves every one of those five stars. The food's magnificent."

700 Drayton was part of the Mansion in Forsyth Park, and Francesca had chosen well. The restaurant had a series of smaller dining rooms on the second floor that were ideal for Bree's introduction to Savannah legal circles. The walls were painted a deep eggplant. The dangling light fixtures had various shades of gold and red, and silver lamé draped the windows. The interior shouldn't have worked, but it did.

Francesca poked Bree in the side. "Now, who's that good-looking young man talking up a storm with your sister? You suppose he's with one of the big law firms from Atlanta? He looks so downtown."

Bree craned her neck. Antonia, splendid in a black cocktail dress with no back and a plunging front, was in close conversation with a stunningly handsome man with long hair and a black leather jacket. "Sorry, Mamma. It's the lead actor from the Savannah Rep. I met him when she hauled him in here. Cute as bug and poor as a church mouse."

"I should have guessed it," her mother grumbled. "How come all the good-looking ones are broke?"

"Daddy was broke when you married him," Bree pointed out. "I hate to mention it, Mamma, but the money's all on your side."

"There's broke and then there's broke," Francesca muttered. "Your daddy had *prospects*."

Bree prowled the room, feeling like a sliced potato on a red-hot griddle. John Stubblefield held court at the small mahogany bar. Every so often, his little gray eyes slid sideways in her direction. Payton skulked at his elbow. Douglas Fairchild was conspicuous by his absence; Hunter had decided to press obstruction charges, and either Fairchild or his wife had decided to skip the whispers that would follow a public appearance. The gossip wouldn't last for long; with the possible exception of a murder indictment, Southern society tended to be most forgiving of its own. Bree accepted condolences on her uncle Franklin's death from a fellow judge and the senior partner in a local accounting firm, fielded some nosy questions about Jennifer Skinner from a mutual friend, and ducked questions about the actual whereabouts of her current practice.

"You'll think about moving into Franklin's old offices as soon as the restoration's done, if you mean to stay here in Savannah," Royal said during a lull in the chatter. "This address on Angelus seems pretty out of the way. I've been telling people it's temporary."

"I may split my time between the two," Bree said, deliberately vague. "That's Carlton Montifiore over there."

Her father was tall, and he squinted over the heads of the crowd. "Yes, I believe it is. Franklin's old colleagues did right well by you, Bree. There's a lot of money and power in this room."

"Excuse me, Daddy. I'll just go say hello."

Bree wound her way through the mass of people. Montifiore stood with his back to the wall. His gray sports coat strained over his broad back. He'd loosened his tie. Unsmiling, he watched Bree's approach. Her relaxed and genial guide to the Pyramid Office Building had disappeared. In these surroundings, he looked tense and angry.

"Is there anything I can get for you, Carlo?" she asked politely. "I hope you're finding everything to your satisfaction."

"Stubblefield tells me you're the woman who nailed Doug Fairchild's butt to the floor."

"I guess I am."

He smiled, shifted his Manhattan to his left hand, and squeezed her by the upper arm in a congratulatory way. His grip was hard. Irritated, Bree shook herself free. "It's time someone took Dougie down a peg. Glad to see it."

"You thought he was getting a little too big for his britches?" Bree said.

"Let's say his eyes were bigger than his ability to borrow."

"Your company's listed as one of his chief creditors," Bree said. "Must be a bit troubling for you." *And,* she added silently to herself, *you lied like a rug, Carlo*. Plenty of money around, indeed.

Montifiore's eyes darkened, but he said genially, "Oh, we end up getting our pound of flesh, one way or the other. Don't you worry about us."

Bree bet that the banks were real worried about Montifiore. But her mother would skin her alive if she started a brouhaha at a social event. She said merely, "Maybe we should talk about that, Carlo."

He stiffened, glared at her, and turned on his heel to walk away.

Someone struck a wineglass with a fork. The "ting" rose above the clatter, and conversation slowed, then stopped. The waitstaff began circulating through the crowd with trays of champagne. Bree turned and faced the hors d'oeuvres table. Her father and mother stood hand in hand, smiling. Royal cleared his throat, raised his wineglass, and said, "Bree? Come up here, darlin'." Bree nodded to Carlton Montifiore and made her way up to the front of the room. Her father clasped her hand, and tucked it into his arm. "I'd like to welcome you all to this celebration. It's a happy day for Francesca and me. Our oldest daughter has taken up the reins of Franklin's practice, and begun a new life and a new career here in Savannah. My family and I would like to thank you all for being here with us. Here's to you all. And to the fine practice of law in Georgia!" He raised a glass in a toast.

"To the law!" Everyone followed his lead and drank.

Francesca turned with a flutter to the towering cake that occupied the center of the table. Ron had outdone himself. The cake was a miniature replica of the Hall of Justice on Montgomery. A gust of wind rattled the windows as Francesca cut into the cake, and she shuddered dramatically.

Then, with a slow, crumbling slide, the cake toppled

onto its side. Francesca turned to the crowd with a look of mock dismay and laughed. Antonia called out, "Now, sister! I sure hope Georgia law's got a firmer foundation than that!" Bree turned around to make a face at her aggravating little sister.

Carlton Montifiore stared back at her. He drew his teeth back in a feral grin. Malice glittered in his eyes.

Bree stood stock-still. Foundation. When she'd been hit on the head, she was kneeling in front of the basement foundation. She had a plastic bag in one hand, and she was exploring the base of the wall with the other. As if she was going to take samples of the concrete?

She was surrounded by whispers, too faint to hear clearly. The staticlike sound rose to a peak, then trailed off.

...murder...

She shook herself free of the tormented sounds. Facts. Logic. Reasoned analysis. That's what Professor Cianquino had taught her, and that's what she needed to apply now:

The building inspector was dead.

Skinner had desperately wanted out of what should have been a very lucrative deal. He was in the process of stopping the project in its tracks.

Fairchild was in a lot of financial trouble.

Montifiore had been in trouble with building inspectors before.

Bree didn't know much about construction, but she did know that the new hurricane codes were ruinously expensive. You could save hundreds of thousands of dollars by substituting sand for concrete in a foundation; and thousands more by reducing the bolts and supports in the walls by half. Or even more than half.

She set her champagne glass on the table and started toward Montifiore. He turned his back and forced his way through the crowd. Bree started after him, and then stopped short, as if she'd slammed into a wall. The whispers rose around her in an agonized cry: *Save her ... save her ... save her ...*

The wind belted against the side of the Mansion and a roar of rain shook the windows.

Bree came to herself with a jolt.

She had to get Chastity out of Island Dream—before it turned into an island nightmare.

❊

"How sure are you of the facts?" Sam Hunter drove with seeming indifference to the wind rocketing around his car. Rain sluiced down the windshield like an incoming tide; Bree could barely make out the lights of the emergency truck in front of them.

"You should have seen Montifiore's face. Guilt all over it like kudzu in a field of wheat."

Sam grunted, unamused. "Facial expressions aren't admissible proof in any court in Georgia. Texas, maybe."

"Very funny. The proof will be in the building itself. Will you *hurry*?" Bree's impatience was edged with guilt. Publicly, her mother had taken Bree's abrupt abandonment of her own party with her usual grace. But she was sure to hear about it later.

"You'd better have a damn good reason to get the rescue crew out on a night like this one. The whole island's been evacuated. There's nobody left there."

"Chastity's still there," Bree said stubbornly. "She said she wasn't going to leave unless she got thrown out, and I got cut off before I could tell her the whole building was

going to fall down around her ears. She doesn't have a
cell phone, the lines are down, and the wind would knock
a helicopter six ways from Sunday. We've got to save
her."

"But you haven't any proof that she's in danger."

"That building isn't going to stand up to a storm like
this one."

Sam's sigh was both exasperated and annoyed. "You're
arguing like a revolutionary. All emotion and no facts.
Maybe you could try looking at it like the lawyer you
are?"

"Okay, it's an educated guess," Bree said impatiently.
"But no other explanation fits the facts as well as this one:
Montifiore and Grainger Skinner were skimming money
from the project. Montifiore indulged in the fine old practice of chiseling on the quality of the building materials."

"I can think of at least two other reasonable explana-
tions," Sam said. He steered the car expertly through a
knee-high drift of water.

"Well?" Bree said after a long silence.

He glanced at her with a grin. "Okay. So I can't think
of anything else that doesn't leave some loose ends.
Damn!" Both of them ducked involuntarily as a tree
branch whirled by the driver's door. "And Chastity's just
brainless enough . . ."

"She's not stupid," Bree snapped. "She's just never
had a chance."

Sam muttered something that might have been "heard
that one before." Bree hoped not.

The wheels took on a thrum of tires on metal. They
were headed over the bridge. Bree looked out her window. Huge waves lashed at the bridge pilings. "I'm not

very good at estimating heights," she admitted. "Did the weather report say anything about the surf?"

"Up to twenty feet. The storm surge is estimated at fifteen." He glanced at his watch. "It'll be along in about twenty minutes or so."

Bree leaned forward and peered into the darkness. She couldn't see a thing. She leaned back in the seat with a sigh. Sam's car was a mess. Old Styrofoam coffee cups, crumpled burger wrappers, and empty bottles of water cluttered the floor. She nudged a Dunkin' Donuts box aside with her toe. "Have the Skinners talked yet?"

"Just through their lawyer. Stubblefield's a sleazy son of a bitch."

"No kidding."

"The story goes something like this: *If* Dad was dead before they took the *Sea Mew* out—and they aren't admitting to a thing—it was because they got a panicked phone call from Fairchild to give him a hand disposing of the body. And *if* they felt it was incumbent upon them to help an old family friend, it was only because everyone's investment was at risk. If Skinner had succeeded in pulling his money out of Island Dream—and his new lawyers were planning on going ahead with that, even though he was dead and gone—Fairchild stood to lose everything. Grainger isn't admitting how much he personally was going to lose, but I'll bet it was a lot."

"And Fairchild didn't kill him?"

"Fairchild has an alibi. Grainger and Jenny have an alibi. That dumb-ass Tiptree found Skinner's body, called Fairchild in a panic, and Fairchild called Grainger, since Grainger was already two minutes away at the arena."

"You don't suspect Calvin Tiptree."

"Nope. He was there at the right time, all right. But he was with a sales prospect until ten o'clock, we verified that. And he called Doug from his cell five minutes and thirty-two seconds after the suckers left. The ME says it's highly unlikely he had time to clout the poor guy over the head, pump his lungs full of water, and arrange his death. Besides, he doesn't fit the profile."

"You have an instinct about these things, do you?" Bree asked dryly. "Well, so do I. It's pretty clear to me that Montifiore's behind Skinner's murder and the murder of that poor Elphine Mather's stepson."

"Hang on." He put his arm out across her middle and braked hard. The car skidded, turned, and stopped. "Tree down," he said briefly. He cut the engine, but kept his headlights on. The emergency truck ahead of them hadn't been so quick to respond. The truck was piled nose first into the trunk of a huge live oak that lay across the road. The red lights blip-blip-blipped through the sheets of rain.

"Where are we?"

"About halfway up the back road to the building. Can you see it? It's about a quarter mile ahead of us."

"I'll be surprised if I can see my hand in front of my face," Bree said. She retied her raincoat around her, pulled on her rain hat, and prepared to get out.

"Whoa." Sam grabbed her arm. "Where do you think you're going?"

"Up to the building, of course."

"Are you crazy?"

She looked at him. He scowled, shook his head, and began to mutter under his breath. But he shrugged himself into his rain gear, and pushed the driver's door open.

At least it isn't cold, Bree told herself. The air was

thick and humid and the rain seemed to be everywhere at once, up her sleeves, down the back of her neck, in her eyes. Three rubber-suited figures clumped around the emergency truck, clearing debris away from the tires. Bree and Sam struggled past them and scrambled over the tree trunk. Abruptly, the rain lessened and the wind dropped off. Bree was able to breathe again. With the flashing red lights behind them, they were able to see the dim outline of the marina a half mile to the east. Many of the boats had been moved farther inland in anticipation of the storm. Those that were left were inundated with waves.

Directly ahead, she made out the towering outline of Island Dream. Against all odds, the electricity was on, and the building was ablaze, like a giant cruise ship in the ocean of the night. Bree made out the lights in the penthouse, even at this distance.

Suddenly, Sam drew her to his side. His voice was grim. "Look out. Here it comes. The storm surge."

A huge wall of water traveled up the causeway. It swept over the boats, toppling the masts into the water. It swept over the docks and the piers, onto the sand, and up the dunes.

Bree grabbed Sam's hand and held it.

The wall of water surged like a slow, lazy beast of huge, immeasurable size. It rolled across the drive, a juggernaut. It flowed up the drive, surrounding the building, and slapped against the foundations. A second wall of water followed the first, and boiled against the building.

A huge groan rolled through the air. And with painful, agonizing slowness, the building listed, tilted, and began to fall.

The death of the Island Dream was a noisy one. The

roof tiles tumbled into the sea. Windows smashed and sprayed glass into the air. The steel girders shrieked as they were torn from the earth.

Then all the lights went out.

The growling of the destruction continued in the dark. Bree trembled with shock, and sudden cold. Her knees gave way, and she sat back against the bole of the tree. "Too late," she said quietly. "Too late. I'm so sorry, Mr. Skinner." Her teeth began to chatter. Sam pulled his cell phone from his pocket and spoke urgently into it. He jammed the phone back into his pocket, and helped her to her feet. "Come on," he said gently. "Let's get you back to the car."

Bree pressed her hands to her eyes, then straightened herself up. "That poor girl," she said fiercely. "I'll never forgive myself, never! We should have done something, Sam!"

"We did what we could." His voice was low and so quiet she almost didn't hear him. "I called this in. We'd better get back before the rain and the wind pick up again."

"Wait a minute." Bree grabbed the sleeve of his coat. "Did you hear something?"

"Something like what?"

There it was again, a cry like a cat's. A thin thread of sound barely audible in the rising wind. "Don't you hear it? She's yelling 'Wait! Wait!'" Bree cupped her hands around her mouth and shouted, "Over here!"

"Wait for me!"

Chastity McFarland stumbled out of the dark and fell into Bree's open arms.

"It was the weirdest thing!" Chastity, again in a T-shirt and low-rise jeans, was soaked to the skin, which probably, Bree reflected, spurred the rescue workers to eager efforts to dry her off. She sat in the back of the truck, shuddering with fear and excitement. "It was the weirdest thing," she repeated. "I was all set to wait this ol' storm out and you know what?" She stared up at Bree, her eyes huge. She accepted a cup of hot tea from one of the techs with a grateful smile and gulped it down.

Bree had a notion about "what," but she said, "Something made you decide to leave?"

She leaned over and whispered in Bree's ear, "Bennie showed up!" She sat back and brushed her sodden hair out of her eyes. "I didn't have a drop to drink, either. I was like to die, I was so shocked."

"But not scared?"

"Nope." She grinned. "The old coot didn't scare me when he was alive, and certainly not when he was dead." She glanced from side to side. Sam was outside, rapping out orders on his cell phone. The wind and rain picked up, and the techs prepared to leave. She lowered her voice. "Do you think I'm stark raving crazy, or what?"

"I think he loved you enough to cross the divide between us and the dark," Bree said. "And you can't ask more of a man than that."

Twenty-three

For, as thou urgest justice, be assured
Thou shalt have justice...
—*The Merchant of Venice*, Shakespeare

"You know that Montifiore's skipped town." Bree dropped the *Savannah Daily* onto her desk. The headline read: "Construction Magnate Disappears: Police Search Five State Area." "It's maddening."

"That it is," Ron agreed. "But we can wrap up the Skinner case very soon now."

"I'm wrapping it up even as we speak." Bree stacked the paper reports on Benjamin Skinner's death into a neat pile and slipped them into the file folder. She handed the file to Ron, who looked at it with some bewilderment.

"What do you want me to do with this?"

"Maybe file it?" Bree asked sweetly. She leaned back in her swivel chair and stuck her feet on her desk. "Sam Hunter seems to think they'll catch up with Montifiore eventually. I wish I had that much faith in the system. He could be halfway to Aruba by now."

Ron flourished the file at her. "We've got a court appearance coming up. Or have you forgotten?"

Bree put her feet on the floor and sat up straight. "I'm

pretty sure I don't want to ask you what you're talking about. As a matter of fact, I know I don't."

"You remember that Mr. Skinner is our original client," Ron said. "He's got this little problem? He's been accused of Second Degree Misdemeanor Greed? He's hired us to defend him? We can't let him twist in the wind here, Bree. He's looking at doing some hard time in purgatory."

"Well, yes," Bree floundered, "but . . ." She waved one hand in the air. "I thought we took care of all that. I mean, we've found his murderer. We've exonerated him from any culpability in the Island Dream debacle. It's very clear he was trying to stop the project once he discovered Montifiore was using adulterated concrete."

"That's not going to cut any ice with You-Know-Who." Ron looked at his watch. "We've got a court date in thirty minutes. Time enough for you to go over the pleadings." He opened the file, sorted through the papers, and handed Bree a Response to a Summons and Complaint. The Summons and Complaint itself was beneath it. And sure enough, the heading read:

Ninth Sphere Circuit Court
In the matter of the Celestial Sphere v. Skinner

"Petru's listed all of the relevant citations. There's quite a few, fortunately; I think our most compelling argument is *C.S. v. Rockefeller*, 1915. The man gave a significant portion of his net worth to pretty good causes. Despite some compelling evidence for the prosecution, the judge found for the plaintiff."

"Who's sitting today?" Bree asked faintly.

Ron flipped through the file. "Azreal. Hm. Don't know him."

"Maybe he's a she," Bree said flippantly.

"Angels are nongender specific," Ron said. "Are you ready?"

"Where?" Bree cleared her throat. "Where are we going?"

"The County Courthouse," Ron said. "Where else?"

"Where else?" Bree echoed. She stuffed the files in her briefcase, smoothed her hair, and dusted some lint off her skirt. "I'm glad I didn't dress down today. I almost wore my jeans."

"You wear robes in court," Ron said reprovingly. "Lavinia finished them last night. They're in my briefcase." He rocked back and forth on his toes. "Do you want to walk or drive?"

Bree looked out her tiny window. The tropical storm had swept through the city and left Savannah sparkling. "Let's walk."

The courthouse was a huge, six-story concrete block building at the corner of Montgomery and Martin Luther King Boulevard. It was yellow, and had that indescribable air of earnestness that seemed to characterize municipal buildings. Bree and Ron went through the metal detectors and stopped in front of the elevators. Bree examined the white boards that listed the court activities for the day: Probate. Magistrate. Juvenile. State. No Ninth Sphere. Azreal's name didn't appear on the list of sitting judges, either.

The cars were crowded. Bree got shoved to the back. Ron positioned himself near the callboard and the car lurched up. The car emptied out at six.

And continued up.

"Seven!" Ron said cheerily.

The hallway looked just like the hallways on the six floors below, with one notable exception: The medallion on the wall was not that of the state of Georgia. It read "Court of Celestial Sphere" and the logo was a pair of golden scales cupped by two feathery wings. Except for the two of them, the hallway was empty.

"Slow day," Ron observed. "Here. Since no one's around, you won't have to duck into the ladies' room." He put his briefcase on the floor, opened it up, and shook out a long, crimson robe. It was velvet, with panels on the front worked in gold embroidery. "Lavinia does such nice work," Ron said. He held it out and Bree stepped into it. It was exactly like her graduation robes, except for the needlework. Bree smoothed the fabric with one hand. Lavinia had worked nine Spheres rising to a single point on each panel.

Ron tapped briskly down the hallway and stopped at an elaborately carved wooden door. A wood board to the right of the door read:

COURT G
AZREAL PRESIDING

"I'm nervous," Bree said.

"P'shaw!" Ron said. "You'll do just fine." He opened the door. "After you."

Bree adjusted her robes, smoothed her hair, and stepped inside.

───※───

"It wasn't quite as intimidating as I thought it might be." Bree felt lighthearted. The two of them swung along

Montgomery at a brisk pace. The air was clear, after the storm, and the sky a brilliant blue. "Do you think I presented the case"—she paused, searching for the right words—"decisively enough?"

"No question," Ronald said promptly.

"I thought it might be a little grander," Bree offered after a moment. "I thought a Celestial Court would be, I don't know, more harps, maybe."

"There were no harps," Ron said, slightly shocked. "This is a lower court, Bree. The lesser felonies, misdemeanors. It's more like a justice court."

"A justice court!" Bree stopped on the pavement, dismayed. "You mean, I just pled the equivalent of a traffic ticket?"

"No, no, no, of course not," Ron murmured reassuringly. "Much more important than that, of course. But don't forget. Pride goeth ..."

"Right," Bree muttered. Then, rather crossly, she said to herself, "Justice court."

"There will be time for more significant cases, later."

"What about the disposition of the case? When will we know if Ben Skinner went to—wherever it is he wanted to go to rather than where he was?"

"We'll check the *Ultima* when we get back to the office. The judgments are filed there."

They halted in front of the little house at 66 Angelus. "I do wish we hadn't let Montifiore get away," Bree said. "I'd like to know the disposition of that case, for sure. I'm not happy at the thought he's wandering around here somewhere free as a bird. The man was a murderer twice over. And I don't know that if the cops do find him, there'll be enough evidence to convict."

Ron leaned over the wrought-iron fence and nodded toward the live oak tree.

"It's a new grave," Bree said, in a troubled voice. "And it's empty."

"Not for long, I hope. You see the headstone? No date, of course. But he'll end up there eventually."

R. I. P.
CARLTON MONTIFIORE
THE MILLS OF GOD GRIND SLOWLY
YET THEY GRIND EXCEEDINGLY SMALL

Epilogue

"How was your day?" Antonia lay flat on the couch, raised both legs over her head, and lowered them.

"Fine." Bree set her briefcase by the fireplace, bent to pet Sasha, and threw herself into the leather chair. "Interesting."

"Yeah?" Antonia continued her exercises. She swore they kept her stomach flat. "The parents got off okay after you left for the office." She swung her feet to the floor and sat up, her face flushed with effort. "They came this close to pitching a fit over my staying on with you." She held her thumb and forefinger a scant eighth of an inch apart.

"I'm glad there wasn't too big a hoo-rah," Bree said.

"So what did you do today?"

Bree smiled at her. "Won my case. Very satisfying. My client's in seventh heaven."

"Is that a fact? Congratulations. You want to go down to the Shrimp Factory and celebrate?"

Bree unpinned her braids and let them swing free. "Let's do that."

A Note on
the Origin of Angels

The cosmology created for Beaufort & Company is based on eleventh- and twelfth-century medieval theology. This was a time in the history of Christianity when influences from three of the world's great religions—Christianity, Judaism, and Islam—began to show up in documents in Europe's monasteries. The monks were especially fond of angels, and there are hundreds of them listed in these old manuscripts.

Many angels were assigned responsibilities for temporal phenomena, such as earthquakes, rain, moonlight, and sunshine.

The angels in Beaufort & Company benefit from contributions from several of the great Chinese religions; Mahayana Buddhism is one.

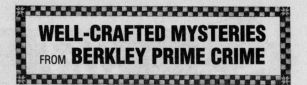